The Sp

"So many spells," said Lauris to her familiar. Shadow swiveled a gray ear in her direction. "I wonder what happened to Blayne. Surely such a powerful wizard wouldn't be taken by surprise."

Unless the Dark itself devoured him, came a thought that did not originate inside her own head.

At once, Shadow was on his feet. His back arched, and his yellow gaze fastened on something Lauris could not see.

Lauris went bone cold. "Make yourself known," she whispered. But she already knew who it was—didn't she?

You grace this house, came the external thought. *Such beauty...such compassion...*

And then something cold as the grave itself brushed past her, through her. Lauris gasped, feeling icy tendrils of nothingness stroke her body, take shape, though remaining invisible, and become cold, strong arms, and she felt the press of lips that were not there on hers....

And then he announced his presence a second time. As she watched, the pages of the book lying in front of her began to turn, as if flipped by a gentle wind, then stopped. Her heart nearly shaking her with its pounding, Lauris glanced down at the spell.

"A Spell to Reanimayte the Dead."

from "Summer Storms" by Christie Golden

LAMMAS NIGHT

CREATED BY
MERCEDES LACKEY

Edited By
JOSEPHA SHERMAN

LAMMAS NIGHT

This is a work of fiction. All the characters and events portrayed in this book are fictional, and any resemblance to real people or incidents is purely coincidental.

A Baen Books Original

Baen Publishing Enterprises
P.O. Box 1403
Riverdale, N.Y. 10471

ISBN: 0-671-87713-5

Cover art by Victoria Poyser

First printing, February 1996

Distributed by
SIMON & SCHUSTER
1230 Avenue of the Americas
New York, N.Y. 10020

Printed in the United States of America

CONTENTS

Introduction

First there was the song.

Several years back, Mercedes Lackey wrote "Lammas Night," a spooky, supernatural ballad that ended with the wizard protagonist facing a very perilous choice that was left to the listener to decide.

Then came the birthday present that wasn't.

Bill Jahnel and friends put together a collection of endings for the song, intending to offer it as a tribute to Mercedes, known to her friends as "Misty." However, the best laid plans often don't come off as intended. The project was shelved for a time, then offered to Baen Books for possible publication. Unfortunately, while this project, in its original form, made a lovely tribute and Misty was quite touched, it was felt that a book made up strictly of endings to a song would have made for rather limited reading.

And so the book now known as *Lammas Night* was born.

What you hold in your hands is an all-new collection of fantasy stories by some of the brightest stars in the field. Each was given a copy of "Lammas Night" and was told to use it as a springboard for his or her imagination. The only restriction was that their stories must show some tie-in to the original song.

What resulted is a wild range of stories, some

1

traditional, some outright bizarre. *Lammas Night* is both a tribute to the song and to Misty herself. It is also a chance for readers to enter new worlds of fantasy and see the creative imagination at work.

—**Josepha Sherman**

Lammas Night

MERCEDES LACKEY

A waning moon conceals her face
Behind a scudding wind-torn cloud.
   (a wind-torn shroud)
She wraps herself in its embrace
As in a tattered cloak.
   (a shadow cloak)
The wind is wailing in the trees.
Their limbs are warped and bent and bowed.
   (so bleak and cowed)
I stand within my circle now
To deal with what I woke.
   (I wake—I see, but not yet free.)

A wanderer of wizard kind
I was, until a month ago
   (so well I know)
The headman of this village came
And begged that I should stay.
   (so cold and fey)
"For since our wizard died," he said
"And why he died we do not know—
   (so long ago!)
We have no one to weave us spells
And keep the Dark at bay."
   (the dark, so deep: so cold the sleep)

3

"His house and books are yours, milady,
If you choose but to remain."
   (remembered pain)
His offer was too tempting
To be lightly set aside
   (remembered pride)
I'd wearied of my travel, being
Plaything of the sun and rain—
   (choose to remain—)
This was the chance I'd hoped for—
And I said that I would bide.
   (I hope—I pray—and you must stay)

Perhaps if I had been a man,
And not a maid, perhaps if I
Had been less lonely, less alone,
Or less of magic folk—
   (the spell-bound broke)
Whatever weakness was in me,
Or for whatever reason why
   (my reason why)
Something slept within that house
That my own presence woke.
   (You dream so much—I try to touch)

A half-seen shadow courted me,
Stirred close at hand or by my side.
   (to bid you bide)
It left a lover's token—one
Fresh blossom on my plate.
   (a fragrant bait)
I woke to danger—knew the young
Magician still to Earth was tied—
   (for freedom cried)
And tied to me—and I must act.

Or I might share his fate.
　(I need your aid, be not afraid)

I found a spell for banishment—
The pages then turned—and not by me!
　(look now and see)
The next spell differed by one word,
A few strokes of a pen.
　(and read again)
The first one I had seen before,
The spell to set a spirit free;
　(so I will be)
The second let the mage-born dead
Take flesh and live again!
　(one spell and then I live again)

Now both these spells were equal
In their risk to body and to soul.
　(I shall be whole)
And both these spells demanded
They be cast on Lammas Night.
　(the darkest night)
And both these spells of spirit
And of caster took an equal toll,
　(task to the soul)
But nowhere is it writ
That either spell is of the Light.
　(to live and see and touch, to be)

Can it be wise to risk the anger
Of the Gods in such a task?
　(yet I must ask)
Yet who am I to judge of who
Should live and who should die?
　(don't let me die—)
Does love or duty call him?

Is his kindness to me all a mask?
   (take up the task)
And could I trust his answer
If I dared to ask him "Why?"
   (give all your trust—my will [you must])

So now I stand within the circle
I have drawn upon the floor—
   (the open door)
I have no further answer if
This spirit's friend or foe
   (nor can you know)
Though I have prayed full often, nor
Can I this moment answer if
I'll tell him "Come" or "Go."

Hallowmas Night

MERCEDES LACKEY

The moon is on the wane tonight, and her light is fitful and hard to work by. There is a chill and bitter wind tossing the bare branches of the trees; had there been any leaves left upon those sad, black boughs when the sun set, they would have been ripped away by now. That same wind shreds the thin, fraying clouds that scud across the moon's face, so that she seems to be dressed in the tattered remnants of a shroud. The sound of it among the trees is like the wailing of a hundred thousand lost souls.

And while my hands busy themselves with the preparations I have rehearsed in my mind too many times to be counted, I find myself trying to trace the path that brought me to this night, and these perilous rituals.

Was it only last month, a bare moon-span of days ago that I came to this place? It hardly seems possible, and yet that is indeed the case. It seems so strange, to look back upon the thing I was, so sure of myself and my place in the world—

A wizard I was and am, for my talents lie with the manipulations of energy, and my knowledge is that of the doors to and creatures of other worlds. Unlike some of my fellows, I do not hold that witchcraft is the lesser art—oh no; I have seen too many things to

7

believe that to be the case. Faced with an elemental or the need to bring fertility to man, beast or field, I should be as helpless as a witch given a wraith to exorcise, or a demon to subdue. And the healing arts that come so easily to the witch born were slow and painful for me to learn. To each of us her strengths and her weaknesses, say I—but in my craft, I count myself no weakling. I long ago attained the Master's rank and staff—and yet, I wandered, ever wandered, as if I were a Journeyman still.

At first it had been by choice, for I took joy in the sights and sounds of new places—but that was no longer the case. I was long wearied with traveling, with the hardships and mundane dangers of the road, with being the plaything of the weather, the pawn of the seasons. But I, having been hurt too many times by my fellow man—fellows in my art, let me say— had grown shy of their company, and would settle only in some remote place, far from other prac- titioners of my art, in some rustic habitat where I might meditate and study at leisure, and use my skills to the mutual benefit of my pocket and the well-being of ordinary folk.

But we of wizardly kind are often of that frame of mind; and it seemed that no matter where my feet carried me, there were others settled there before me.

Until, one autumn day, my wanderings brought me here—

It was a goodly village I saw, nestled in a quiet little valley. The gold of freshly-thatched roofs blended with the brighter gold and red of the autumn leaves; there was a mill clacking and plashing the water of the stream (always a good sign of prosperity) and from the row of carts next to it, the harvest had been an ample one. Even more cheering, I could see from my vantage point where my road crested the hill that the mill wheel was being used to power a cider press at the side of the building. Three or four village folk were tending it, and an errant breeze brought the scent of apples to me even as I determined to descend into their valley.

The inn, though small, was cheerful with white-washed wall, red shutters, and smoke-blackened beams. I took my seat within it at a trestle table and nodded in a friendly fashion to two or three broad-shouldered lads (farmers waiting for their grain to be ground, I judged). I had waited no more than a breath or two before the portly, balding, redcheeked inn-keeper appeared to ask my desires.

I told him; he served me my bread, cheese, sausage and cider—then stood behind me as if he wished something of me.

I let him wait for a little as I eased my parched and dry throat with his most excellent drink, then looked up at him with a sidewise glance out of my eye—I have found that common folk do not like to be looked at directly by a practitioner of arcane skill.

"Your fare is quite satisfactory, good innkeeper," I said, giving him an opening to speak.

" 'Tis all of our own, milady," he made answer. "Well, and it may be humble by some folk's lights, but 'tis proud we are of it. Milady—might I be askin' ye—be ye a magiker?"

I nodded at my staff, that leaned against the wall beside my table. Carved with silver-inlaid runes, and surmounted by a globe of crystal clasped in an eagle's claw of silver, it told all the world what my calling was. "As you can see, goodman. I am of wizard-teaching."

"Then, milady, would it be puttin' ye out of yer way to be speakin' to our headman?"

I was a bit surprised by the question, but took pains not to show it. "I have nowhere in particular to go, good sir; I am a free wanderer, with my time all my own."

He bobbed his head at me. "Then, if ye'd be so kind, I be goin' to fetch him."

And to my astonishment, he trotted across the rutted dirt street to the chandler's shop.

He returned quickly enough, and by his side walked a thin, sallow-faced fellow clad in brown homespun, who might well have looked disagreeable but for the lines of good humor about his eyes and mouth.

He came straight to my table and wasted no time in coming to the point.

"Jesse tells me you are a magician—and a wanderer," he said. "Forgive my impudence, but—milady, we have strong need of one such as you."

Again, I was astonished, for this seemed the perfect place for wizard or witch to settle, and in truth I had been somewhat expecting to be greeted by another such as I with a subtle hint that I should let my feet carry me further.

"How so?" I asked, still not letting my astonishment show. "I would have thought that so charming a place as this would have a resident mage."

"We—did have, milady," the man said, looking anxious. "He—died. We don't know why."

By the Powers of Light, *that* had an ominous ring to it!

"Was he old?" I asked cautiously. "How did this happen?"

"Nay, lady, he was young, young as you, I would reckon. He just—died. Between sunset and sunrise. The dairymaid found him, sitting up at the table, when she brought the morning milk, with not a mark on him."

My mind worked furiously; such a death could have any number of causes, some arcane, some as simple as an unguessed heart ailment. "And why do you say you have need of one such as I?" I asked while I thought.

"Because of the forest, lady," he said in a half-whisper, gesturing northwards. "East, west and south, it's just woods—but northwards—nay. It's haunted, belike, or worse. Uncanny things live there, and sometimes take a notion to come out. *He* kept 'em bound away, so that we never even heard 'em squall on black nights, but since he died—well, we hear 'em, and we're starting to see 'em again just beyond the fence he put 'round 'em, when we have to travel in that direction. We need another magiker to keep 'em bound, and that's a fact."

That made sense; whatever their mage had been holding off, and however he'd done it, the spells he'd set would be fading with his death.

I looked at the headman a little more closely, this time using a touch of mage-sight. "I would say you need one for more than that—or haven't you got a healer hereabouts?" Mage-sight told me his sallow complexion came from a half-poisoned liver; something a simple healing spell could deal with readily.

"Have you skill at healing, too?" He looked like a child with an unexpected abundance of Yule giftings. "Nay, we've no healer; our herb woman died a good three years ago and her kin hadn't the talent. And Master Keighvin, he didn't have the knack, either, though he tried, I'll give him that. Milady, we built him a house; we've kept it cleanly and snug, hoping one such as you would chance this way. If you choose to stay, milady, the house and all he left are yours; keep the evil in the forest bound, and we'll provision you as we did him. Do aught else, and you'll be well repaid, in cash or kind."

The offer was far too tempting to resist. This was

just such an opportunity as I had longed for; and whatever it was that had killed Keighvin, I was certain I would be able to deal with it.

"Done," I said.

Perhaps I should have been more cautious; if any evil power had wanted to lay a trap for me, this was the perfect bait. Yet such was my weariness, my longing for a place to settle, that I threw all caution to the winds.

Headman Olam led me to a snug little cottage set apart from the rest of the clustered houses of the village. It was exactly the kind of dwelling I would have built for myself, far enough from the village to allow me to feel undisturbed, yet near enough that isolation would not become a burden. Three rooms below it had, and one above—and I knew without his telling me that the one above was the former wizard's room of power and knowledge. I could feel the residuum of magics worked there even from below. For the rest—a bedroom, a sitting room, a tiny kitchen, all showing the subtle carelessness of a bachelor. I probed about me carefully, paying closest attention to the area where the wizard had been found dead, and felt—nothing. Nothing at all. I stood quietly in the very center of the house, and still felt nothing. The house was empty. If Keighvin had been killed by something here, it was long gone. And I was certain *my* wardings would be proof against any second such intrusion.

I spent the remainder of that day cleaning out all traces of the former owner—although I somehow could not bring myself to destroy his possessions. Instead, I packed them away in three barrels brought me by the miller, and stored them up in the attic. My own few possessions were soon augmented by gifts, brought shyly by the village women—a bunch of bright autumn leaves and grasses in a homely pottery vase, a bright bit of weaving to grace a chest, an embroidered cloth for the table, another in a handmade frame to adorn the wall, some soft pillows to soften the wooden settle. I surmised that they would gladly have gifted their former mage with such things, but that his bachelor austerity seemed to forbid such presents.

More substantial giftings came over the course of the next three days from their spouses: firewood, smoked meat and fish, cheese and meal, ale and cider, root vegetables. In return I began my own work; curing first the headman's ailing liver, then the miller's cow that had a tumor of the womb, then casting half a dozen finding spells to recover lost objects.

By week's end the little things that had needed doing since their wizard had gone were all taken care of, and I had the greater work before me—to determine just what it was that he had kept in check. And, if I could, what had killed him.

I went out northwards into the forest; by night, for if I was going to confront evil, I wanted to know it at its full strength. There was a kind of path here, with a touch of magic about it; I surmised that he had made it, the Wizard Keighvin, and followed it.

Deeper and deeper into the inky shadows beneath the trees it led. There was a little breeze that murmured uneasily among the dying leaves, but there was no sign of animal or bird. At last it grew so dark that even my augmented sight could not avail me; I kindled a witchlight within the crystal on the end of my staff, and forged onward by the aid it gave me. The branches of the trees seemed to shrink away from the cold blue light. My own steps crunching through the fallen leaves seemed as loud as those of a careless giant. The sharp-sour scent of them told me that few, if any, had taken this path of late.

When I had penetrated nearly half a league, I began to feel eyes upon me—unfriendly eyes. And more, I detected that magic had been worked hereabouts, somewhere. Powerful magic, wizardly magic, akin to mine, but not precisely of the school I had been taught in. Soon enough thereafter I came upon the source of that magic.

It lay before me like a wall that only wizardly sight could reveal. It was a great circle-casting, fading now, but still powerful. Nothing material of evil birthing could have passed it; only wraiths and shades, and they would have found the passage difficult and painful. When Keighvin had been among the living, it must have been impossible even for them to cross. I found myself pausing to admire the work; it was truly set by the hand of a master, and I wished I could have known him. Such an orderly piece of work bespoke an orderly mind—and the strength of it implied a powerful sense of duty. Both are traits I find admirable, and more pleasing than a fair form or comely face.

Vague shapes lurked at the edge of the light cast by my staff; I could see only their eyes, and that not clearly. My mage-senses told me more than enough—the villagers feared them, with good sense. Whatever it was that spawned them, they hungered; some for flesh and blood, others for death and pain. And now beneath the casting placed by Keighvin, I could sense the faint traces of others, older and older—it was plain that one wizard had always guarded the people of the village from these creatures of the Dark, passing the task on to a successor. I guessed (truthfully, as I later found) that the Things had broken loose enough times that the villagers had come to value their wizards, and to fear to be without one.

I opened my shields to the casting, for to reinforce it I would have to take some of it into myself. No wizard's workings are the same as another's; were I to impose my powers alone upon that circle of protection I would surely break it. I must blend my own magics with it, as all the others had done before me.

I ignored the looming presence of those Others—they could not harm me, double armored as I was by the circle and my own shieldings. I tested the flavors of Keighvin's magic: crisp and cool, like a tart, frost-chilled apple. I felt the textures, smooth and sleek; saw the color, the blue of fine steel; knew the scent, like juniper and sage. And beneath it, the fading flavors and colors and scents of the others, cinnamon and willow and sunrise, ice and harpsong and roses, fire and lightning and velvet—

When I knew them, knew them all, I built upon them my own power. I reached into the core of myself, and wove a starsong melody, blending it with pinesmoke silk and crystal rainbow; knotting it all into a cord stronger than cold iron and more enduring than diamond; for those were the hallmarks of my own powers.

When I opened my eyes the circle glowed at my feet and reached breast-high, so brightly even the untaught could have seen it; glowed with the same blue as the witchlight of my staff.

I felt exhausted, utterly drained, yet elated. To test the efficacy of my weaving, I dropped my shielding, and waited to see what the creatures of the Dark trapped within it would do.

Seeing me unguarded was too much of a temptation for them. A half-dozen wraiths, thin, filmy arms outstretched and claws grasping, flung themselves at the barrier, wailing. For the first time I saw some of what the magic barrier had held at bay, and despite that I had been expecting something of the kind, I shuddered inwardly.

If you have never seen a wraith, they are hardly impressive. They seem to be mist-shadows, attenuated, sexless man-forms of spiderweb and fog, with great gaping mouths and hollow eyes. If you know what they can do, however, you will fear them. They can tear the heart from the body with those flimsy-seeming claws, and devour it with that toothless mouth. When you know that—when you have *seen* that, as I have—you know them for the horrible creatures that they are, and know that they present a greater danger than many birthings of the Dark of a more solid form.

They struck the barrier, and rebounded, and fled back into the darkness beyond my witchlight.

I laughed in my pride, and left them.

But that night something began—

It was little more at first than a simple, vague dream, insubstantial as smoke, hardly more in the dawn than a distant recollection of something pleasant. But the next night, the dream was stronger, clearer, and more compelling. I am no virgin, I have known the loving touch of a man, but it was long, two years and more, since I had shared such pleasures, and until now I had thought I did not miss them.

But the dreams, as they became stronger, drew me more and more, until one night they were as full of reality and solidity as my daylit world.

I dreamed of a lover, gentle, considerate, a lover who took as much care for my pleasure as for his own. And we joined, not once, but many times, body to body, and soul to soul, as I had never joined with any other.

I woke late, with sun warming the foot of the bed. I was tired, but I had been working late into the night, constructing a set-spell to keep vermin from the village granary. But—I was also curiously sated, as if the dream-loving had been real.

I rose and stretched lazily, and dressed. I entered my tiny kitchen to break my fast.

Beside the plate I had laid ready the night before lay a single fresh blossom of spring beauty.

This was autumn.

Still, I rationalized after my first surprise, many of the villagers had forcing frames. Some kind soul, or admiring child, perhaps, had left it there.

Thus even the wisest can delude themselves when they do not wish to face the truth.

I walked through the next two weeks in a waking dream—by day, doing my duty to the now-contented villagers. *They* were well pleased, for now not even the faintest hint of the creatures of the Dark reached to the lands they called their own. Their needs (those that I could tend to) were few, and simple, and quickly disposed of. In my free time, I studied in Keighvin's library. He had owned a treasure trove of wizardly lore, a cache of some three or four dozen books. Some I was familiar with, but some were entirely new.

I studied also those notes he had made on the nature of the "haunted forest." It seemed to him that there was a heart to the evil, a spawning ground, where the normal was taken in and perverted to evil. He referred often to the "heart of darkness," and reading between the lines, I surmised that he intended to confront this "heart," and attempt to defeat it. A worthy intention—if he could remain untouched by it. *If*—that was the operable word. Something so powerful might well corrupt all it touched, a mage included.

By night I dreamed those erotic dreams, in which

I was possessed by my lover and possessed him in turn. Each night they were clearer; each night the murmuring of my lover came closer to understandable words. Each morning I woke a little later. And yet— and yet, I recovered quickly, nor was the heart of my magic touched in any way.

And each morning, there was another fresh blossom by my plate—now, invariably, a red rose, symbolic of desire.

It seemed to me that the autumnal light did strange things within this little house, for as I moved about it I was followed by a shadow, not *quite* a double of my own. And never could I see it when I looked straightly at it—only from the corner of my eye. It danced attendance on me from the moment I crossed the threshold to the moment I left.

I really don't know why it took me so long to realize the danger I was in. Perhaps—if I had been a man, this never could have happened. I was so lonely, and had denied my loneliness so long that I was, I suppose, doubly vulnerable. Nor, had I been less of a mage, could I have been so ensorceled, for a lesser mage would not have been able to merge with Keighvin's magic as I had been able to do.

For whatever reason there was, for whatever weakness lay in me, I had woken something in that place with my presence.

I ventured at last a second time into that haunted wood—this time by daylight, for I meant to cross the boundary.

I found the "heart of darkness" indeed, just as Keighvin had written of it.

It was a grove in the center of the haunted circle, a grove in which the noon sun did not even penetrate the unleaving branches of the trees. I did not venture into it, for there was a deadly cold about that place, and I took warning by it. I sensed something buried beneath the font of an ancient willow; something older than *my* art, something that hated with a passion like knives of ice. Something so utterly evil that my very soul was shaken to the roots.

Not death—that was not what it longed for—corruption, perversion of all that lived and grew was the goal it sought. It was bound—but only half-bound. The magics that held it were incomplete. And they were Keighvin's; I could sense this beyond doubting.

He had come here, then, but had left his work unfinished. Why? What had disturbed him? Had he fallen ill, or worse than ill? The orderly man I intuited from his work and writings would not so have left something incomplete, unless—

Unless he had no choice.

And I dared not try to complete it, not without knowing exactly what he had done, else I would loose what he had sought to bind.

But to leave it half-bound—that was dangerous, too. If this thing should break the half-bonds, and absorb them into itself, it would be powerful enough to pass the boundary of the circle so many had cast.

I left that place more awake than I had been since I came to my village, and returned, sobered and not a little frightened, to the home I had come to call my own. I sat, my thoughts chasing themselves around in circles, until the last light died and I lit a candle, placing it on the table in the sitting room. As I did so, I glanced at the night-darkened glass of the window, looking not at the landscape beyond, but at the reflection.

And it was only then, only when I saw the shadow standing behind me in that reflection and recognized him for my dream lover, that I truly woke to what had been happening to me in my own home.

How, why, I did not know, but I knew this—the shadow that courted me, the lover of my drams, and the wizard Keighvin were one and the same. He was still earthbound—tied to me, feeding on me. A benign, harmless relationship—now. But unless I acted, and acted quickly, I could easily find myself being drained by the ghostly lovemaking. With every dream-tryst, he was growing stronger, and had been for some time. For the moment the relationship was harmless—but there was no guarantee that it would remain so. I stood in mortal danger of becoming exhausted, until I became another such wraith. Like Keighvin, unliving, yet undying.

I dropped the candlestick I was holding, and the chimney shattered at my feet.

Heedless of the shards of glass I trod upon, I ran for the stairs and the library. I knew I must act, and act quickly, while I still had the resolution to do so.

I remembered one book, a huge, hand-lettered tome, that held the spell I needed. I pulled it down from its place on the shelf, coughing a little from the dust that I disturbed, and set it on the table, flipping hurriedly through the pages to find the one spell I needed.

I found it three-quarters of the way through the book; not a spell of exorcism, but a different sort of spell. A spell to open the door between this world and the next so that an earthbound spirit would be drawn through it and into its proper sphere. It was a most dangerous spell, risking both body and soul of the caster. The danger to the body lay in that the caster must leave it to open the door, and that it would cause a deadly draining of physical energy. The danger to the soul lay in that the spell left it vulnerable and unshielded, and the temptation of that doorway would be very great.

Yet—I could not drive my gentle lover away by brutal exorcism; no, I could not be so cruel to him who had only been (thus far) kind. This was the only spell I could choose—

And then, in the draftless room, an unseen hand turned the page of the great book.

I thought it was the same spell at first. Then I saw that it differed by one single word, a few strokes of a pen. That first spell I knew, but this—this was another totally unknown. And its purpose was—

Was to let the mage-born, if they had died before their appointed time, take flesh and live again.

Both spells were equal in danger to body and soul. The second, in point of fact, placed a tolerable amount of danger on the spirit involved, for if he was judged and found wanting, it meant utter dissolution. Nowhere was it written that either spell was of Dark path, or Light; they were utterly neutral.

Both required they be cast this night of all nights; Hallowmas, the perilous, when Light magic and Dark are in equal balance, and either result is likely from any spell made—and most particularly when, as now, Hallowmas falls under a waning moon.

This is risking the anger of the gods, to take upon oneself the restoring of the dead—yet what and who am I to judge who is fit to live or die?

Since that day, one week ago, he has not come to me by night; does he judge that I would repudiate him (do I have the strength?) or is he letting me make my decision unsullied by his attentions?

What of the "heart of darkness?" Did he try to bind it, and become corrupted by it? Why did he leave the task half done? Did it murder him, to keep him from destroying it? Is this why he begs life anew? Duty? To see the task through to its end?

Or—does he love me, as he seemed to? Is it me

that calls to him? Never have I melded so with another's magics as I did with his—never has my soul or body responded so to another's touch.

Or does he seek to use me, corrupted by that foul thing that lay beneath the willow's roots? Will he use me, and then destroy me and set that evil free?

Could I trust his answer if I were to attempt to ask him why?

I have sought for an answer, and found none, but in heaven nor hell nor all the lore that wizard-kind knows. No gods have made their will manifest to me, not even at this final hour, as my hands go through motions that I have rehearsed so often that I could perform them sleeping or near-dead.

I stand within my circles now; my preparations all are made. I can see him, a shadow among the shadows, standing just outside the boundaries I have made. I can almost make out his face. I cannot tell what expression he wears. The hour of midnight is drawing closer, and I have begun my chants. In a few more minutes, I will speak that single word—

And I cannot at this moment answer if it will be "come" or "go."

Harvest of Souls

DORANNA DURGIN

"Kenlan died a year ago," the woman told Dyanara. "And things've gone from bad to worse."

Dyanara looked into the stone-lined well; a sulfurous odor wafted up to sting her nose. She stepped back from the wooden housing of the well, her booted feet sinking into ground softened by spilled water. The local wizard should have taken care of this long ago, along with some of the unhealthy crops she'd seen as she walked into the community of Churtna.

That is, if he hadn't been killed, and somehow gone unreplaced.

The woman—her name was Parrie—squeezed one hand with the other, quietly anxious. "We'll pay you the best we can. I . . . I just don't know how much longer we can drink this water. The new well Tavis dug out back gave us just the same, only less of it." Her light brown hair was graying, her face browned and wrinkled by the sun, and her expression tight.

And no wonder. The house garden was stunted and browning, in this late spring when it should have been growing its fastest. The cow was ribby, the chickens had pecked at each other until fully half of them were bald, and the hayfield boasted sparse and stingy grass that would never be ready for first harvest. The entire homestead looked blighted, down to the thatched little cottage that served as home for this family.

The oldest was a youth almost ready to be out on his own; there were a handful of boys and girls in between, and then the youngest, a girl who looked to be ten or eleven and brightly interested in the arrival of a wizard. A woman wizard, with well-worn trews just this side of patching, and a loose, long tunic with the symbols of her House of Magic embroidered on cuffs and around the neckline. At thirty-four, Dyanara was hitting the strength of her powers, and the strength of her body had not yet started to wane; she was, if neither willowy and graceful nor plump and well-endowed, at least hardened by her travels into something of clean lines and self-assured movement. She looked down at the girl. Dyanara wondered if she, too, would have had such a family, had she chosen other than a wanderer's path.

"I will cleanse the well," Dyanara said, "but I do not work for nothing." Parrie's already tight lips thinned even further; she wrapped her arms around herself and waited for the bad news. They were strong arms, showing signs of hard work—a bruise here, a scratch there, an old thin scar that went from wrist to elbow. "If your wizard died last year," Dyanara added, "there will be others in need here. I must have someone to guide me to them." She looked at the girl. "My fee will be the services of your youngest."

"Jacoba? You want ..." Parrie trailed off, dropped her hand to the child's shoulder. Jacoba's hopeful face looked up at her with *please* shining through.

"Do you agree?" Dyanara asked, putting a little starch into her voice.

"Why, yes," the woman said, sounding a little bewildered. "Of course you may have Jacoba as guide while you bide here." Relief slowly relaxed her features.

Dyanara nodded briskly, and turned to Stumble, her pack donkey and travel companion. Purification of foul water ... she'd have to try to follow the water to the source and take care of the problem there, or she'd be back here again before summer was over.

Stumble's pack yielded a few fragrant herbs and a crystal Dyanara used to trigger the state of deep concentration she'd need. She gave the herbs to one of the middle children, a daughter who'd been watching from behind Stumble. "Tea," she said sternly. "Hold it for me."

Dyanara pulled a bucket of water and carefully soaked the well rope with it; she tossed the bucket back down into the well. Parrie and the girls watched, saying nothing.

Then Dyanara turned away from them, turned away from the noises of the little homestead, the call of one child to another, the mutterings of the chickens. Kneeling at the wooden well cover, grasping the sodden rope with one hand and the quartz in the other, she turned inward. Bonding with the water in the rope, she followed it to the pool of water that held the bucket. With the acrid tang of sulphur permeating her senses, she traced the water back as it seeped between rock layers, now a slow trickle, now a sudden free rush through open space. The smell/touch/taste of sulphur thickened, coating the inside of her mouth, stinging her eyes. There. A space that had been open, a little arch of rock above the water—now crumbled and fallen, a cave-in of nearly pure sulphur.

Dyanara held steady in the flow of the water, considering the choking rock. Then she turned to a new chant, and neatly, with no more energy than the task required, she *moved* the rock aside and anchored it in place, shielding it. Gently, she let herself be swept back in the current of the water, sending out tendrils of clarifying energy that expanded and grew until they and Dyanara arrived back in the well, in clean, sweet water.

She took a direct hop back to her body and opened her eyes to see the pink flare of light fading in her crystal. Setting it atop the well housing, she stood, brusquely brushing off knees grown damp from kneeling in front of the well. "There," she said. "That should do it." She wished she could as easily fix all the homestead's ills, but Parrie was delighted.

"Look, Jacoba, Sissy—we've got *water*!" She bent over the well and inhaled deeply. "It even *smells* good!"

"Draw some of it," Dyanara said. "We'll use it for that tea." The last of her tea, but a fair trade for the company, after the lonely days of the road. Parrie gladly bent to follow Dyanara's suggestion, her whole body shouting of her elation.

Dyanara looked past the well and into the stunted fields beyond. Something else needed fixing here. She felt its touch—and felt it flicker out of reach, beyond her ability to follow, or even to name, leaving only a lingering taste of decay in her mind.

Dyanara stood in the middle of the cart path with Jacoba beside her and Stumble browsing the roadside behind her. Before her was a man who was taking her entirely too much for granted, somehow assuming she'd leap at the chance to give up the patterns of her wandering life.

"You don't even know me," Dyanara said pointedly. She, Stumble and Jacoba were on their way to one of Jacoba's neighbors. She wasn't overly pleased to meet someone who wanted to sidetrack her. "Or I, you." He said his name was Balbas. He said he was Churtna's mayor. And he said he wanted her to stay.

"The wizard Kenlan . . ." said Balbas, and hesitated, apparently realizing he'd taken the wrong approach with his confidence. He was tall and brawny and in his strength, with furred arms and ginger chest hair poking out the top of his shirt. But signs of long-term strain grouped in frown lines between his brows, and Dyanara wondered if his forwardness merely spoke of how much he had to lose.

"Kenlan is dead," she said, and her tone gentled somewhat. "This, I know. What I don't know is how, or why." She flipped her long braid, brown with glints of sun-bronzed highlights, off her shoulder and down her back, and made a conscious effort to remove the stern traces from a face that took them on all too easily. Long straight nose, lean cheeks, a long jaw saved from plainness by the fine curve of her chin . . . all she had to do was lower her brow a touch and her expression went straight to imposing. Sometimes that was hard to remember.

"None of us know just how Kenlan died," Balbas said. His mouth tightened into a grim expression, and then, through obvious effort, relaxed again. "All we know is that it was magic, and he's dead, and we've had a hard year because of it. You, Mistress, will probably learn more than that, simply by examining his home. A home, I might add, which can easily be yours. A library that was Kenlan's pride, a good deep well, and a large number of customers who are not above begging if it means you will stay, if only through the winter."

Winter under shelter of her own. That *did* sound like a nice change. "I have a job to do now," she told him. "If you come with us, afterward you may show me this house."

Balbas was pleased to accompany them to Sennalee's house, where Dyanara put a simple charm on the family's new plow. The work was quickly done, and the walk to Kenlan's house only a few miles.

The house greeted her almost as though it were alive, with an odd air of eagerness, a forlorn sigh of cobweb. A small gray cat crept out from a cranny in the woodpile and met her before the door, tail held high and aquiver with pleasure. Dyanara scooped the creature up without thought, letting it settle against her chest. It purred, its eyes half closed, giving her the occasional loving nudge-rub with its chin.

Balbas eyed her askance, and she looked back at him, brow raised, eyes demanding.

"No one's been able to get near that wild thing since Kenlan died," he told her, and opened the door of the house for her. He, she saw, obviously intended to stay outside with Jacoba and Stumble. No matter. He felt only that the house was different, while she knew it was safe.

When Dyanara stepped through the threshold, the house folded itself around her with the air of a long-lost friend. Though the dried remains of Kenlan's last meal still sat at the hearth, and the braided wool rugs were moth-eaten and musty, Dyanara's first impression was of welcoming warmth; she would have sworn the air held the scent of spicy tea instead of mildew.

But she blinked, and focused herself, and thus *saw*. It would take days to clean this house. Its roof was in dire need of repair, the rugs and bedding were ruined, and she wasn't sure the chimney was safe to use.

But it wanted her. And it made her think wistfully of her fifteen years on the road, and all the *likes* in her life that could have turned into *loves* if she'd given them half a chance, and the fact that if she'd allowed it, she could have had her own daughter's eyes watching her through the open doorway instead of Jacoba's.

She'd always been independent; fiercely so. It had

served her well as she traveled from town to town,
picking up bits of wizardly lore that her House had
not provided, curing ills and warding homesteads
against the kind of malaise that had somehow perme-
ated every home in this area. And while fierce inde-
pendence had protected her from the normal
heartaches of life, she wondered about all the things
she'd missed as a result, and if it had been a price
too high.

Dyanara snorted, startling the cat against her
breast. She looked down at it and murmured, "Never
mind. I'll stay, but it's not because of the glamour
you"—meaning the cat, the house, and whatever else
might have had a part—"tried to work on me. It's
because . . . maybe it's time." Gently, she set the cat
on the floor, and then turned to face Balbas through
the door. "I'll stay," she told him, matter-of-factly.

The relief that lit his face reminded her that
Churtna was in trouble, and that Kenlan's death was
still a mystery—and that she had just agreed to step
into the middle of it.

Dyanara opened the house to the summer breezes
and tossed the molded, useless bedding out for the
birds to pick apart. She swept out the corners, bar-
tered repair for the chimney, and sent Jacoba around
to inform the village inhabitants that they could find
her here.

What had killed him, and left this house for her?
Such an odd little house, one the bright Jacoba
entered unwillingly and only momentarily, where
Dyanara found herself turning around, mouth open
to speak to someone she was certain was there. Where
the evening shadows sometimes held peculiar shapes,
and where the brush of a breeze against her arm felt
so much like the transient touch of a gentle hand.

She supposed she should be concerned; instead she felt flattered, even . . . courted. She enjoyed the rare quiet moments of her evenings, when she took the small gray cat into her arms, sitting in her mended rocking chair by the door and the fresh air. The cat sat quietly, kneading Dyanara's lap gently with her paws—except for those moments when she suddenly lifted her head, gave a small *mrrp* of greeting, and followed something—nothing that Dyanara could see—with her big green eyes. And then would come that touch, a breeze to ruffle the fine hairs of her arm.

The villagers, so long bereft of their wizard, had many needs. She gathered quickly enough that while Kenlan had been a good man, a trusted ally in the daily struggle for survival, his interests had been weighted toward study and innovation. Her own ability to sift her mind's store of practical spells and come up with the right chant for cleansing a crop of black blight or repelling a certain grub won her the instant respect of her customers.

And yet, while bartering slowly stocked her pantry, filled her woodpile, mended her roof and plowed her late garden, Dyanara realized she was not making enough of a difference. How had things gone bad so fast?

A summer morning found Dyanara crouched by the fireplace, patiently waiting for the water to boil her breakfast eggs, picking at a threadbare spot on her knee and knowing she must barter for clothing next. The steeping tea filled the cottage with beckoning spice, and the air was thick and already hot with the promise of the day. Dyanara thought she would cool the tea before she actually drank it. Practical thoughts, all of them. She ran from one to the other, trying to avoid the dream she'd woken from.

The dream—and the man in her dream. Kenlan?

He was sandy-haired and several years younger than she, with suppressed excitement in his sharp-edged blue eyes—excitement mingled with something sterner, something that spoke of the knowledge of dark things. And then, fading around the edges and clear reluctance on his face, he'd left. He'd walked by her, brushing against her arm in an intimate way. A familiar touch, as gentle as a breeze.

As gentle as a breeze.

But no memory of a breeze had ever raised such goosebumps on her arms. Dyanara briskly rubbed those arms, and spooned her eggs from the water, knowing they'd still be too soft for her liking but needing to *do* it, to move away from her thoughts. She went to the table, bowl in hand—and there she froze. She almost dropped the bowl.

There was a blossom on her plate. Fresh white petals edged with scarlet, a mist of dew still lining the inner throat of the bell-shaped blossom . . . it sat there, a fragrant and flagrant impossibility. A spring offering in high summer. A lover's token.

She touched it. She gently scooped it up in her free hand and brought it close to her face, breathing its scent. And she finally admitted she was not alone in this house.

Jacoba stood in the doorway. "Sennalee's corn's got silk rot," she announced. They came to Jacoba, now, and let Jacoba take the news to Dyanara. Dyanara would have taught the girl herb lore anyway—it was nice to have help in the gathering—but it was clear that the girl liked to earn her way.

But not today. Dyanara said as much, sitting at the table with a stack of Kenlan's books in front of her. "Today, I'm trying to figure out what killed Kenlan."

"Magic he couldn't control, says Balbas," Jacoba

offered. She lingered in the doorway, only one small bare foot venturing over the threshold to toe at the board floor before retreating again.

"Does he?" Dyanara said, saving her place in the book with a finger. "Not to me, he doesn't."

"He's afraid of you," the girl said simply.

Dyanara hid her smile and instead raised an eyebrow.

"He *is*. Ever since the cat liked you. And the house, too." She hesitated, then added, "Lammas Night is tomorrow. It'd be a hurtin' bad sign if Sennalee had to start the celebration with silk rot."

Lammas, the month of ripening. Lammas Night, the dedication to renewal of life and earth. No, Sennalee would not be happy to start the celebration of harvest and life with her corn sickening. "Then we'll have to make sure Sennalee's corn is all right before then," Dyanara said. "But this morning, I'm working on something else."

Jacoba gave her an uncertain look, unused to such delay. "Go," Dyanara said gently. "I'll take care of the corn."

She bent her head back to the book. Another moment's pause, and she heard the careless slap of Jacoba's feet as the girl ran down the path. *Sennalee's corn*, she told herself, and went back to her reading.

Though the rest of the cottage might have fallen to ruin around them, the books rested untouched on sturdy shelves against the back wall. Spelled against damage from fire, damp, and creature, the books almost hummed to themselves as they waited to be read. Kenlan's neat, tiny script filled the book margins, detailing his thoughts about the theories and spells within.

Dyanara chose volumes at random, skimming, hoping to trip or stumble over something that didn't seem quite right. Something that he shouldn't have been fooling with—and something that might tie into the community's miserable growing season. Something dated from last summer. . . .

In early afternoon, she paused for tea and cornbread, and to return her first stack of books to the shelves in exchange for her second. In the middle of a deep yawn and well-deserved stretch, she smelled a hint of a newly familiar fragrance. A spring fragrance, bringing immediately to mind a belled, scarlet-fringed blossom, and coming to her on an intimate breeze.

Dyanara dropped out of her stretch, her gaze darting around the cottage. Nothing. She gave the bookshelves a critical eye, and then she saw it. Another blossomed token, sitting atop the spine of one of the thickest books, waiting for her. Dyanara hesitated, and scooped it up with a gentle hand.

The flower turned to mist and fading scarlet; the scent lingered. She looked at her hand, looked at the book again. "I can take a hint," she said aloud, and pulled the book from the shelf.

"Mrrp," said the little gray cat, winding between her legs. Dyanara stepped over it and put the book on the table, opening it to thick pages. The calligraphy was ornate but exacting and easy to read, and when she came to the spell for banishment, she recognized it immediately. No wonder Kenlan was getting pushy; it was a spell for Lammas Night—for releasing souls to the heavens. Souls like Kenlan's, as benign as it seemed to be, that haunted this cottage.

But meddling in souls was no wizard's business.

She stared at the page, thinking about that school-bred injunction. A breeze brushed against her, a suspiciously convenient breeze, and it flipped the thick page over. The next spell was identical to the first but for a single word, which immediately caught Dyanara's eye.

Meant for the mage-born, this spell would not free
Kenlan's soul, but would instead bind him to the earth
again. Give him flesh, and bring him back to Churtna.
To . . . Dyanara. She thought again of her dream, and
the look in his eyes as he'd touched her arm. *Please,* the
breeze whispered, playing with the loose tendrils of her
braided hair.

Dyanara's hand was shaking as she abruptly closed
the book on both forbidden spells. "Meddling in souls
is no wizard's business!" she said, out loud this time,
and loudly as well.

But could she leave him stranded, forever tied to
this cottage and the little gray cat who loved him?
Had he done anything to deserve that, which she
would not have wished on her most evil foe? And . . .
she was a practitioner, quick and efficient. *He* was
the scholar, the seeker. Alive, could he help her heal
this place?

She couldn't know. The real question was, did she
dare to find out? Dyanara looked from her shaking
hand to the thick book of spells. No. She didn't have
time for this. Tomorrow was Lammas Night, and Sennalee's corn was ailing. Dyanara swept out of the cottage, snatching up her pack on the way. She didn't
turn around to eye the piteously mewing cat, or
respond to the beseeching breeze that slipped through
the thick, still air of summer, renewing her goosebumps. As she stalked away from the cottage, the
breeze faded, leaving her with nothing but her
thoughts.

And those thoughts, unfortunately, kept those
goosebumps right where they were.

"Kenlan?" said Sennalee, while Dyanara prepared
to deal with her corn. "He was always a little distracted, but he was a good man."

"Kenlan?" Balbas said, looking up from the wax tablet he was laboring over, surprised to see Dyanara in town. "Had his mind on something the last month or so he was alive. Seemed worried. But yes, I trusted him. He was a good man."

"Kenlan?" Jacoba's mother prodded a hen away from the side of her house and retrieved the egg the noisy bird had been sitting on. "Why, I liked him well enough, what I knew of him. He was always kind to Jacoba. He asked an awful lot of questions about the season's crops right before we lost him, now that I think about it." She sighed. "The best any of us could figure—the way we found him inside that circle on the hill—he was fussing with magic that was too big for him. That was a sorrowful thing, his death. He was—"

"A good man," Dyanara finished for her. "Do you think . . . Jacoba could show me that hill?"

The bright moon disappeared behind another clump of fast-moving clouds, taking light from what had been a bright night; in another moment, it was back, flirting, washing the hillside with silver light—and then not.

The wind lifted Dyanara's loose hair and sent the ends dancing into tangles, pulling against the circlet at her brow. She had exchanged her trousers for a long, loose dress of gauzy linen, belted at her waist with woven hempweed. Spellcasting clothes, as dictated by her need to formalize any casting so serious as this one. The dress skirt snapped and belled with the wind, but the rustle of the material was lost in the sound of the trees—creaking as they bent, leaves flipping and hissing against one another, fluttering to the ground when they lost their grip on parent wood.

I should be with the village. They need their wizard

on Lammas Night of all nights. But she wasn't. She was here, and she was still facing her decision. Send him on his way, or. . . Or trust him. Bring him back. Find out if his sweet touch on her arm felt as good in person. Find out if his sharp blue eyes looked at her the same way they had in her dream. If he could, at least, help her.

Dyanara closed her eyes tightly, and turned into the wind, letting it tug the hair away from her face, feeling it streaming back behind her. She'd spent too many lonely years on the road to be making this sort of decision—and to be making it wisely. Were the tokens, the gentleness—the look on his face—all a ruse?

She took a deep breath. She didn't have to decide now. She'd be in contact with him, she'd *know* him by it, before she finished the spell. She just had to be strong enough to make the right decision when the time came.

She'd made her circle of rocks, the only thing that wouldn't blow away in this fitful wind. The book of spells rested by her feet, but she wouldn't need it—she knew the spell by heart. Both versions. She raised her arms above her head, standing tall and straight, feeling the power gathering at her very intent, letting it wash up from the ground at her feet through her body to spill out to the heavens. *Don't let me down, Kenlan,* she thought, half prayer, half warning—and began. Chanting softly under her breath, the words a mere touch of her breath against her lips, she drew Kenlan's earthbound spirit to the circle.

Prepared to tame the power itself, she was taken by surprise at the pull of Kenlan's spirit on her own. His gratitude at her effort, his admiration of her skill, his . . . his *love.*

She struggled to pull away from him. Love, for someone he didn't even know?

*But I do know you. I know you well. I've been with
you all summer.*

"But I don't know you!" she cried.

Then learn of me now.

Bring him back, then? He wanted to come back,
to break those wizardly rules and walk twice upon
this earth? Her chanting lips faltered, wavering with
her decision.

*No! Not yet! I need your help. Churtna needs
your help!*

She blinked against the wind, not seeing hair that
whipped into her eyes, nor feeling it snatch at her
clothes. Did he know, then? Did he have answers?

Meddling with souls is no wizard's business. He
whispered her own words back to her. *The price is
high when you blunder—and someone did.* And in a
quick fold of time, he showed her the night he'd died.
Standing on this hill, enclosed in his own circle, lost
in his own spell. She followed his loosed spirit as it
traced the faint path of evil showing in the spirit
shadow of the earth, marveling at his skill. As though
a hunter after game, he spotted each slight sign and
leapt upon it, knowing it would lead him to whatever
was threatening Churtna.

She was with him when he found it, a solid core of
hunger, dark and unfathomable in its need, blackness
seething to a rhythm of its own.

And you tried to stop it, she thought. But she knew
right away he wasn't strong enough to do it alone.
And she knew he knew—and that he had to try, for
on this Lammas Night, it reached to steal the power
and lifefood that the villagers dedicated back to the
earth. An illicit harvester, snatching their next year's
bounty.

So he tried. And . . . he died.

But he hadn't gone.

How could I go, and leave my village undefended?
He was silent a moment, as his warmth coalesced
around her like a lover's embrace. *We can stop that
sinkhole, that harvester of life. Now. Together.*

She staggered then, in body and soul, her upheld
arms jerking against the fear of knowing he was right,
her unseeing eyes going wide in the sudden wash of
moonlight. He *was* right. Nothing she did for this
village would help them in the end, not as long as
that harvester was still sucking away their lives. And
next year would be worse than this last, and the year
after that . . .

Dyanara, he whispered, his voice soft against her ears,
tracing a shiver down the back of her neck. *I know you,
Dyanara. I've watched you. You can do this thing—we
can do this thing. An end to the harvester . . .*

Yes, she thought, and reached up to take his hand,
leaving her body behind, just as she had left it when
she'd cleared Jacoba's well of taint.

This time Kenlan knew where the harvester hid.
He held her to him, guiding her, easily finding the
dark presence, and then holding them both back to
circle it warily.

Weave a shield, she thought, remembering the well
again, and the sulphur fall she'd closed off.

Ahh, he thought, brushing up against her presence
with a mental kiss. *You always have those spells so
close at hand.* Do it, he meant, and the silent pause
that followed meant they both knew it wouldn't be
easy—wouldn't be anything like shutting off spirit-
less rock.

Do it, she told herself, and began to shape the spell
with him.

And the harvester reared up, stronger than she'd
imagined, a parasite with a year of nourishment in its
belly. Like a great mobile splash of ink against a

psychic sky, it reached for them. It lashed out, gouts of power capable of obliterating anything so frail as a human spirit. Kenlan shielded Dyanara while she tied down the frame of her barrier, then added his strength to hers while she built it—built it and rebuilt it, while the harvester destroyed what they created, hissing and spitting like an angry cat.

Buffeted, unused to resistance, Dyanara tired. Kenlan, wearied by a year's vigil, seemed to fade from her side. Ever hungry, the harvester reached for them, tendrils of darkness drawn by their souls.

Dyanara! Kenlan cried, echoing resolve despite his waning presence. *We must finish this.*

"I won't have the strength to bring you back," she whispered out loud. Not without risking another blunder, another harvester.

We must *finish this.*

Dyanara thought of Jacoba's bright eyes and quick feet, and saw those eyes dulled, those feet stilled. She reached back to her own body, and she took from it—she *stole* from it—and she found the strength she needed. Shored by Kenlan, she threw up the walls of the shield, a quick latticework of energy that expanded and spread until it was whole. Until the harvester, trapped behind walls made of her life essence, was left to consume itself in an inevitable frenzy of hunger. Until her body, wrung dry, collapsed within its circle, empty of everything but the slender thread that still tied it to Dyanara.

She reached for Kenlan, and knew that there'd been as much gain as sacrifice. Then, too tired to do anything else, Dyanara whispered a few final words to free them both.

"Mrrp?" A quiet feline question came clearly in the still night air. The trees were quiet, and the moon

shone unobscured upon the hill, silvering the gray fur of the small cat. Its feet flashed in rapid movement as it trotted up the slope to the circle of stones, and the lifeless woman that lay there. Her long traveler's legs were quiet beneath the thin fabric of her dress, and her face, full of strong lines and practicality, was softened by the hint of a smile.

Dyanara, no longer traveling.

The cat reached her and stopped, every muscle stilled but for the twitch at the tip of its tail, and the quick movement of its eyes as they followed the flutter of the ethereal, scarlet-edged bellflowers settling to the ground around Dyanara. Tokens.

Dyanara, no longer alone.

The Heart of the Grove

ARDATH MAYHAR

I hear strange echoes as each word falls from my lips, and outside the house the wind is rising, beating the branches of the shrubbery against the walls. Almost, the sound distracts me, as if some force from that haunted wood is trying to keep me from my task.

Before me lie the elements needed to form a new body for this lost spirit: earth and water, flame and wood. The bowl of soil stirs uneasily as if a breeze riffles its surface. The water quivers deep in its transparent jar. The blaze leaps at the candle-tip as if that wind outside reaches even here to stir it. Only the wood is motionless, as I go forward with the chanting, the ritual motions, the deed that may mean my own doom.

As I near the utterance of that final word, my lips slow as if dreading to give it voice. Does anyone know—can any being judge the cleanliness of its own spirit? Am I worthy or will I be cast as dust upon that fitful wind?

But there was no turning back, for taking no action at all was now as dangerous as the completion of my task. My voice rose, as if in defiance, as I said that final, irrevocable Word.

Reflected in the warped mirror before me were the

flame of my candle, my pale face, and the table laden
with elements intended to form a house for the spirit
I hoped to restore. Between my face and the mirror
hovered a shadow that seemed to waver between visibility and disappearance. Keighvin? It must be!

The Word hung between us for an endless moment,
and it seemed even to still the wind and the whisper
of leafless shrubs against the walls. The shadow was
pulled toward me by some force I did not understand;
the elements in their containers stirred and began
rising in little spirals, as the flame of the candle went
out, leaving me in darkness.

I could hear movement, sighs and groans and
sloshings and crackles, but I was searching for my
staff and the witch-light by which I could see what
was happening. When the blue light flared into being,
I stared, stunned—appalled by the thing on the other
side of the table.

The shape was comely. My gaze met that of the
wizard for an instant, and in his I saw gratitude—and
despair. "Save yourself!" came his cry, as some other
spirit quelled his and looked out at me from those
eyes. ·

A darkness, a hatred, a coldness like no other ever
met in all my wanderings stared out at me, and I
knew that Keighvin had been compelled to quench
his own life in order to subdue the evil that had overtaken him among his labors. Yet the wizard was still
there, drowned but still struggling in that overwhelming spirit which had conquered him at last.

I straightened, holding that commanding gaze with
my own. I had proven my own soul to be strong
enough, clean enough to meddle with the stuff of
life. Surely the gods were guiding me, shaping me all
through the years of my travels and my studies.

I would not submit to the heart of darkness or allow

the warm and loving person Keighvin had been to be imprisoned and used by this monster. The body that my spell had formed would dissolve if the spirit was removed from it, and that lay within my power.

The lips, red-brown as the soil that colored them, widened into a smile, as if this not-Keighvin thought me enspelled by its beauty. The eyes sparked with life that grew with each passing moment. There was no time to tarry; I must act instantly.

I smiled in turn, moving around the table with my arms open to embrace him. The other stood, waiting confidently as I approached, the witch-light still burning from the staff in my hand.

Was I strong enough? Brave enough? Dedicated enough to accomplish this lonely and all but impossible task?

Remembering those nights when Keighvin had visited my dreams, I felt a vast emptiness. I thought of the villagers, apt to suffer if I failed now. Without hesitation, I put my arm about the newly-risen wizard and raised my lips to his.

It was an old art, known from the earliest of times: I sucked the spirit from that false body as the first Dark witches had drawn the souls from their unwitting victims. Yet because I intended only good to come of this, I received that essence into myself and felt the anguished amazement of that cold Other as he found himself trapped once again, inside my iron spirit.

The light in the crystal dimmed as the dissolving body flung the whole of its strength against me, trying to fight free. The cold spirit drained into me, and I set my wards and the guardian spells to confine him. But I expected that, and provision had been made.

Clinging to the table, leaning on the staff, I bent to the fury unleashed inside me, as it surged and burned and struggled. At last it quieted, leaving me drained and exhausted.

A cup of wine restored something of my energy, and I turned to the stair and sought my bed. This was the most terrible task I had undertaken in all my life as an Adept, and it had almost been the end of me.

As I pulled the embroidered cover, a gift from the headman's wife, about my ears, I had a moment of intense sadness. The tender dream that had warmed my nights ... what a loss to one as lonely as I!

And then I felt a thrill of recognition within my inner self. Keighvin was there: he would not company me in flesh as I had hoped, but in essence.

A voice whispered inside me, "Well done, milady. Do not grieve, for now I am with you totally, and together we will hold that dark well of hatred in thrall, locked behind the gate of your will and my guarding."

Warmth flooded through me, and I crossed my arms over my breast, hugging myself tightly. Never again would I be alone as I went about my duties to the village; I would carry with me the potencies of two wizards, allied and yet differing in capacity. The nights would not be cold and solitary, for his spirit lived with mine, housed in my own flesh as together we held captive the hating thing we had trapped.

Tomorrow I would go back into that haunted wood and feel through it for the leering presences I had known before. The heart of darkness must now be drained of energy, and surely we could ring it with power, confining any remaining potency within that grove.

My task is done. And my work is just beginning.

Miranda

RU EMERSON

Miranda drew a deep breath—her first in hours, it seemed. Her feet ached; her legs wanted to tremble. *No,* she thought dully, and forced her knees to lock. Silence in the small hut, save for the distant, whispery crackle of fire; she couldn't feel the warmth of it, was barely aware of ruddy light on the far wall—beyond the silvery shifting barrier between her—and That.

That: Good or evil? She sighed, very faintly. How many times had she asked herself that, this night? And what answer save the first—no way to tell, unless she spoke the final word. If she chose to speak the word of release. "Wait longer, if you will, Miranda," she whispered. The colored mist that stopped just short of small bare feet shimmered, the pattern once again changing. She didn't dare eye it directly; it would trap her, if it could—lull her into a half-daze otherwise. Traps within traps. The very lure of that inner barrier should convince her to speak the word of banishment. What man—what Thing—would set such movement upon the air before her—unless it sought to control her utterly?

Soon, you will be too exhausted to decide—or to pronounce either word. And then it will have you as well. Proud fool.

She *had* been a fool: To remain in this village

when the headman begged the favor of her—a woman of sense would never have taken such heavy responsibility, even if it came with the promise of shelter. But for a woman sought as she was to assume any burden so near Naples! Well, perhaps that much hadn't been entirely a fool's dare. Thus far the dusty little collection of goats, grapes and impoverished huts had proven safer than the open road, where any noble or high-ranking Naples churchman might espy her. King's widow, duke's daughter—she'd surely seek sanctuary in a nunnery, from a relative, from another royal in another land, never in a poor high country village, mere days' straight travel from her former life. A full year and more by her own wanderings.

No woman of that court—no man, either—would have done what I did, to find a niche here among the grapes and goats. Amid peasants scrabbling for a living amid stones and poor dirt. But I am also the Miranda of that island; I know how to live rough, if I must. Pray god Naples continues to forget that.

Still, to take the headman's offer of a hut and the living which had belonged to a curiously—mysteriously—missing wizard had been foolish enough. Not that she hadn't tried to discover where the man had gone. But the village headman wouldn't speak of the previous tenant and he looked so angry when she pressed the matter, it seemed better to leave it be; the villagers seemed afraid.

But why of her? She had done nothing these past months that was not to their benefit; she'd been polite, kindly—still most had been wary of her at best. Why?

No answer, either, what things remained in the small hut—it was as though the one who'd last slept on that rough cot had never been. Still. Her dreams from the very first night had been of someone else in this place . . .

Those dreams were proof that her heritage and her own childhood dabblings in Prospero's magics—the influence of her childhood companions—had left her vulnerable to dreams, if to no other influence.

Then, to attempt magician's books once more! The books weren't necessary for the kinds of protection these peasants needed: she should have been more surprised, and wary, to find such volumes among the possessions of a simple village mage. She hadn't been; she hadn't given the matter thought at all, until now. Any more than she'd considered tossing them into the village pond. The safe course—but there never had been 'a safe course for the daughter of Prospero of Milan.

Still—did you learn nothing all those years about the ultimate cost of magic, Miranda? Prospero had gained what he sought through his books: resolution of his exile, return of his ducal chair from a usurping brother, and a royal mate for his only child. He had lost all, including his life, within a year—dead, it was said, of one of Milan's winter fevers. *Dead of a traitor brother—or the mage hired by that brother—who first stole his throne and palace and gave him exile in return, then took his life after he returned triumphant to Milan. I know my uncle and I sensed what passed in father's palace, though I knew too late to be of aid to anyone. Father drowned his books too hastily.* And he trusted too much. She, his only child, would not make such a mistake again. A drop of sweat fell from her chin, slid down her breastbone; she shivered.

Decide. Though her earlier efforts to bring herself to this moment had created the greatest drain on her strengths, the final word would be a test of strength in itself—free or banish. No mere pronouncement, an act of power that would ask much of her. And what followed, however she chose, might require even greater strength.

Unpleasant thought indeed.

"Either way you are dead, then, Miranda," she whispered. Well—what matter? Father and husband dead—what did she have left? What cause to prolong her own life?

She caught her breath; her heart lurched painfully. There again, the faint glimpse of gaunt, drawn features before the inner circle shrouded what was held within. The face that had haunted her dreams since she'd taken this hut for her own. "That is not Ferdinand." The words carried no weight. Ferdinand was dead—like Prospero, either of fever or a slow poison, his physicians had claimed to be uncertain. *And so, the young king had died within weeks of ascending his father's throne—a king who now slept with his fathers—and a young queen fled from Naples to escape the stake. Better you had remained, and saved yourself this moment, Miranda. That is not Ferdinand.*

Yet somehow—somehow if there were life beyond the tomb as the priests had dinned into her after her reintroduction to Italian nobility. If Ferdinand knew the torments she had suffered since his death. If he sought to soothe her pain, to reach her in the only way possible, if he wished to gather her to him . . . If that were he . . . *Ah, beloved.* She closed her eyes, drew a deep breath and spoke the final word. Sudden wind shrilled through the hut, showering her with hot ash from the fire. She cried out, fell back a pace, brushing furiously at her arms and hair.

The encircling spells were gone, vanished with the sudden wind. And in a pool of faint and fading yellowish light, the sprawled figure of a man.

"Ferdinand?" The faintest of whispers; but even as

she spoke the name she knew the still form in the middle of her floor was a stranger. She stared down at him; dread slid up her spine with chill fingers.

He was tall and slender, but dark, as though burnt by long summers under the hot sun. His hair appeared black in the uncertain light of the dying fire, as did the line of beard outlining a squared jaw. Long hands and fingers. She sighed; her eyelids sagged closed. *So tired.* But she dared not sleep: *eat something, regain a little of the strength you spent this night.* Preferably before That—before *he*—woke.

High summer it might be but this high in the hills the nights were cool. Chill wind whistled through the closed shutters. She built the fire back up and put her pot of herbed water on the hoddle to heat, then lit a fat candle and set it on the wobbly table before fetching her shawl from the end of the narrow straw cot that was the room's only other furniture. "Tea first," she murmured. It scalded her tongue but fragrant steam cleared her mind, a little. Enough. She refilled the wooden cup, carried it with her and caught up the candle.

The stranger hadn't moved. She knelt beside him, set the candle on the floor so she could observe him more closely. He slept, she thought, by the rise and fall of his shoulders; by the look of his face, he'd sleep for hours. *Trust, Miranda; trust to that if you dare!* A deep frown furrowed his brow, and now she could see a few silver hairs in his beard; silver at his temples. But he wasn't an old man, he couldn't be above thirty. The hands—a dark splotch on the web between thumb and forefinger, the blue thumbnail marked him for what he was: wizard. Miranda had such a dark splotch on the palm of her hand, where she'd been careless with a particular potion.

Was this the village's missing—? She shrugged,

didn't complete the thought. When he woke, she'd ask questions, possibly even receive answers. Or not. Fruitless to speculate.

He had no visible wounds, no other mark on him that she could see by straight vision, and the other—no. The power would not respond for some hours, after a night such as this. "I must sleep." The man shifted at the sound of her voice and she edged away from him but he sighed deeply and was still once more. Sleep—how could she possibly sleep with this unknown quantity sprawled across her floor? She drank a little tea and considered the possibilities.

Bind him—but physical bonds against a wizard? Or a spell of binding, if she had the strength for it. "Oh, yes, Miranda, and if he's a stronger mage than you? With a temper to match that frown?" She'd be the first thing to hand if he chose to lash out. By rights, he'd be grateful to her for his release—if he was nothing more than what he seemed. "More than—no. He's man. I can still tell demon from man—but clean man from foul? And what was he doing where I found him?"

She shook her head. If she'd had *that* talent, telling clean from otherwise, Ferdinand would still be alive, and his chief counselor exiled or lying dead in a head-foreshortened coffin.

She staggered to her feet, caught up the candle as she rose and snuffed it, set it upon the table along with her now empty cup; the room swam. Off balance, she staggered back; the cot was hard against the backs of her legs; it would be soft against her back. Miranda's eyelids flickered, sagged shut; her legs sagged, dropping her to the prickly mattress. Already unaware, she smiled faintly, licked her lips, snuggled deeply into her shawl. Between one breath and another, she was asleep.

* * *

Pale light of early day washed the hut. Sun touched the foot of the cot and then her feet; Miranda drew a deep breath, rolled onto her side. *So tired.*

Why?

'Ware, Miranda. The warning touched her, was gone.

She woke to the crackle of fire, and the not-quite-right odor of tea. Someone else's mix of herbs, that. A board creaked nearby; a second. *Stay very still and seem yet sleeping.* She felt a shadow cross her body. Silence, not even the sound of breathing, save her own. The board creaked again, the shadow moved on. Sun nearly too warm upon her shoulders.

"She's still asleep." Stranger's voice, coming from near the hut's narrow doorway; deep and very quiet. Had she not been breathing quietly, she'd never have caught the words.

"That's certain?" The headman's equally low response; impossible to mistake the faint whistle in his speech.

"I said it." Impatient, perhaps angry. *Familiar as well; the headman is no new acquaintance. What have I done?*

"Good. You—look—"

"Yes. Don't bother to say it, I can well imagine how I look. You look dreadful, old man. Didn't you get what you wanted, after all this time?" Definitely angry. She let her eyes open the merest slit. The newcomer leaned into her table, cup in hand; the headman facing him at arm's length. He shuffled back, visibly nervous, stopping only when he fetched up against the wall. The newcomer laughed quietly; it wasn't a pleasant sound. "Afraid I'll want payment now?"

"It wasn't my fault, Alfonso," the older man mumbled. He eyed the other resentfully. "Those books weren't for a mage of your class—"

"No. Still, I've had plenty of time to consider those books—and your 'kindly' way of warning me away from them. You wanted me to—"

"No!" The headman slid along the wall, one cautious step at a time; the newcomer was at the door before him, blocking it.

"It *is* true, then, isn't it? You were jealous of me; jealous the power came so freely into *my* hands, that I could work spells that evaded you, that little was denied me even from the first—oh, save your lies," he added flatly as the headman strove to override him. "I can see it in your face. You set a drawing spell to ensnare me, and when I took hold of the book, it opened to the page *you* had chosen!" Silence. The newcomer—Alfonso—glared down at the headman; the old man's shoulders sagged and he nodded. "It did you little good, though, did it? Entrap me in that place between places so you could draw upon my power—don't deny that, either."

"Sssst! Keep your voice down, you'll waken her!" The headman cast an alarmed glance toward the bed; Miranda drew a deep breath, let it out in a quiet sigh.

"It's all right; after what she did last night, she won't waken soon." But Alfonso lowered his voice; for some moments she could hear the low, angry tone but not the words.

"All right. I admit it. But it wasn't for the reason you think; you're my dead brother's son, after all, I would never harm you, I swear—"

"Swear by what, Uncle? Is there anything you could swear by that I would trust?"

"You remember only how easily the magic came to you," the headman replied sullenly. "Not how insuf-

ferable you were, how certain of your skills! I merely
thought to teach you a lesson, and a degree of caution,
nothing more." His companion laughed shortly. "It's
true, I tell you! And then, once you were properly
ensnared—there was nothing I could do! Do you
think I made no effort to retrieve you? Look at me!
Last Lammas Night, I attempted what *she* accomplished, and since that night there's been no power
in me! Why do you think I allowed such a gifted
outsider into this village?"

"I remember last Lammas Night," Alfonso replied
grimly. "And the word *you* meant to speak." Miranda
was watching them once more, cautiously. Alfonso
abruptly stepped back from the door. "Go, get yourself out of here."

"Remember *she* nearly spoke that word, last night,"
the headman growled. "If you think to make an ally
of her against me—she owes me for this sanctuary, I
know who and what she is and I've not acted on that
knowledge. Before you put any trust in her, be aware
she's poisoned one husband already." He slid along
the wall to the door and vanished abruptly. Alfonso
caught himself in the doorway and swore under his
breath; Miranda let her eyes close.

Now, before you lose your nerve entirely, she
ordered herself. Her mouth was very dry. She shifted,
stretched like a woman just waking from a long, deep
sleep, and yawned.

Startled exclamation from her perforce guest; he
retreated to the far side of the hut as she sat up,
mumbled something she couldn't make out. "I'm
glad," she said mildly. "And I'd welcome some of that
tea, it smells good." He muttered something else,
sighed faintly and went to the fire to pour steaming
liquid into her cup. He almost dropped the cup as
she took hold of it and her fingers brushed his. She

kept cutting remarks behind her lips and drank. Was he trying to lull her into a false sense of superiority? This was nothing like the arrogant, hard young man who'd just been threatening the headman.

She finished the tea as he turned away, got to her feet and spread the shawl across her cot. The silence stretched uncomfortably. *Say something.* "Was—this your home?" He nodded sharply once; his shoulders were tense and he wouldn't look at her. "I see."

"Don't worry, Lady. I won't ask this place back from you."

"Not 'Lady.' Miranda."

"A—Alfonso." He was quiet for a long moment, finally turned to face her. "Miranda—it's not a common name." She shook her head. She could see the thoughts cross his face: he flushed, and turned away.

"I knew the reports had come this far," she said after a long moment. "And the warnings against sheltering the murderess who had been Milan's queen." Another silence; he might have been stone, or wood. "I didn't poison the king," she said quietly. "I'd say that, either way, possibly, but it's truth."

"I didn't intend to give you away," he mumbled; he sounded angry now.

"I never thought that. I won't poison *you*, either."

"I didn't—" He stopped, shook his head. "The others know—?"

"I think so. The headman does, I think. Things he's said, the months I've been here—but he's no threat."

He shook his head again. "You don't know him well enough, if you think that. Or—or others here, in this village. It is dangerous for you, staying here."

To her own surprise, she laughed. "Danger?"

"Don't laugh at me!" He turned back to face her, his brows drawn together, eyes black under them.

"There are some here who'd show you a pretty face and hide a black heart behind it."

"Ah. Whereas you—"

"I told you—!"

"Nothing!" Miranda shouted him down. "And don't dare look at me so! Do you resent it so much that I rescued you from a trap that you couldn't break?"

"I—you needn't have bothered," he snapped and spun away from her again. "I would have found a way, eventually." His voice was muffled and sounded sulky and furious both.

Miranda cast her eyes heavenward and bit back a sigh. Silence again. "All right. You've certainly found a way to anger me, if that's what you wanted."

"I never—"

"Be still, let me finish, so please you," she broke in crisply. "However, if you planned to make me angry enough that I'd storm out of this house *and* this village—or was that your uncle's plan?" She smiled grimly as he whirled around, mouth agape and eyes wide. "I didn't hear all of the argument, Alfonso, just enough."

"Ah—ah, *hells*." His shoulders slumped. Miranda waited. "You weren't part of anything *I* wanted," he said finally. He glanced at her, quickly away again. "Not last—last night, what you did. Certainly nothing *he* suggested just now. He's—Lady, he's no one to trust, he thinks in coils, always one plan behind the one engaged, and another behind that. You can't— you can't anticipate what he'll do, save that it will benefit old Gaetano, and that he won't care if it causes harm to anyone else."

Miranda laughed, silencing him. "You think I know nothing of men—*and* women—like that, after a year and more at court? Plots within plots, fair faces and black hearts. Only a babe would remain pure of

thought after what I've seen of the Napoli noble
houses! And only such a child would think such folk
are born only to the noble and royal."

"All the same, you trusted Uncle—"

"No. I accepted what he offered, nothing more.
I haven't trusted anyone since—well, that's not your
business. And I know to keep watch over my food
and drink, and to check my spellbooks with care
before using them." He scowled, turned to slam one
hand hard against the wall.

"And I don't—"

"Do *not*," Miranda broke in flatly, "presume to read
your own meaning into my words, I won't stand for
it."

"Ah. I see." His words sounded strangled, all at
once. "Well, then! Since I annoy you so, perhaps *I*
had better begone!"

She swore under her breath and moved to block
the doorway as he stalked toward it. "Is it utterly
necessary for you to create scenes? I don't take them
well so early in the day, thank you!"

"Thank *you*," he replied sourly, and gave her an
overly broad bow.

"This is—or was—your home. You've every right to
remain if you choose, but in any case, you won't leave
until you've properly rested and regained your
strength. I didn't endure Lammas Night simply to
deliver a half-dead man to the night vapors, and I
won't have another death linked to my soul, either."

"You need not—what's that?" he demanded
sharply, and turned away from her to catch at the
window sill. Miranda shook her head, came up behind
him. Noise in the yard—

"It's only the geese," she began; she fell silent as
he held up a warning hand. The birds were making
that irritating, shrill honking noise that was geese at

their worst, but beyond them she could now hear the clamor of voices.

"Look," Alfonso said grimly, and leveled a hand at the road. "My uncle hasn't waited for either of us to move. Don't say I didn't warn you!" Miranda caught her breath as men came into view: a crowd of angry-looking men bearing ancient pikes, staves and cudgels—and shouting them on, the village headman.

She couldn't think what to do, what to say—but the villagers gave them no opportunity: the hut was suddenly full of angry peasants who caught hold of the two mages, bound them tight, and dragged them back down the road to the village square.

There were women here—some of the elderly and a widow in crow's black. No children or maidens anywhere. Miranda's heart sank as the village men parted to reveal a huge stack of brush and lit torches. "I told you!" The headman shoved his way through the angry guard; he stopped prudently short of Miranda, waved an arm to indicate her and her young male companion. "I told you all she had begun to work against our village, did I not? That she was no common sorceress seeking a keeping, but a dread wizard, a noblewoman, daughter of the black island sorcerer Prospero! Even now our new king seeks her, for the foul murder of her husband!"

Someone in the crowd cried out; an elderly woman pushed her way into the open. "Alfonso—!"

"That is *not* Alfonso!" the headman roared. "That is what she wrought last night, when we all saw strange lights in that hut! Ask her! She will claim the man is indeed Alfonso, I have no doubts of that! But it is not true, my beloved nephew is dead two years." He caught his breath on a sob, turned away to blot his eyes against his sleeve. But the triumphant glance he cast Alfonso was chill and tearless. "I told you all

how it came to pass, remember? A beauteous sprite
upon the wind, we both saw it, but my poor half-
tutored nephew was caught in the drawing spell and
pulled over the cliff and into the river!" He sniffed,
blotted his eyes again, cleared his throat. "*She* was
already fled from Milan—perhaps even then she plot-
ted to take this village and yoke all of you—all of
us!—to her will!"

"Ohhhh—nonsense!" An elderly woman's voice cut
through the ensuing babble. "This is no woman like
any of us, Gaetano! The least girl-child in the village
could see it, she could live rough if she must but she
wasn't born to it! And the sorrow she bore—why, any
woman could see that, too, and understand it—it
spoke of loss nearly too great to carry."

"You will be silent!" the headman howled; the old
woman's cackling laugh silenced him instead.

"What will you do to me, Gaetano? I'm old! I've
outlived my husband and all but one of my children;
I've seen brothers and sisters die of fever or hunger
or cold, I've lost grandchildren to dark things or priva-
tion. What can you do to me that the pain of living
hasn't already done? You all know her!" she shouted.
There were more women in the square, Miranda realized all at once: girls and maidens carrying infant sisters or brothers, young women barely old enough to
put their hair up, young women wed but not yet
quickened. All eyeing her or the old woman—or, in
surprise, Alfonso, who was a glowering bulk at her
shoulder. "What woman in the village didn't know her
immediately? This is Miranda—Queen Miranda, *our*
Miranda! Since she came, she's done nothing but
good: blessing the crops so none starved; blessing the
young women carrying first babes—how many such
young women have we lost since she came here?"
Silence. The men began edging away from the bound

pair; Gaetano stared at the old woman as though frozen. "None! Not—one! Nor any other quickened woman, either!" She turned to glare at the headman, who fell one step away from her. "How dare you even suggest a woman who cares for the least of us would *ever* conspire against us?" She shoved her way past him, laid a wrinkled old hand against Miranda's cheek. "Don't fear, my lady. There's not one woman in this village who'll permit harm to you." She turned to glare at the armed men, but they were already backing away, muttering among themselves. The old woman gestured imperiously, and at her gesture, the other women came forward to undo the bonds on both prisoners.

Miranda blinked tears aside and swallowed. "I— thank you, Madam Ella. I—"

"Aunt." Alfonso brushed by her to take the old woman in his arms. Ella sighed happily and caught him around the waist.

"You're too thin, boy. You'll need feeding."

"Never—never mind that, Aunt. But—" He pressed her gently aside; Gaetano was gone. "My uncle—who saw him just now?" No one had, it appeared; many of those around them looked quite worried because of it.

Miranda cleared her throat. "Never mind, good people! He can't harm you so long as one of us remains to guard the village!"

"One?" One of the younger women stepped forward and took hold of Miranda's hands. "But—but which of you?"

"I will not force her to leave," Alfonso began angrily. Miranda shook her head.

"You do not leave this village! You are the one born and raised here, it's your family, your people! And I—if word somehow reaches Milan where I've come to rest, there's danger for everyone here, not just for me!"

"I will not have it!" Alfonso shouted.

"Silence!" Ella roared. Silence she got; even the men eyed her with caution and were suddenly still. "None of us will betray this woman! Swear it now!" And as some of the men cast each other dark looks and hesitated, "When ever did Gaetano do *you* favors?"

One of them stepped forward, dropping his long pike into the dust as he did. "All right, Ella! Anything to stop your bellowing! But she's right, isn't she? The man sought ever a new book, a new liquid or powder and whose coin bought it all? Ours! And who received the good of that liquid or powder when it worked? Gaetano! Whatever she may be, this woman has cost us nothing—"

"Ahhh, such praise, Sebastian!" old Ella snarled. "Did she not save your son from a lifelong laming, this past winter?" Silence. "Swear!" Ella shouted. A murmur of voices answered her: "Swear."

Miranda eyed her companion sidelong. He still looked worried, possibly at the edge of anger as well. Under all, she thought, confused. *He's young yet*, she reminded herself. He glanced her direction, caught her eye and blushed a deep, mottled red right to his hairline. She smothered a smile. Young, and capable of emotion beyond anger, given the chance. Not Ferdinand—but that same height and bone structure, a pleasant combination. And, she thought, a boy with the right emotions, in there somewhere. Waiting for an elderly aunt like Ella—or perhaps another, younger woman—to free them.

Ferdinand, will you blame me if I find happiness— if I try to find happiness with this green boy?

No answer, of course. She hadn't expected one. But

something deep within her was suddenly at peace. Alfonso gave her a rueful smile and took her hand.

"Lady—your pardon, *Miranda*—the hut is yours, of course."

"It's not so small as all that," she replied mildly. "And your books are there, as well as mine. It's a good-sized village with a new need for protection. I'd be remiss if I sent you away, don't you think?" He eyed her doubtfully; she smiled. "You know the headman, after all—better than I. The village needs us both."

Silence. When he nodded and bent to kiss her fingers, the women around them—and no few of the men—cheered. Miranda blinked aside tears. To be wanted—*needed*! This was a new thing, indeed. She gazed at Alfonso thoughtfully. He wouldn't completely trust her just yet, of course; possibly she wouldn't entirely trust him, either. They'd manage, eventually.

Demonheart

MARK SHEPHERD

For generations my family had kept the demons of
the northern wood in check, and never before had
the spirits succeeded in overtaking one of our kind.
Until now.

Whether or not the demon found my prison ironic
escaped my sharpened senses, as I was still grappling
with the anger, and humiliation, of being defeated at
my own game. How dare this demon imprison the
soul of Wizard Keighvin and torment me with prom-
ises of freedom?

The prison was simple, effective. In this place of
dark thoughts and ghostly beings—indeed, I *was* a
ghost—my captor made a sphere from which I could
not escape. With no sense of up or down, my soul
floated freely in this cage, having forgotten already
what it was like to have a body, to be able to touch,
to walk, and to breathe in cool night air. And the
irony was, this prison drew its power from the very
circle-casting I had forged in the northern meadow,
with which I'd intended to imprison, or at least ward
away, the being which kept me under lock and key
now! I wanted freedom, but whoever or whatever was
responsible was slow to inform me of its motives.
Years seemed to pass before I understood the extent
of my hellish fate.

I knew I had to forget the happiness I had enjoyed in the small village if I were to avoid total madness, and focus on what was happening to me now. If indeed I had any purpose left, it was to defeat this demon with whatever I could. But to do that, I had to learn about it. And the easiest way to do *that* would be to feign an alliance. . . .

As I entertained these devious thoughts I became aware of a deep shadow that mirrored my mood all too well. It resembled the wraiths that I had, for a time, kept successfully at bay, but it was much larger and darker than those faint ghosts that had clustered at the edge of my erstwhile shields. It stank of evil, and of a power behind that, a collection of magics I never dreamed existed. I comforted myself with bleak reassurances that I was already dead, that no further harm could come to me. Since I had failed to subdue the demon in my own world, I would have to do so in his—for it was indeed male, I saw, its ugly shape, its horned head. It parted great stormclouds to reveal my prison, and stood over it, tall as a tree.

The demon regarded me silently for a time, like an overgrown lad contemplating a newly caught rodent in a cage. I sent forth thought forms of confusion and complacency, all the while hoping this creature didn't dig too deeply. This was a new venture for me, tricking demons in their own kingdoms, and I doubted my work would hold up under much scrutiny.

"What are you?" I asked, my words only thoughts, and for a time I didn't know if it understood. "What happened to make me a prisoner of my own magic?"

Its face contorted into something approximating amusement. *I am your captor, your victorious enemy. I am your master, and you are my slave.*

I am Demonheart . . .

Images of the grove and the circle I had cast within it flew at me as if caught up in a storm.

It was the heart of evil you found, and tried, like a fool, to imprison. I am that heart. I am Demonheart.

There was gloating in the creature's words, but I detected a sense of simplicity about it; it might know the magical world but it might yet be fooled by guile. I conveyed a feeling of helplessness in manner and thought. In apparent response to this my prison walls thinned somewhat, and Demonheart came into sharper focus. It was a monstrous wraith, yes, but one that still had a sense of naivete about him, if such things were possible in a demon.

Would you serve me in my work? Demonheart asked.

"Of course I would," I said readily. "Not because I appear to have no choice, but because I would gladly serve one as mighty as you. What would you have me do?"

Demonheart didn't tell me immediately what he had in mind, but over the course of time I learned that, despite his power, he lacked something mortal humans take for granted: life. Not spiritual life, of which he obviously had plenty, but a physical life, with birth and death and all the joys and miseries in between. Whether he had lived before he never said, but if he had, it was a long time ago. How he was to be reborn remained a mystery, as he was no mere soul; I also had the impression that he had tried before, with no results other than a hasty death for the newborn infant. He would need something other than a mere mortal body, and I was beginning to suspect I was going to be his means of achieving this dark purpose.

This I could not do, to create a being in which this evil thing could live. It was against my oaths as a wizard;

even though I was quite dead, I was still bound to them: *I would not do harm, nor would I create something that would do any harm. Do what thou will, but harm none, that will be the whole of the law.*

Demonheart began to let me out of my cage from time to time, allowing me explore this new world of phantasm, only to bottle me up once again. I found myself ensnared by bindings the demon created, thin but strong silver threads that kept me tethered and at the demon's whim. I thought that with time the demon might become more trusting and let me explore other regions with greater freedom. I might travel distances his bindings could not sustain, and I would be free—to go where, I did not know, but if I were to be an earthbound spirit then so be it. At least earthbound I might find a wizard who could send me onward to the divine light, from whence I might return and be reborn.

First things first, I reminded myself. *To fool the demon . . .*

This plan might have served its purpose if not for the arrival of an unaccounted-for presence: the wizard who came to take my place as the village magiker.

Beautiful, she was, with long red hair. I did not know what tradition she learned from, but from her competent air, she seemed highly learned in whatever school had taught her. She also seemed eager and wanting a place to practice, and I remembered all too well the pleasant working conditions I'd had in my previous life. These people were kind and generous, and if she had any degree of compassion she would stay on whatever terms they offered, and help them. When I sensed her gift for healing I rejoiced, knowing the town needed a good healer. My poor attempts at the healing arts had produced little result despite the village's great need for them.

As she took up residence, going through my former belongings with respect, but also with a determination to wipe the slate clean, so to speak, I realized she was in great danger. My demise must concern her, if she be a magiker of any merit. She would investigate, and soon she would discover the demon, and perhaps make the same mistake as I in underestimating it.

Only if I could contact her, warn her . . . My reins tightened the moment she took up residence in my former home, and Demonheart let me from my spherical cage only rarely, and when he did he kept me under constant watch.

Beautiful, is she not? Demonheart asked, from a point directly over my shoulder. She had already healed the headman's ailment, whatever it had been, and had started work on the miller's sickly cow. *She would make a suitable wife for anyone, don't you think, my young slave?*

I agreed with the demon's observations. It was at this point that I began to suspect his intention, although I was not convinced he was shrewd enough to pull it off. *He would have to know . . . what I know. My books, my spells.* With a sickening realization I saw that was what he had done; Demonheart had absorbed my knowledge as he had absorbed my soul.

I tried to pretend ignorance of my magical abilities, but it was to no avail. Demonheart already knew what I could do, and he knew where the important volumes were in the cottage. Helplessly I watched him follow her about, just at the edge of her magical vision. My plan of presenting an illusion of cooperation would, I feared, endanger her more than it would help me to escape. But at the time I had no other plan, and I had for the most part convinced Demonheart of my sincerity. I bided my time.

Meanwhile, she did everything she could to thwart

my attempts at protecting her, though of course she had no way of knowing. Her curiosity about my death got the best of her, I saw clearly. On this night she set out northwards, towards the grove—a brave one, she was, to face a power when it was at its strongest. She followed the path directly to my former magical work, which had all but drained into the reinforcement of my cage, though there was still some residual power. The expertise with which she studied and deciphered the circle . . . I was complimented when I sensed her appreciation of *my* work.

I felt Demonheart's uneasiness; he had already dispatched his army of wraiths and other creatures of the dark. He was afraid she was going to attack! I knew better, but I was not going to enlighten the demon. *Now, to test his resolve,* I thought.

The demon was a coward. One single human mage kept him at bay, this Demonheart who sent his minions to flail harmlessly against her shields. I could tell she was no stranger to beings such as these; she barely flinched when the most hideous of the lot attacked her, and my estimation of her increased threefold.

She left the circle with hardly a backward glance. Her casual demeanor visibly angered and insulted Demonheart, and it was all I could do to conceal my own amusement. Simple-minded and a coward Demonheart might be, but it still had the power to imprison me, and would likely do the same with her, if given a chance.

Demonheart took up other tactics, of which I was the principal instrument. I agreed to this only because it permitted me more intimate contact with this powerful, and beautiful, wizard.

I discovered much to my dismay that whatever tradition this wizard studied had neglected to show her the basics of dream shielding. Her mind was amazingly open to attack while she slept, a fact of which Demonheart was unaware since he would have taken advantage of it otherwise.

That night something began, something that changed everything. . . .

As I've said, my imprisoned soul had begun to lose touch with what it was like to have a body, to be alive, to eat, to sleep. These things happen when one is discorporate; the memories are there, but they become vague with time. Perhaps Demonheart sensed this when he dispatched me to enter her dreams. When night fell and the wizard retired I entered her unguarded sleep easily, like a thief walking into an unlocked house.

I am no stranger to the company of females, but my sudden contact with her reminded me how long it had been, and how much I had been secretly yearning to be with her. Granted it was only my soul that was with her, but very quickly the memory of former sensation was made painfully sharp. Over the next several nights I became more daring, tempting her with erotic pleasures in which she seemed all too willing to indulge. I would have considered myself in heaven, save for the appalling discovery I made on the third night.

Demonheart had stolen into the dream with me! Using my soul as a shield, he hid behind my essence while I seduced her, watching us make love from the shadowed edges of her dream. I might have objected if I had thought it would do any good, but I knew I was free on the demon's terms, and that I risked ending these ecstatic trysts if I so much as hinted I knew of the demon's presence. For I was in love with this woman, whose name I still didn't know, and would do nothing to jeopardize our time together, tenuous as it was.

Then Demonheart did something maddening—he left fresh flowers for her to find the next morning, and she thought they had been left by me! However, I still didn't understand the *true* plan, at least not yet.

But then she decided to explore the haunted grove again, and I knew this made the demon nervous. A secret remained hidden in the grove, one I had been close to revealing myself before the demon robbed me of soul and life, what seemed like an eternity ago. I had described the demon as a "heart of darkness" in my notes, and this curious wizard was determined to succeed where I had failed.

In daylight she ventured into the haunted wood. I noted with no small interest that Demonheart had difficulty summoning his wraiths in the full light of day; this time he made do with simply observing from a distance.

She indeed found what I had tried to bind. From my peculiar perspective, however, I saw with startling clarity what evil had been buried there. It was a grave, exceedingly old, possibly dating back to a primitive time when our kind lived in caves and migrated in animal like bands. Such evil . . . Demonheart had never been able to return to the living, so evil and alien his soul was. And here he had lurked, for millennia.

Once she discovered the grave, everything changed subtly. The demon feared for its existence, and rightly so; she was out to bind it, to complete the task I had begun.

I had to warn her, even if it meant betraying my ruse. I was finished, but she was still among the living, and I was determined to keep her there, gods willing. When the demon wasn't paying attention, I appeared to her in a reflection. She must have known the danger she was in, for she ran for the library, for a particular book of spells I knew quite well.

She will ruin everything! Demonheart shrieked. *Stop her, you fool, or she will destroy us both!*

This I doubted, but I took advantage of my brief freedom by directing her to a spell that would send me on, far away from her, where I could be of no use to the demon.

No, you don't! the demon shrieked, and surprised us both by turning the page of the spell book.

This is the spell she must work, you fool Demonheart said. *You must create a child, so that I would live again!*

I saw the spell the book had fallen to. If performed correctly, the working would bring me back, not only in spirit, but in flesh. It was a necromancer's spell, one I had never done, and had sworn never to do.

The wizard seemed uncertain as to which spell to work, and I saw why: they were identical, save for one word. Uttering that one word made the difference between summoning or banishing my spirit. And this night was *Hallowmas* night, the only night upon which either could be worked.

I resigned it all to the fates, but the demon seemed to think he had won. *We'll see,* I thought.

The wizard's magical circle appeared at the edge of our domain. I felt the spell pulling at me, urging my attendance. I obeyed, not knowing where I would be sent.

Then the hour of midnight was upon us, and she looked at me directly and commanded, *"Come."*

I would have shrieked in rage had I the voice, but the magics that descended upon me at that moment drowned any such attempt. But I heard Demonheart bellowing in victory as the darkness surrounded me.

I found myself standing in her circle, very much flesh and blood. The wind had whipped up a frenzy of dried leaves, and I smelled rain, and the rich earth beneath me, so sharp were my senses now that they had been thrust upon me.

She regarded me with something like awe, or perhaps it was lust. For a moment I was taken by her beauty, the flow of her robe as the wind blew it about her. I wanted to touch her, to be with her again . . . but I knew it could not be.

"So you are the wizard Keighvin," she whispered. "How nice of you to attend."

"And it is my honor to attend," I replied, uncertain of my voice. I looked at my hands and arms, found them to be close replicas of what I once was . . . but my body was dead and decaying in the ground somewhere. I was only a facsimile, and one which I doubted would last.

Ah, but likely last long enough to sire her child! I heard Demonheart call from behind me. He was deep in the shadows, kept out by the effective circle she had cast, but near.

At least, for the moment, I was free. Demonheart had no control over me here, within her circle. I must act quickly . . .

"I am not what I seem," I blurted out. "The evil I tried to defeat took my life while I sat at the very table at which you have dined many times, and he means to use me to conquer you! You must rework the spell! Send me on, I cannot live again. This," I said, holding my arms up, "this isn't real. I am not alive, really. I am flesh only for the moment."

No! You cannot do this . . . Demonheart howled, but he could do nothing.

"I see," she said, and I saw with relief that she really did. "I trust you. The evil could not have come from you."

"Please. Send me on." Demonheart was summoning his forces back in the shadows, and for a moment I doubted her circle would keep them all out. "For your own sake, rework the spell!"

I wanted to hold her, make love to her, amid the swirling leaves. Behind me Demonheart was encouraging me to do just that, and I knew that to give in to my wants would mean certain victory for him. And that could not be.

"Do it, now," I said. "For the sake of the folk of this village. It must be defeated."

"Yes," she said.

The relief I felt was tainted with the pain of knowing I would not, after all, hold her as a man would. So be it. I would win in the long run.

Demonheart's silence was ominous, and as the wizard worked essential points of her spell I looked back to see an army of wraiths ready to attack. Whether they would be successful or not, I did not know.

With a tear in her eye, the wizard said the final word.

"*Go.*"

The world collapsed around me. I felt pulled upwards, my body dissolving into nothingness. I became aware of a light, bright light.

With the force of a million storms, I was pulled into the light of the waning moon.

Sunflower

JODY LYNN NYE

Vinory dreamed again of the sunflower: tall, yellow-fringed, with a strong, thick stalk bowing slightly under the weight of its heavy head. Everything about the dream flower seemed normal, except that instead of tracking the sun throughout the day, its face followed her.

There were plenty of sunflowers in the garden outside, but why would she dream about them instead of the roses or asters or herbs? All this place was new to her. She had come here only a few days ago. Glad for the promise of shelter against the coming winter, Vinory had not questioned too closely the circumstances under which the position of village wonder worker became vacant. Otherwise she might have shouldered her pack and pressed on farther down the road, regardless of the holes in her boots.

Now, those boots had fresh, entire soles, and winter receded to far away in the future. Moreover, there were whole woollen blankets on the feather bed, also blessedly hers, and free of vermin, thank all gods! The three-room cottage was not merely nice, but sound, well-proportioned, and well-built. It smelled of dry herbs and dust, but what of that? Half an hour's sweeping and dusting, and some of her own herbs scattered on the air or boiled for the scent had driven away the ghost of dead parsley and sage. The headman's wife had made her guesting gift of oats, tea, honey, salt, a new loaf, some dried meat, and a small crock of wine, with the promise of good food every day. Whatever she needed, they would give. Somewhere, they told her, there was a black and white cat for company, but he tended to go about his business as he chose. This could be a nice sinecure, all the benefits to stay with her, or go, as she chose, if only Vinory would at least stay through until spring. The people of Twin Streams had no one else to weave the spells to protect them from the storm or the spirits who rode it. Their last mage had died in the spring. Vinory was a gift to them from the gods, and they treated her as such.

The dream symbol of the sunflower kept preying at her mind. This was no ordinary bloom. It had a distinctively masculine presence, teasing at her with a faint, fresh-washed scent and the insouciant flaunting of mature sexuality. Did a god's presence touch this house?

If such a visitation was troubling her, she wanted to see it off! Vinory needed a whole mind and a whole heart to take care of the villagers. Some of them had been saving up a list of spells and nostrums they needed, against the time that this cottage would house a mage again. Vinory would be busy from morning 'til night for weeks to come.

"Good morning, Mistress Vinory," the headman said, when she came to take care of his youngest daughter, who was suffering from night terrors. Bilisa also had a head cold and was breaking out in webbing between her toes and fingers from handling an enchanted frog, but those were quietish maladies, not calculated to make her scream in the dark and wake the house.

"Now, think of something bright," Vinory told the girl, a mite of six, with big dark eyes and long braids framing a pale, moon-shaped face. "Something that gleams. Keep it in your mind." Vinory spun a disk of metal between her fingers, gathering sunlight from the beams that came in the window to store in the girl's mind. "Think of yellow, like buttercups and primroses."

And sunflowers, a quiet voice said in the back of her mind.

When the girl's mind was eased and her other problems treated, Vinory returned to her cottage and hearth. She mustn't start thinking of the cottage as hers, she warned herself, as she started a pot of porridge to cook. The mage-born really belonged nowhere in this world. They were only loosely tied to physical existence. Love of possessions made it more difficult to travel across the Veil to accomplish their spells and curses. But how easily she could get used to earthly comforts! Her cup and bowl, spoon and knife looked very homey on the mantel beside the goods of the departed Master Samon. The reflection the mirror showed her had silver threads showing near the scalp in the black wings of her hair; and fine lines ran in patterns on her weathered skin beside her dark blue eyes and the corners of her mouth. Her body would one day grow old. Would this not be a nice place to stay until the time came when she abandoned it? Hastily, she put the thought aside.

Next to the hearth was a wooden chest that Vinory hadn't dared to open as yet. It was unlocked, and the hasp was flipped upward as if its owner had been about to open it when. . . . The villagers said that the last mage died unexpectedly. Could it have been poison, or was the latch made of a deadly metal? Vinory prayed to be shown the truth, whispering a few words to the void.

The wind howled outside suddenly, making her gasp with its ferocity. But she saw no black spots or shining, sickly greenness on or about the lock or the chest to suggest that it would do her harm. She reached for it again.

It seemed to her that a warm hand brushed hers when she pushed the heavy lid open. Cobwebs, Vinory told herself. You're imagining things.

To her delight the chest was full of books. That made sense. It was placed handily so one could reach for a book and read by firelight. Vinory hummed with pleasure as she took the clothbound volumes out one by one and laid them on the fleece that served as a hearth mat. There was a *Geographicus Mundi*, a handsome herbal in Latin, and several books of charms and spells. Some of the books were handwritten, all in the same strong, beautiful hand, and peppered with tiny illuminations. Among the goods on the wall shelves were pots of paint and brushes made of twigs and hair. Had these drawings been the work of Samon? Then he was a scholar and an artist! She was sorry now not to have met him. And now these lovely things were hers to use. Vinory felt an unexpected sensation of warmth, as if the house gave her its blessing.

The dream of the sunflower came again that night. The seed-heavy head leaned closer to her; its leaves rustling, whispering. If the flower had had eyes, it would be looking deep into her soul. The image grew larger until it took up all of her mind's eye. Vinory woke in the dark, panting with fear. It wasn't that she disliked sunflowers, she told herself, except that the damned shells kept getting stuck between her teeth,

but what was the meaning of the recurring dream?
She sought peace as she concentrated on it.

Her mind had to be affected by some stimulus
around her. Vinory thought again of the unseen hand
that had touched her when she opened the box of
books. It was almost as if someone had brushed her
arm lovingly. She put her hands up into the shadows,
feeling, sensing. The air was empty, as it was supposed
to be.

Movement near the fire startled her. Vinory sat
upright to see what had thrown that shadow against
the wall. No one else was in the room with her. It
must be the cat, she told herself.

No. The thought came unbidden. Vinory started.

There *was* a consciousness here. Who—or what—
was it? Vinory crawled from her bed and flung a cloak
around her, determined to learn more. From her basket, she took a thin copper ring and a thread, and
crouched by the fire. She set the pendulum spinning,
catching glints from the faint embers.

"Are you malevolent? Do you mean me harm?"
she asked the pendulum. Without hesitation, the ring
began to rock back and forth. No. Twice. And the
shadow fluttered into the light again.

"Who are you?"

That question the pendulum could not answer. The
intruder could have been from anywhere and any time
in the beyond. Vinory reached outward with all of the
delicate fingers of consciousness that she used to
touch the other side of the Veil. The presence seemed
to have a connectedness to the place in which it was
now. Was it an entity called here by the previous
owner of the cottage, or an unfortunate spirit tied
here by who knew what bonds? She couldn't guess
what had gone before. Perhaps in the daylight she
could peruse the books and notebooks for a clue.

An unexpected rush of air flowed past her cheek and brushed her hair. Chilled, Vinory crept back to bed and tucked the blankets around her.

She treated the presence with careful reverence, in case it was the tendril of a god's mind. When Vinory rose in the morning, she greeted it, and put the first crumbs and drops of her breakfast on a dish to one side as an offering. If it was not a god, then it had another name, and she meant to find it out. As she worked on a charm for a spinning wheel for Lenda, the village fine-weaver, they chatted idly.

"What sort of man was Samon?" Vinory asked, tying threads together through the spokes of the wheel.

"Oh, he was a fine-looking man," Lenda said, rocking her plump self back on her three-legged stool. "Not as big as some, but with white skin like a girl's, and dark eyes and lashes that looked painted on. I wanted to picture him in a tapestry, but he wouldn't let me make an image of him. Said it tied him down."

"That's true," Vinory said. "How did Samon die?"

"Caught a chill sitting up for six nights in a row to cure a sick child," Lenda said. "Or at least, that's what I thought it must be. The next day, I was bringing him food, and found him. I thought he was sleeping, but he was dead. Not a mark on him. Such a shock it was." Lenda clicked her tongue.

"Six nights! Such devotion to healercraft," Vinory said, impressed. "He must have been most caring."

"Oh, well, any man would do the same, since it was *his* child," Lenda said, peering at the mage-woman under her heavy lids. "The girl he got it on was too young to marry, our headman said, but plenty old enough for dalliance among the daisies at the spring planting, in Samon's eye. Said it was the god's doing.

He shouldn't have taken her, but what could the parents say? You can't make a cow back into a heifer."

"Oh," Vinory said, disappointed. "Too true." The wretch. Her image of a lost scholar and saint tarnished around the edges. Technically Samon had been correct. Mere mortals could not dictate whom the god said should play the spring queen in the planting dance, but one could temper his whim by leaving unwed children out of the range of choice. Had the god stayed around too long after the dance, and swept Samon away while leaving a thought-shadow in his place?

"No, indeed," Lenda said, reminiscing. She sounded fond of him, as she stared past Vinory through the door at the bright autumn sunshine. "Couldn't keep hands to himself, no, not if they were tied behind him. He needed a strong woman to keep him in line. Not that women here aren't of sound mind," she added, warningly, in case Vinory would think they were all vow-loose, "but none *wanted* to say no to him."

I could, Vinory thought.

The presence teased at her the next day as she rooted through the cottage's storerooms. It seemed to have a courtier's manners, going here and there with her, moving aside while she was walking, crouching close as she knelt to examine a box or basket. It certainly was not a god, since when Vinory had chosen to ward herself the night before, she was not troubled by the dreams or the mysterious touch. Instead, Vinory could feel the presence hammering unhappily at the wards she had set up, pleading to come in until she drew a veil across her thoughts so she could sleep. Who or what could the presence be?

"I don't know whether it would have been a pleasure to know you or not, Master Samon!" Vinory said, sorting through a bag of dyed threads. "Dallying with children, though I grant you lived up to your responsibilities afterward. You stood right on the fulcrum of the great Balance, didn't you?" The presence said nothing, but she was beginning to feel that it might indeed be Samon lingering here.

What *had* taken his life? Over the years, she had sat up many nights with patients. Sometimes she'd caught what disease they had, but she always manifested the usual symptoms. The women said there were no signs at all, and yet Samon's soul had fled. Vinory's mind spun with unanswerable questions. Could Samon have been ripped from his body by some powerful force? A curse? Could what happened to him happen to Vinory? Should she flee this place while she could? No wonder the townsfolk were so desperately glad to have her stay.

When she went to bed that night, she surrounded herself with wards and protections so thick that the cat couldn't find a place on the bed. He hunkered down next to it, grumbling.

The next morning, the sun poked a gleaming finger through the curtains of the cottage window and tickled Vinory's nose until she woke up with a sneeze.

Goodness, she thought. I hope I'm not coming down with Bilisa's cold. A few experimental sniffs proved that her nose was clear. That was a relief.

The cottage was tidied nearly to the homey stage. Vinory thought that today she would ask the fuller or the blacksmith for a little polishing sand to shine up the fine metalwork that decorated the doors and cupboard fastenings. That would be the finishing touch that would make all perfect. She could perform some small service for the craftsmen in exchange, but so far everyone had been too shy to ask their due. That courtesy would pass soon enough, Vinory knew, so she would keep offering so as not to seem arrogant in her power.

Vinory thought a slice of bread and some broth boiled from the dried meat would taste nice this morning. The black and white cat wound between her feet while she put the pot onto the fire and made her toilet for the day. She gave him a piece of the meat. He gulped it down and begged for more.

"There, now," she said, picking up a cloth to swing the hook holding the pot out of the fire, and flicked it at him. "You've had your bounty. Go and catch something for yourself. Fresh meat's better for you anyhow." The cat sat down and nonchalantly washed his shoulder to prove to her that he didn't care. Smiling, Vinory ladled broth into her bowl and took it and the remains of the loaf to the table.

Beside her plate was a yellow flower. Vinory hadn't noticed it before, but that did not mean it hadn't been there when she arose. She was touched by the gesture, thinking that a villager had decided to show her a kindness by leaving her a posy of autumn flowers. Then she took a close look at the bloom. It was a daffodil. Another sunflower, not heavy with autumn, but fresh with the dew of springtime. She'd always known it as a gage of the laughing young god, in his youngest and most playful incarnation. And yet, she reminded herself that the dancer was also faithless, flitting from woman to woman, whoever would have him. There were no daffodils in the village. They withered by May. July was long past their season. Who had reached through time for this lovely thing?

I, the voice said. *I would please you.* The warm touch brushed her hand again and encircled her wrist with a lover's touch.

Vinory started, afraid. Samon *was* still here, and not only was he tied to this place, he was now tied to her as well! Abandoning bowl, loaf, and hunger, Vinory rushed out into the sunshine.

At least the ghost didn't follow her beyond the walls. She ran down the hill toward the fields where all the able-bodied villagers were helping to bring in the hay. The good folk greeted her gladly, offering her bread, cheese, and meat from their own breakfasts. She accepted only enough to keep from getting lightheaded.

"Now you're here, will you bless the coming harvest, lady?" the blacksmith said, leaning heavily on his scythe. He swept a hand around to show her a valley filled with dusty gold and dark green. Poppies of that astonishing red clustered at the edge of the cropline.

"How hard you have worked," Vinory said, sincerely. The villagers straightened up with pride. "Of course I will give the blessing. The gods have been good to this place. It will be a bountiful year. I need a handful of each of the young produce." Two boys ran off and came back with handfuls of grain, fruit, and tiny, perfect vegetables. Vinory exclaimed over their beauty. "Good. And now I . . . I need wine, salt, a small bowl, and a crust."

There were a few odd glances exchanged, and one or two people looked up the hill at her cottage, only a few hundred yards away. Vinory was ashamed to admit she was afraid to go back for her basket, so she waited and smiled politely until somebody gathered the components of the harvest prayer for her. At least her knife was in her belt.

Beckoning the workers together, Vinory sprinkled salt in a circle around them, then advanced to the sunrise side with the wine and bread. The headman, who had witnessed many a harvest rite, came forward with a large, flat stone, which he set down at her feet.

Chanting the ritual words, Vinory poured the wine into the bowl and crumbled the bread into it. She held up the bowl to the sky, and let the Veil open ever so slightly.

The powers of nature were formidable, but most folk only saw the merest wisp of that influence. It was only during rituals and festivals that they had the opportunity to see what Vinory and the magekind saw every day. The headman and his villagers were agog as a mouth opened in the sky and drew the wine and bread up to it in a garnet stream. A beam of light issued down on Vinory and her makeshift altar. The offering was acceptable. Now she filled the bowl with the fruits of the harvest. As she continued her chant of praise and entreaty, the golden light covered the bowl. In a blinding flash, the offering was gone. The light faded into Vinory, leaving her glowing in front of the stone, ponderous with the weight of godhead. She was silent for a long time. The villagers waited respectfully until she spoke.

"The gods hear us, and they are pleased," she said, feeling both god and goddess resounding in her chest and brain. "Blessed be this place and these people. The work that they do shall prosper."

The villagers muttered "thanksgiving," and Vinory ended the ritual by touching the point of her knife down to the flat stone, earthing the gods' power as a symbol of the unity of the planes. When she broke the circle, she drew a little of the godhead into herself to protect her as she walked back up the hill to the cottage. It was hers now. She had earned it. No ghost would dare to keep her from it.

The bread on the table was stale now, and her broth was gone from the bowl. The cat must have lapped it up as soon as it cooled. Vinory's movements were abrupt as she prepared another meal to restore her after the drain of rending the Veil.

The spirit presence was immediately at her elbow, offering concern. She pushed away at it with her thoughts, trying to find some peace to think. The spirit kept trying to get her attention.

"Leave off!" she said, irritably. "You're worse than the cat." It drew back perceptibly, hovering near the book chest. Vinory ate her meal and took a little rest on the bed with her back propped up against the wool-stuffed pillow. The presence stayed at a distance from her, but she could still feel its regard.

"What do you want?" she demanded at last. Protected by the fragment of light, she let her consciousness open up to the presence. Immediately a sensation of need flowed over her. Vinory raised the godhead as a shield, and the presence withdrew a little. It continued to broadcast to her its feelings: pain, fear, frustration, and despair.

"You are trapped here," she said. "That I had already guessed. But what do you want of me?"

Her soul was suddenly flying, feeling wings stretching out to either side of her, feeling the air cupped beneath them as strong as a hill. Terrified, Vinory threw up her shield and cowered behind it. The sensation stopped at once. The spirit sent contrition, and she glared in its direction.

"You wish to be free," she said.

Beside her on the bed, another daffodil appeared, fresh and golden yellow. Vinory reached for it, but her fingers stopped halfway. She could sense the spirit's anticipation, but she was afraid.

There were spells to free spirits of the dead who had become trapped in a place. But she did not dare to try one of them without knowing how it was Samon met his end. Could his fate drag her along with it?

Neither the headman nor her neighbors had mentioned anything haunting this cottage before her arrival. She, the mageborn, must have reawakened him. Now he radiated hope towards her.

"Go away," she said, leaving the flower untouched on the blanket. "I must think."

Ignoring the desperation she felt at the perimeter of her consciousness, she drew up wards of protection that she wore all day.

"Oh, yes," the blacksmith said, scooping polishing sand into a cloth for her. "Master Samon demanded the best from us, but he gave champion service. Saved my cow when she was in calf with twins. Told me his price was I owed him ironwork for a year after that. I saved no money. He had gauged exactly how long it would take me to pay off two more bullocks. Ah, well," he said, twisting the corners of the cloth into a knot, "fair measure's fair, after all."

"What about the child he left?" Vinory asked, tucking the parcel into her basket. The blacksmith put his own interpretation upon her question.

"She's all right. Shows no signs of acting like one of the mage—like one of your good folk, lady. Just eight months old, she is. The girl was much too young when he picked her to dance the spring goddess with him, just into womanhood, but she's turned out a good mother for all that. She's wed to my son, now."

Fair and foul, Vinory thought, as she lay abed that night. The spirit offered caresses and favors, but she kept him firmly at arm's length. Every one of the folk here have a story or two to tell about him. He's trustworthy. He's not. He's generous. He's mean. I don't know what to believe. And none knew how he died.

*   *   *

"He was kind, mistress," the girl said. The house was small but very tidy. In a corner a baby slept. Vinory glanced at it and noted the dark eyelashes and hair, unlike its mother, who had hair red as a fox's fur. "He was good to me, so kind and gentlelike. The husband he got for me I have now isn't nearly as . . . nice to be with. Though he tries." She gave a helpless shrug, and a shy smile.

The girl lifted her sleeping infant for Vinory to bless. Halfway through the incantation the child woke, and watched her with eyes far too wise for its age. They reminded her of the sunflower.

Over the following days, the spirit of Samon kept up its wooing. Every time she sat down, it was at her elbow. It stood at the end of her bed at night, and attended her at table like a servitor. She began to find its constant company oppressive.

"I can never be alone with my thoughts while you're here," she complained to the invisible presence. It had grown stronger and more distinct as the moon waxed. Tonight the moon was nearly full. She could almost imagine she could hear Samon speak from the other side of the Veil. She shooed him away so she could think.

Vinory had now been in Twin Streams two weeks. In another two it would be Lammas. She began to think of the harvest festival. It would be nice to have a strong male to play the corn king in the reaping dance. Vinory had studied all the available men, and confessed herself disappointed. The only really attractive man of exactly the right age, Robi the tanner, had a jealous wife whom it would be bad to cross. The blacksmith looked likely, too, though he was very heavy handed. Vinory was speculating idly on the identity of her partner, because it didn't matter whom *she* liked. The goddess would choose for herself when she possessed Vinory's body. Luckily there was no such stigma on a young man as there was on a young woman in joining the sacred dance. If he could perform, he was old enough.

"I could dance the autumn and the spring with you, if you set me free," the spirit told her that night in her dreams. Vinory felt the warm touch of a man's body against hers, strong muscle, questing hands. She squirmed against the caresses, enjoying them. She brushed against a smooth swell of muscle, which shouted, "Yow!" Vinory's eyes fluttered open to see the cat scooting across the floor between her and the fire, tail lashing furiously.

I'm just dreaming about the dance because I was thinking about it today, she told herself. Because I'm lonely.

When Vinory settled back to sleep, she forgot again to raise her wards. A tall, dark-haired, dark-eyed man came to her and showed her visions of the times he'd led the dance. He was graceful and slim-legged, with broad shoulders and narrow, strong hands that he used to lead his partner to and fro in the complicated patterns. Vinory felt herself tapping her feet, wishing she could join in. It looked so tempting. The man passed within arm's reach of her. She called him by name.

"Samon?"

He turned as if to answer, stretching out a hand to her, his eyes agleam. . . . Then she woke up, with the fitful light from a lantern in her eyes.

"Sorry to wake you, mistress," said Tarili, the baker. "My wife's baby's coming. She needs you. The baby's turned wrong."

"I'll come at once," she said. groaning, Vinory roused herself, and let the dream fade from her mind as she gathered her medicines and paraphernalia. She could now feel the presence standing in the corner, disappointed.

When she returned after daybreak, exhausted, the spirit resumed its campaign to get her attention, hovering around her like a bee on a lilac bush.

"Oh, go away, Master Samon!" she groaned, half asleep already. "I'm too tired to argue with you."

"That's why I'm pushing you now," he said, to her dreaming mind. "Wouldn't you like to have someone to warm you? Winter is coming. You could have a babe of your own next summer."

"I have a dozen babies! The villagers' children are my responsibility. You must not tie me down." She could see his face again, an inverted triangle of ivory, with those dark, long-lashed eyes. She was afraid even in her dreams, but tempted. Samon was very strong-willed. And handsome.

When she woke several hours later, she was refreshed, and also resolute. Samon was dead. She, Vinory, must stay alive and clear her mind. That meant banishing the spirit who continued to trouble her.

She felt panic. But knew at once it wasn't her own.

"If you won't, or can't, go on your own, then I must help you along," Vinory said, brutally. "It's only logical, Master Samon."

The presence sought to get between her and the book chest, but she just walked slap through him, ignoring the psychic shock she got from the contact.

She had seen a spell for setting free a trapped spirit in one of the handsomely made volumes that Samon had scribed for himself. Vinory thumbed through the books until she came to the one she remembered. It was a harsh enchantment. The rebound of the working would be hard on her, Vinory knew, but she could be rid of this nettlesome presence who awoke all sorts of feelings in her that she had no time for. She had what components were needed at hand. The text said the working must be done on Lammas Night. After that, he would be free, and so would she. She felt lucky that she had not come after Lammas. Otherwise it would be a whole year before she could send him away.

The spirit's panic was stronger than ever. Then, as she watched, the very pages of the tome turned over one by one, past the banishment spell, to another text. Vinory bent her head to read.

It was almost the same as the first, ridding a place of a troublesome spirit—but by locking it again into human form. The difference between the two spells was only a single word. She looked up involuntarily, as if Samon was sitting there across from her.

"You want me to re-embody you?" she asked. Feelings of joy and hope washed over her, then retreated at once, lest she chide him again for overwhelming her consciousness.

I could do it, Vinory thought, rereading the text. But do I want to? Samon has had his life—he's led it! But was his work done? Do I dare to make that decision, for or against? I serve Nature. But do I want so strong a man to push me out of my place just before the weather begins to turn?

Perhaps she was not as young as once she was; the thought of sleeping in cold caves and under the brush at waysides now bothered her. You're getting soft, she told herself. You're becoming too earthbound.

I was not earthbound enough, the presence felt at her. I lost my hold. It was too soon. Help me! It is my will.

She read the spells again, both of them, hoping for

clues to what she should do. The spells lacked reference to the high gods, and took part of her as well as of the one who sought reinstatement in life. Were these evil spells? Would she imperil her soul by performing one or the other? And yet, she had to do something, or the dead mage would drive her insane with his fretting and pleading. Either banish or restore, but she must do one of them, no matter what it cost her. To harvest one must sacrifice, so the Lammas rite went. But did she want this harvest? A mage who was neither good nor evil, and yet neither dead nor alive. And yet he was a living being, deserving of her aid.

Vinory's sleep that night was troubled by Samon's entreaties. "I will hold you in honor," his spirit said in her dreams. He dropped to his knees before her, the dark eyes pleading. "I will give you pride of place, and let you lead in all things, if I may live. Oh, lady, let me through!"

Honor. Samon could see all her thoughts. He knew the turmoil in her mind. How could Vinory hide anything from him? But did he mean it?

"I . . . I don't know if I can trust you, Master Samon," she said at last, conscious even though her body was asleep. "I'm afraid of what admitting you back into life will mean to me. I dare not undo what the gods have done. You should go on to the Summerlands beyond the Veil."

"Not yet! Oh, I will be kind, lady. On pain of eternal condemnation, I swear it. I will give you all honor."

"How can I believe it?" Vinory asked. "You'll say anything so that I will open the Door on Lammas Night and let you through instead of banishing you forever."

"See for yourself," he said, taking both her hands between his as he continued to kneel before her. The impishness touched his eyes, and she felt like melting. He was so very handsome. "If I lie, you can take other revenge upon me. To be mortal again has its own discomforts. It will at least be interesting to stand with you, for fair or foul."

She took chances; why else would she be a witch and a mage if she was not ready to face the unseen and call the unknown by its name? A challenge like that appealed to her more than any of his blandishments, but she was still uncertain.

"I will think about it," she promised.

The candles burned as she swung open the cottage door to allow the night breeze to enter. The villagers of Twin Streams had gone off to enjoy the rest of their harvest night. Now she was left with only one task to do. The spirit of Samon waited at the perimeter of the room, full of fear and anticipation as to his coming fate, for it was tonight or never.

All the materials Vinory needed were laid out. She lit each one of the candles in turn, praying to the gods that what she was about to do was right. The warm breeze caressed her bare skin as she chalked the circle on the floor and stood inside it. She took up the book and read aloud from it by the light of the candle in her hand. Her voice trembled through the first syllables, then grew stronger, though she felt the pull of unseen forces at the very stuff of her existence.

The golden light broke from the candles at the points of the compass and joined together to form a ring of fire which grew and grew until she was surrounded by it. And then it died away, leaving an arch at the north side of the circle. Through it she could see a shadow. It was a mature man with dark hair and eyes, and milk-pale skin. She smiled at her tentatively. Vinory knew at once that this was Samon. She must send him away or answer his plea *now*. There was no more time to decide.

"I will give you all my honor, no matter what you decide," Samon said. He looked hopeful, like a puppy who did not dare to wag its tail. "May I come, or must I go?"

He held out a daffodil to her, as a token of the beginning of new things for both of them. At least it would be an interesting life from now on, she thought. A considerate lover, so the girl had said. He would have to be, to make up for the part of her life the restoration of his life would take. Vinory smiled. For fair or foul.

"Come," she said, and held out her hand to him.

Summer Storms

CHRISTIE GOLDEN

It was one thunderstorm too many for Lauris. She had just gotten her cloak, her clothes, her *juya* bag and her familiar, Shadow, dried from the last deluge when the warning rumble caused her to glance up at the rapidly clouding sky. Lauris wrapped her stiff cloak around her tall frame. Shadow crouched at her feet, his gray tail swishing. She gathered the cat in her arms, doing what she could to shield the animal with her cloak.

The rain came. And kept coming as Lauris slogged her way along the dirt path that rapidly changed to mud, threatening to suck off her boots with each step.

There were weatherworking spells. Lauris knew some of them. But they were tiring, and the materials were costly, and it was easier to bundle up against the wet than defy it. Though, Lauris admitted as the rain began to soak through her cloak yet again, if she did indeed have the materials, she'd put them to good use right now.

A weathered sign announced that the village of Greenhaven lay two miles hence. The thought of a dry bed, hot food and perhaps a pint of ale cheered the weary young woman, and there was a spring in her step despite the hungry mud.

The little inn, the Blue Bell, couldn't have been

more welcoming. A fire glowed brightly. The few customers inside glanced up, then back down at the games in which they were clearly engrossed. Lauris stepped inside, shivering.

"Good day, miss," came a voice. Lauris glanced up, heaving the thick, sodden mass of her dark hair off her pale face. She smiled at the innkeeper, who took her cloak. He inhaled swiftly at the sight of the gray cat and the unmistakable sigil that marked the *juya* bag. His bushy eyebrows shot up.

"Yes, I'm of wizard-kind," Lauris replied in answer to his unvoiced question. "My home is the road, but I am happy to leave it behind in such weather!"

The innkeeper relaxed, and a spark of avarice sprang to his eyes. Lauris could tell that he was already wondering what to ask for in return for shelter and food. She strode up to the fire with a sigh of pleasure.

"You are a welcome sight, Lady Wizard," came a voice from the nearest table. Lauris turned. The man who had addressed her lounged in his chair. Dark hair flowed down his broad shoulders. A mustache and beard hid most of his face, but his piercing blue eyes regarded her steadily.

"And why is that?" she asked.

"Our own wizard died two months ago, and we've been lost without him." He rose and strode toward her, graceful as Shadow despite his bulk. "The crops alternately burn or drown. Our herds grow thinner. And there have even been reports of disappearing children."

"And who are you, to credit such rumors?"

"I am Aelfric, headman of Greenhaven. They are *not* rumors, I assure you."

Lauris turned her gaze back to the fire. "And what would you have me do, Headman Aelfric?"

"I would have you stay, and protect our village as Wizard Blayne did." Startled, she glanced back at him. "His home stands empty. None of us dare go inside. All is as he left it—books, tools, garden. We're poor folk, but we will recompense you fairly. Will you consider my offer?"

Her eyes searched his, seeking out the lie. Lauris knew how to sense deceit and malice—it was all part of her training. She found none. Aelfric's offer, as far as her skills could tell, was both generous and genuine. Lauris thought of the rain, the mud, the loneliness that had been her life up to now, and nodded. His face relaxed into a smile. "I am so glad. When you are warm, sit and eat with me, and I will tell you of Greenhaven."

Two days later, Lauris knew she had made the right decision. No lady in her manor home could have been happier than Lauris in the four-bay, stone-walled house with fresh thatching for its roof. Behind the house was a garden, overgrown (no villager would dare weed a wizard's garden!) but planted with all manner of useful herbs. And the books! The solar that had served as Blayne's bedroom was crammed with them.

Lauris was leafing through a pile of old tomes when a knock on the door startled her.

"Come," she called.

A lad of about thirteen summers poked his head in shyly. "Good morning, milady," he murmured. "My name is Tomas. I served Master Blayne before he—when he lived here, and I'm to serve you as faithfully. I've brought you some food, and I've come to clean for you."

Lauris quirked an eyebrow. "Aelfric said nothing of a servant," she said.

The boy shrugged. "Headman Aelfric doesn't know everything about Master Blayne."

She regarded the youth for a moment, from his tow head to his scuffed boots, sensed only shyness and sincerity, and decided she liked him. "Very well. Come in, and I'll sit in the garden while you clean."

He smiled, and it was like the sun coming out from behind the clouds. She had made the right choice.

She left him to his chores, smiling herself as he burst into an off-key rendition of the latest drinking tune as he made a fire in the hearth and set a pot to boil. Outside, the late summer heat made the garden seem hazy to Lauris's eyes. She stretched in the sun as Shadow might, then knelt on the good, clean earth and began to weed.

He's planted everything, she thought as she worked. Yarrow, agrimony, lady's mantle, angelica, woodworm, mugwort, chamomile, meadowsweet, lavender, feverfew—every herb she was familiar with seemed to be growing here, as well as several she'd never seen before. She'd have to go back over Blayne's books to see if he had one on herbs.

Eventually, Lauris rose, wincing as she straightened, and noticed that the sun had traveled quite a way across the sky. Clearly, she'd lost track of time, poking around in Blayne's—no, *her*—garden. But that was all right. She couldn't recall when she'd felt so . . . carefree.

She realized she was smiling as she walked back into the house. Tomas had gone, but he had set out food for her—and something else. A rose, pink and soft as a baby's mouth, lay across the metal trencher.

How sweet, and yet how awkward. She'd have to handle the youth's infatuation gently. She picked up the rose, inhaled the sweet fragrance, then ate heartily of the fare Tomas had provided.

Suddenly Lauris saw a shadow move out of the corner of her eye. She jumped, then told herself it was surely no more than poor young Tomas, blushingly eager to see how his token was received. But when she turned around, there was no one there.

"Who's there?" she called, but no answer came. The wizard glanced around for Shadow, trusting the cat's senses more than her own, but the feline had gone—off hunting voles in the garden, no doubt. Where was a familiar when you needed him? "Tomas?"

No reply. Frowning a little, she moved to the opened door, and peered out. Only the dirt road, winding its way from the village to the forest trail, met her gaze. A breeze rose, stirring up dust, and Lauris firmly closed the door. She was annoyed to find that her heart was beating rapidly. An idea was starting to take shape in her mind, an idea that, if true, would spell trouble, caution, and fear.

That idea's name was *ghost*.

Lauris had never seen the ocean, but now she stood on the white sand, her naked shoulders turned to alabaster by the radiance of the full moon, and flung back her head. The wind took her long, dark hair and gave it new life. She shivered at the zephyr's cool fingers as they caressed her skin, then walked into the warm, welcoming water.

Though she did not know how to swim, she merged effortlessly with the ocean, a mermaid who yet kept her legs. Shark and octopus brushed past her, but Lauris was unafraid until she sensed panic in the ocean depths.

Something was here that did not belong, that was afraid, that did not know how to live—that would soon die, its lungs clogged with sea water, if she did not intervene.

Swiftly, Lauris swam toward the panicked creature. Her arms went around it, pulling it to the surface where it shuddered and began to breathe. It was then that she realized she clasped a man to her breast. His pale skin glistened, and when his breath returned and he gazed at her, stars shone from his face. Then she was in his arms, and he kissed her, and then it was she who could not breathe, did not *want* to breathe if it meant ending this sweet, soul-shuddering kiss—

—Lauris bolted upright, gasping. Outside, it was raining again. A flash of lightning illuminated no seascape, only her own room crowded with tools and books. Tears covered her face, trickling into her mouth, where she tasted their sea-saltiness.

"Tell me of Wizard Blayne," asked Lauris a few hours later, sitting with Headman Aelfric at the Blue Bell.

The big man shrugged. "What do you want to know?" he countered, watching her closely.

"What kind of man was he? How did he take care of the villagers? That sort of thing."

"Well, begging your pardon, I don't much take to wizardfolk," said the headman uncomfortably. "They deal with things I don't understand—don't want to understand. You're the first I've ever met that I've felt comfortable around. Blayne—well, he was a loner. Tall, skinny fellow with blond hair. His eyes had this faraway look to them—as if he wasn't ever really here."

Lauris kept her face calm. As before, she sensed no deception—only a mistrust of wizard-kind that was, sadly, far too common. "Any visitors? Other than the villagers?"

Aelfric's brows drew together. "Now that you mention it, yes. There were a few wanderers who came

into town specifically to see him." The frown grew
thunderous. "I didn't trust any of them, not one bit."

"Did they come as friends, or seekers of help?" *Or
did they come as enemies?*

"I don't know. Didn't like the look of 'em, kept
well enough away." Suddenly anger suffused his face.
"Is someone bothering you? Name the bastard, and
I'll—"

"No, no, nothing like that," Lauris soothed, dis-
tressed and yet oddly flattered that it should matter
so much to him. "I'm sure no one in Greenhaven
means me harm."

"If anyone as much as says a cruel word to you,
they'll have me to deal with," the big man growled.
"And that's a promise. I don't like the idea of a pretty
young thing like you, in that house all by herself . . ."

Lauris smothered a smile. Beneath the table, where
Aelfric could not see, her nimble fingers moved in a
conjuration. Aelfric's knife suddenly tore itself from
his hands, twirled around in the air, and then embedded itself to the hilt in the table.

"I can take care of myself," she smiled, enjoying
the shocked admiration on the big man's face.

The night passed uneventfully. Morning brought an
old woman with aching joints, who paid a plump hen
for a salve to ease her pain. The afternoon saw a
young man who blushed and stammered as he asked
for a love potion. The days passed, and Lauris gradually began to win the villagers' trust. She had almost
forgotten about the half-remembered dream and half-
glimpsed shadow until one night, a fortnight or so
later, when she sat curled up by the fire with a pile
of books while a summer storm raged outside.

It was warm inside the house. The fire was more
for light than heat. Expecting no one on an evening

such as this, Lauris had spread out a blanket by the fire and lay on her stomach, naked, and was engrossed in her research.

A foot or so away, Shadow dozed. "So many spells," said Lauris to her familiar. He swiveled a gray ear in her direction. "I wonder what happened to him. Surely such a powerful wizard wouldn't be taken by surprise."

Unless the Dark itself devoured him, came a thought that did not originate inside her own head.

At once, Shadow was on his feet. His back arched, and his yellow gaze fastened on something Lauris could not see.

Lauris went bone cold. "Make yourself known," she whispered. But she already knew who it was—didn't she?

You grace this house, came the external thought. *Such beauty . . . such compassion . . .*

And then something cold as the grave itself brushed past her, through her. Lauris gasped, feeling icy tendrils of nothingness stroke her body, take shape, though remaining invisible, and become cold, strong arms, and she felt the press of lips that were not there on hers. . . .

Gasping, she wriggled out of the specter's embrace, knowing now beyond all doubt that it was Blayne. Or at least, something that had once been Blayne. It was still here, still tied to this world, unable to pass on as it ought.

She scrambled for the book. She'd seen it, just recently, the spell that this frightening *(exciting)* situation demanded. She flipped through the old pages, absently noting in the back of her mind that they were fragile but not caring when they tore, until she found it.

"A Spell to Banysh Spyrits," read the spidery

lettering. Lauris closed her eyes in relief. The spell required that it be cast on Lammas Night—the night of the dying god, one of the high holy days. And Lammas was, thank the gods, only a few days hence.

Suddenly aware of her nakedness, she gathered the blanket around her body to shield her from the eyes of her visitor whom, she knew by Shadow's discomfort, had not yet departed. Lauris couldn't sense him any more, though. Where was—

And then he announced his presence a second time. As she watched, the pages of the book lying in front of her began to turn, as if flipped by a gentle wind, then stopped. Her heart nearly shaking her with its pounding, Lauris glanced down at the spell.

"A Spell to Reanimayte the Dead."

She blinked, confused. This spell seemed identical to the first. Same list of items, the same charge that it be performed on Lammas Night—it was a duplicate. No, not quite. One word was different. One single word—the difference between true death, and new life.

I want to be with you, whispered the voice inside her head.

Lauris knew that when she accepted the privileges of wizard-kind, there came hand in hand with those advantages a terrible responsibility: to always use the magic wisely, and in the service of the Light. She had sworn at the end of her apprenticeship to help, heal, do no harm, perform no spell that was not of the Light. But neither spell indicated if it were for good or ill. She could not ignore the situation. She would go mad. She had to act—but which spell should she cast? Should she send the spirit of Blayne, clearly cut down before his time, to eternal sleep?

Or should she bring him back?

At that instant, Lauris wished with all her heart that

she were married to the lowliest, cruelest, drunkest peasant, with no shoes, no learning, four children to tend and a fifth swelling in her belly. It would be easier than this dreadful decision.

She bowed her head and began to cry.

From a corner of the room where he had taken refuge, Shadow stared at the unseen thing and hissed angrily.

It was fitting that Lammas Night fell when the moon was in her crone phase—dying, as the young god, as the harvest season itself, symbolically died. The winds were fierce and batted the clouds about the heavens, alternately revealing and obscuring the waning moon.

Lauris had moved the furniture into the corners to create a working space. She moved jerkily, her mouth set in a thin, grim line. She did not look like a wizard in control of the spell; she did not feel like one. Murmuring the incantation written in both the spell for banishment and reanimation, she strewed wheat flour on the floor, casting a sacred circle.

The door was open. Though the wind raged outside, it did not penetrate inside to disturb her work.

Now it begins, she thought. *Oh, gods, give me the strength to make the right decision.*

She closed her eyes and began the chant common to both spells, sanctifying the circle and honoring each of the four quarters with a gift: a feather for the East, a lit flame for the South, a bowl of water for the West, a dish of loam for the North.

"I call forth representatives of the forces of Light and Shadow, who would battle for the soul of this man!" she cried imperiously, flinging up her hands. To her right, she felt rather than saw something warm and protective materialize. But on her left, the essence of darkness manifested, and from that part of the room she sensed a deep, deep cold, and a malevolence that extended far beyond the confines of this world. She shuddered, but knew that her circle protected her.

"I summon the spirit of the wizard Blayne of Greenhaven to this which was his home in life!" Her voice was hoarse, and she realized that the wind had risen. In the distance, but growing ever closer, thunder boomed. A storm would be here soon.

Dust billowed, caught by the wind, directly outside the door. No—not dust. It was something else, something that swirled and twisted and out of which grew a shape, a shape that Lauris knew, had held, had kissed.

He was nearly transparent at first, then began to take on color and detail. He stood at least six feet, slender but not slight. His face contorted with the agony of being brought back into form and substance, but it was a face with clean lines and dark, wise eyes. His hair was the color of wheat, his skin milky pale.

Lauris's voice caught in her throat. The next step to complete the incantation—either one—was to issue a Command. One word would send Blayne back permanently into the sleep of death. The other would give him a second life.

Shadow crouched behind her, safe within the circle. He hissed and cowered, spitting angrily. *Does he know something I don't know?* Lauris thought despairingly. But that could not be it; for good or evil, Blayne was at the moment an unnatural creature, caught between death, undeath and true life. She knew that Shadow would have hissed at her, had she been where the other wizard was now. The familiar's hostile reaction was no clue as to Blayne's nature.

She had to speak, choose, or else the circle would collapse and the agents of Light and Darkness would battle for possession of them both. Desperately,

Lauris glanced to Them for aid, but They remained silent. This was her choice.

Let me come, pleaded Blayne silently, warm in her thoughts. The Blayne-thing stretched out its arms imploringly.

If she chose wrongly . . .

She opened her mouth, not knowing which Command would come out, surrendering to that part of her mind beyond thought.

"*Come!*" Lauris cried, sobbing. Beyond all logic, she loved him, and she would take the risk.

The next second was the longest in Lauris's life. Even as the thunder boomed and the heavens opened, there was an equally loud shriek from directly outside her circle. The agents of Darkness and Light vanished. Where they had been now lay, respectively, charred ashes and flower petals.

Blayne shuddered, then collapsed. Color suffused him. He was real, solid, whole—alive. Lauris's own knees gave way beneath her, and she stared, wide-eyed, at the man whom she had given new life.

Groaning, Blayne struggled to his knees. She realized now that he wore the same clothes in which he had been buried; they were partially decomposed, though the human flesh they adorned was whole. She couldn't speak; could only stare.

He lifted his head, his beautiful, wheat-gold head and pierced her with his blue gaze. A slow smile spread across his handsome face. "Lauris," he said, softly, tenderly. "Oh, Lauris, my love . . ."

Then he stumbled to his feet and reached for her, his boots smudging the circle of wheat flour as he entered her sacred space. Lauris's fear bled out of her. Nothing evil could enter that circle, and as his strong arms went around her she eagerly turned her face up for his demanding, hungry, joyful kiss.

Blayne.

It was sweeter than the dream, at once simpler, more human, and more powerful. She melted into him, and if his wise, wizard's hands had moved to remove her magical garb, she would have made the second move to lovemaking herself. She was dizzy with joy and relief. *Blayne, Blayne . . . !*

But he tore himself away from her, panting, and his hands moved from her waist to her upper arms. "I pray to all the gods that there will be a chance to love you afterward . . . but now, there's no time . . ."

"Wh-what?"

He was exasperated, but his blue eyes never lost their gentleness. "Lauris, what do you think happened to me? I was murdered!"

A chill that had nothing to do with the night air shuddered through her. "By whom?"

"Aelfric!"

"Impossible," replied Lauris. "I sensed him . . . every time I talked to him. I would have been able to tell if he were evil!"

Blayne shook his head. "He was able to block your sensing. Who better than a wizard to hide his true nature from another?"

Lauris's heart began to thud in horror. Blayne was right—such a thing could be done.

"Aelfric is an agent of the Dark, Lauris. I discovered his plans and tried to stop him. He killed me; he would have killed you, too. Don't drink from the well in the back; it's poisoned. He did it earlier tonight, just in case he wasn't able to complete the spell."

"But . . . but this makes no sense . . . he was the one who asked me to stay, after . . ."

"He had to! Think how strange it would have looked for a headman not to ask any wandering wizard to abide and protect the town. He never thought you were a real enemy; you're young, and you're a woman." Blayne's lips curved in a harried smile. "This far out of the cities, love, you'll run into that sort of attitude. But we must hurry. Tonight, he completes the ritual. He began it last Lammas. He killed me on Midsummer, a night of High Power for the forces of Light, which is why I was able to hang on to this world." His hand smoothed her hair. "Until you set me free. Come, my love. Together, we can defeat him and hold back the Dark."

Tomas stood naked in front of Headman Aelfric. The dark wizard's powers held the youth motionless, but did nothing to stop the sweat of rank terror that poured off Tomas's body, mixing with the raindrops that hit his skin with stinging force.

Now, he knew why the herds were growing thin. Now, he knew where the missing children had gone. Now, he was about to join them. He stared up at Headman Aelfric, tears creeping out of eyes that were not permitted to blink, and he prayed for reprieve though he knew it would never come.

At the boy's feet inside the bloody circle was a clutter of small objects. He knew their purpose; Aelfric had told him. Each trinket, each bit of nail paring or piece of crockery or baby's toy belonged to one of the villagers. When the dark wizard completed the ritual, sealed his pact with his evil masters by dousing the items with Tomas's blood, the souls of every man, woman and child in Greenhaven would belong to Aelfric. He in turn would then offer them to the Dark, in return for power unimaginable.

Aelfric was unrecognizable. Gone was the stalwart, solid headman Tomas had known all his life. The words spewing from Aelfric's lips were unknown to the boy, but their power and their foulness made his skin crawl. When the incantation was done, the black knife Aelfric held in his left hand would descend, be buried to the hilt in Tomas's chest.

The chant grew louder, the words faster, harsher on the ear. Aelfric's eyes glinted red. His fingers clenched on the evil weapon's hilt.

Tomas wished he could close his eyes.

"*No!*" cried a clear, male voice—a voice that Tomas had never thought to hear again in this lifetime. "I forbid it!"

Tomas could not turn his head, but he did not need to. Aelfric's horrified face, fastened on the figure directly behind the boy, showed all. "It . . . it's not possible," he breathed. "I killed you! You're dead, Blayne!"

Blayne, for surely it was he, laughed. "I *was* dead. But she brought me back—brought me back to fight and defeat you."

"You murdered Blayne by trickery." This was a feminine voice, harsh with righteous anger. Lauris, tall and straight, stepped out of the shadows. "You thought to poison me. You've no stomach for fighting. The Dark will tear you apart. Yield. You cannot face us both!"

For a moment, it seemed as though Aelfric would. Then he drew the black knife across his own palm, laying open a red streak. Suddenly, the knife began to radiate a dull, pulsing purple aura.

"Now the knife has tasted blood!" he crowed. "It must have a human life, or else the full power of Darkness will come upon the land! You speak bravely, wizards, but you know you cannot violate my circle!" And he raised the knife again, resuming the incantation, preparing to slay Tomas even as blood dripped from his own injured hand.

"Perhaps not," Lauris screamed over the thunder. "But if the rain can enter your circle . . ." and she gestured with her hands, "then the lightning surely can!"

Tomas was never certain as to what happened next. One instant, he was standing in front of Aelfric, awaiting his murder. The next he hit the earth a good twenty feet away. His entire body thrummed, spasmed, and for a moment he couldn't breathe. Then suddenly air rushed into his lungs and he painfully turned to see what had happened to Aelfric.

A few yards away, his body smoking, lay the dark wizard. A flash of lightning illuminated his twisted, blackened features. There was a terrible burn in his chest, a second on his feet. By the lightning's illumination, Tomas realized that the boots and skin of the feet had been burned clean away—white bones showed through. He was no threat to anyone anymore.

The knife was another matter. It lay just outside the circle, radiating that eerie purple gleam.

."Dear gods," breathed Blayne, "he was telling the truth. That is a Kitlis dagger, and he has awakened its hunger." His gaze locked with Lauris's. Suddenly he reached for her, brought her close in a fierce, passionate embrace. Then in one fluid motion he pushed the wizard away, lunged for the dagger, and plunged it into his belly.

The storm raged. Rain scoured the crumpling body of the wheat-haired wizard. Wildly, Tomas was reminded of the legend of Lammas Night—the willing sacrifice of the young god, to ensure a bountiful harvest.

Lauris gave a wordless scream of anguish and loss. She crawled over to her beloved, tried to pull the dagger out. But Blayne laid a bloody hand on hers, staying her.

"No," he commanded. "I was already dead. I see that I was meant to die ... that in the end, Aelfric was meant to be my death. I will not give innocents over to the Dark. I ... I am sorry, beloved ... what magic, what love, we could have made . . ." He reached to touch her cheek. Lauris seized him, shook him angrily, but Blayne was already gone. Before Tomas's horrified gaze, the wizard began to decompose. His time in life, as he had intimated, had only been borrowed, not bought. Lauris was beyond caring. She clasped the rotting flesh to her breast, rocked him back and forth, and began to outkeen the howling storm.

The tale of how Lauris and Blayne defeated the worst enemy to have trod Greenhaven soil brought the young wizard fame. She continued, though, to be as accessible as ever. Tomas became her close friend, but as the years passed, he realized that the love he bore her would never be requited. Something quiet and patient sat in her prematurely-aged eyes. Once, he asked her about it.

She was silent for a time, then spoke.

"I have looked into the well of Death, reached inside, and pulled out Love. I could not hold it—no mortal could, I suppose—but I know it is there. I know *he* is there. I see him in the eyes of all those I help. My life, Tomas, is merely a summer storm. It rages long and loud, but I know that soon it will pass. Then I can be with him I love beyond all imagining."

Her eyes were distant, soft, misty. "I can wait out the storm."

A Choice of Many

MARK A. GARLAND

"What do you mean he's dead?" Alluen asked. "What happened."

"We don't know," Jon the miller, who was also the mayor, replied. "We found him . . . that is, what we think was him, smoldering in his house, in a circle he'd drawn. Lennet, his name was." Jon's pouchy cheeked face and easy manner were the sort that could put anyone at ease, but his nervous eyes betrayed him.

"When we hired him he claimed to be a skilled adept, you understand," Thella, the miller's wife, added. She was a bit larger than Jon, and certainly less malleable. "I never thought so. Many make claims, and his claims were many. In truth, he was an ill-mannered, inept young fool."

"So he did it to himself, but you have no idea what he might have been trying to do," Alluen persisted.

"We expect he . . . did something wrong," Jon said.

"Yes, but wrong in what way?" Alluen looked about. Most everyone living in or near the village seemed to be on hand, several hundred of them. A most distracted collection of faces. As though someone had asked them to keep a secret. "Those who court a flame risk a burn!" someone shouted.

Thella stepped closer to Alluen, her gaze steady.

110

"He was a scoundrel, I say. Not a word of truth in him. Too much of that with your kind. So tell us now if your magic is of the Light. If your soul is clean."

Alluen stared back, steadfast. "Yes.

"Good!" Jon exclaimed, with obvious relief. He took Alluen by the arm and pointed her up the street. "You may have the sorcerer's house, of course. And all those books. You do like books?"

"Oh, very much."

"You aren't carrying any," Thella said accusingly. "The others we hired, the men, *all* had books. Even Lennet."

"Many . . . others?" Alluen asked, all the more concerned.

"Only a few," Jon said hastily, glancing briefly at his wife. "But we have had a run of bad luck. People are afraid. Lives are at stake, after all."

But whose? Alluen wondered. "Lives?"

"Thella is concerned that our next sorcerer might be like the last," Jon continued. "And that a . . . a girl, you see, like yourself, and so young, might not be as . . ."

"I know," Alluen said. She was used to this. Even in her own village, where her father had been revered by one and all, his short, skinny, young daughter had been thought of as little more than a hedge witch. She'd been nearly as skilled in sorceries as he, yet when he passed away the many visitors to their cottage in the woods seemed to vanish with him. As if she, too, had died. Leaving that place had seemed the best thing to do.

"Rest all concerns," Alluen said. "I have traveled too far and too long, so my belongings are few. But I am up to the tasks you would ask of me. Trust in that."

"You won't have any trouble getting folks to cook for you, or stock your pantry," Jon explained smartly.

"Not so long as you remain here," his wife sniffed.

"She'll do fine," Jon insisted.

"That is what I intend, but what do I have to do?" Alluen asked in the silence that followed.

"Cast your spells!" the miller told her with a quick, feeble grin. "For the sick, the luck-lost, the changeable seasons; they all need spell weaving."

"That, and the Dark," Thella muttered, folding her arms.

Jon's grin abruptly faded. No one else made a sound.

"Your people are afraid of the dark?" Alluen asked.

"We fear your magic can be turned!" someone from the crowd answered. "We fear the evils we have been cursed with already. Evils you might make worse!"

"If she has any magic at all," another said.

"You can't believe any of her kind," said a third. The crowd seemed to be pressing nearer, their faces tightening.

"I make no false claims, trust in that!" she told them, wondering what evils they seemed to fear so greatly.

"There is no trust for the likes of you!" someone shouted back.

"Just look at you!" called one more.

Alluen instinctively touched one hand to the carved bone handle of the dagger her father had given her, ages ago. "Magic may fail, but you can always trust in a good blade," he had told her. She kept it with her always, and always kept it sharp; still, she had never found cause to use it as a weapon.

"We must give her a chance," Jon scolded them all. "Who else have we?"

This last brought another silence, and a weight in Alluen's stomach.

"Do you have spells that'll keep the Dark at bay?" Thella pressed.

Alluen had been in the village two weeks now, and had yet to notice any strange behavior, day or night. *No matter*, she told herself. She was still weary from the road, and weeks of travel had gained her nothing. In each village it was the same: either she was perceived as a threat to local magic folk, or no one would take her seriously. Until now. She had to give them a chance, and convince them to give her one as well.

"I have many spells, in here," Alluen assured them all, tapping the side of her head. "And my magic is true, as I have said."

"Ah, you see? Well and good!" Jon said, trying the grin again. "You'll get coin, too, what we can give, and trade. And our gratitude ... er, eventually."

Room and board and more sounded wonderful, especially with the winter season approaching. And the needs of these people were small, surely. After all, one could keep the dark at bay simply by building a fire. "Whatever the task, I shall meet it," she promised. Before much else could be said, Jon began to lead her up the street to the wizard's house, leaving most everyone else behind amidst a din of mumbling.

The house itself looked like any other on the street, two stories, wood frame, daub and wattle walls. Jon opened the front door. Alluen entered, but Jon did not. Even when she asked.

"The Dark," he said. "Good day."

The house seemed cozy enough, and the collection of books, some written in exotic languages, was more remarkable than any Alluen had ever seen. Her favorite was the late wizard Lennet's book of spells—she assumed it was his—which Alluen was sure would take her weeks just to look through. Meanwhile the townsfolk brought her ample food and drink, even clothing, yet not one of them was willing to set foot inside her house.

Each time she was needed, which had only been twice in three times that many days, someone from the village would come and knock, then ask her to follow along. She had used an old and simple spell that seemed to help one young girl rid herself of a mild fever, then she'd done much the same for an old man's rash. Each time, she asked those present to come to her house for a visit. "Thank you," the girl's mother had said, and the old man and his wife as well, "but we must not. It's the Dark, you see."

By the end of a week, Alluen decided she had had enough. She asked Jon to meet her at the village inn where, in a quiet corner, she managed to entice Jon to tip first one tankard, then another. When she thought he had gained a sufficiently pliable disposition, she cast a spell that rarely worked, one intended to coax the truth from reluctant lips. Controlling another's thoughts was nearly impossible, even for the most skilled adept, but with enough help from a good brewer the effect could be quite . . . magical.

"Have you ever cheated on your wife?" Alluen asked, just testing.

"Of course I have," Jon boasted, taking yet another swallow. He grinned at her, then wrinkled his nose. "But you are too young and scrawny for me."

"I will trust in the gods to make me worthy, one day," Alluen replied. "For now, you will tell me why no one will enter my house."

Jon's head flopped left as if support had been suddenly withdrawn. "Oh, you'd like me to tell you that, wouldn't you . . . tell you all our secrets."

"Yes, I would."

Jon shrugged. "Very well. A sorcerer by the name of Kimall, a vile old fool of a man, they say, once made our village his home. This was long before my time, and the story is not always the same."

Alluen leaned a bit closer. "Go on."

Jon drew a long breath. "In an attempt to gather more power, he summoned a creature of some sort, a thing of pure darkness as dreadful as Kimall could ever have hoped, but of no mind to tell its secrets, or do Kimall's bidding, alas."

Alluen's father had told her stories of looking over the edge into the dark abyss, of those lured by its vast potential—but the danger, like the pull of the darkness, was always great. "And this is the thing you call the Dark?"

"Aye," Jon said, somewhat chagrined. He finished his third tankard, examined the bottom of the empty vessel as he went on. "Kimall commanded the beast to surrender its powers to him, but the demon apparently preferred the quick harvest Kimall himself supplied."

"It ate Kimall," Alluen clarified.

"So they say."

Alluen beckoned to the innkeeper for more ale. "But what became of the beast after that?"

"It cannot stay in this world for long, we believe. It weakens quickly, fades to nothing, and returns to the nether realms, where it remains until it can renew itself and enter our world once more. Which makes it hungry enough to eat a small family at least, as some of our villagers have learned too well. Most flee, but it finds some of us. Always, it appears in the wizard's house first. So that is where you must stop it. The last wizard, Lennet . . . failed."

"Why?"

"Alas," Jon said painfully, "I cannot say, though my good wife, you see, and many others, they have their ideas."

"You said you think he did something wrong. Tell me what?"

Jon puzzled over this for a moment. "We think he tried to make a deal with the beast. A partnership of some sort. The power of the Dark is great, and a sorcerer who controls it would be . . . greater, I think. Some worry that Lennet believed he could succeed where old Kimall failed. Many of us worry the next sorcerer—you—will try to do the same."

Alluen looked closely into the other's eyes. "And you didn't intend to tell me of this?"

"At length," Jon assured her. "But you would have known about the Dark, no matter."

"How?"

"The Dark comes always on Lammas Night. But they say an adept can sense the creature's coming before that."

"Lammas Night is but a few days away!"

"Many are already preparing to leave," Jon said, verifying.

Alluen wanted to know more, every little detail, but she was sure poor Jon could not provide them. He'd finished with this tankard as well now, and his words were getting too rounded to understand. "No doubt, you will be gone in the morning," he said after a time, more or less. "I can hardly blame you. Thella can, and the rest, but not me." He grinned, again holding his head as if it weighed too much.

"No," Alluen said. She had been in too many places where no one trusted or wanted her, sometimes even when their need was great. Places like home. This village would be different. This time. Jon was different, and Lennet had surely been a fool, or not of the Light to begin with. She went round and helped the miller to his feet. "I will be here," she told him. "And I will do whatever I must do. Trust in that."

"Aye," Jon muttered, and nothing more.

Alluen lay in bed that night thinking about all that the miller had said, until finally she slept. She woke in the middle of the night, aware that she was not alone.

He was just there, in the night. And still there, come morning, though he was nothing seen or heard. Alluen was sure the presence was a "he," though she could be sure of little else. Other than the fact that he was following her through the house. Now she remembered the miller's words only too well.

"I am not afraid of the Dark," she said to the entity that seemed to watch her as she dressed, seemed to shadow her as she stoked the fire, attend her as she ate her dinner, and lie just beside her as she went to bed that night. She felt a chill whenever she allowed herself to acknowledge the subtle apparition. She sensed the other's regard, an earnest devotion, perhaps, though there was something cold and empty about it, too, a gnawing hunger.

"What do you want?" she asked, reaching in the night, sensing the presence fade back out of reach.

No answer. She hadn't truly expected any. Lammas Night was still a few days away, after all. It was quite likely that this creature of the Dark, whatever he was, gained substance as the time drew near, that he did not spring fully formed from the nether realms on his birthday like a gift from a box. *Good,* she thought, steeling herself against the fear that gathered in her throat—telling herself so that she might accept it. *Well and good, for this will give me time and chances to learn more of that which I must face. Time to find a means to abrogate its claims upon this world.*

She slept lightly, finally, though despite the mild night and several blankets, she never got warm.

In the morning she found fresh water in her basin,

and a splash of sweet perfume. Downstairs she found
the fire already stoked, a bowl and a cup already
placed on the table.

"Perhaps you are afraid of me," Alluen mused out
loud. *Or you are full of wicked games ... the more
likely truth.* Alluen's father had raised no fool. The
creature might well have wooed young Lennet in
much the same way—might have been female for
him.

Late in the day, when Alluen left the house to
visit a woman who was suffering dizzy spells, the
presence remained behind. She felt a chill leave her
spine as she realized she was free of him. Though
soon enough it was time to return. She dreaded the
fact, and yet ...

She found water for stew already heating over the
fire, a clean plate on the table, and on the plate, a
single fresh-cut blossom, a lover's token. Few men
from her village had come to court her, her being
born of magic folk, and Alluen had never known a
lover, her father had seen to that. Leaving home
hadn't changed anything. She hadn't stayed any one
place long enough to allow another man to attempt
to measure up.

Love both intrigued and frightened her, to be sure,
but the love of a demon was something altogether
different. A forbidden thing. Unnatural. Untenable.
Yet she could not deny the thought. Could not ignore
the kindness, the ardor this one seemed capable of,
at least toward her.

Alluen lay awake most of that night, sensing the
presence almost beside her, fighting the urge to imagine what forbidden moments might await her on Lammas Night. Or what swift death, she reminded herself,
not for the first time, though this night that warning
seemed less palpable.

Finally she slept, but only to dream. She woke with a start, her head still filled with swirling images. The man in her dream was surely Lennet, the young sorcerer who had died in this very house, and he had come asking for her help, begging to be allowed to die, finally, truly. But he brought a second plea as well, for herself: warning her not to listen to the people of the village, to believe nothing any of them said about the Dark, about old Kimall, about what had happened to him, or she might surely share his fate.

It was not unheard of that the soul of one who died in torment should remain tied to a place, and Alluen was already convinced that this was precisely what she had encountered in her dream. She even had an idea what she might do about it. In the dream she had seen an image of Lennet's own book of magics, open to one particular group of spells. She went straight to the book and found it already opened. As she began to read, she discovered the spell before her to be one of banishment.

This was what all such souls desired, to be set free of this world, to finish dying and find eternity's peace. Whatever sort of scoundrel or fool Lennet had been, he deserved that much.

"I will help you end your torment," she said out loud, noting the structure of the spell, and one detail in particular: this spell, like many, was tied to a single date. There was but one time of the year when she could be sure the spell would work. The night of the beast. Lammas Night.

But abruptly the page turned by itself, revealing the spell that followed. This was much like the first but for one important word. She had never considered the possibility, yet there could be no mistake. Rather

than setting a mage-born spirit free, this spell would
let the mage-born dead take flesh, and live again!

"Not death," she said aloud, seeing it now. "You
want life!"

As she read the spell's fine points she saw the same
stipulations, and the same, most troubling, date. She
looked up as she felt the presence in the house gather
near her again, and felt an overwhelming sense of
anguish and emptiness touch her spirit.

Suddenly all the many implications filled her mind,
rushing in one on top of another until her head ached
and her body began to shake. She slammed the book
shut, and ran out of the house.

Cold rain swept through the night air, chilling
Alluen's flesh, though her own thoughts lent a coldness that ran much deeper. She didn't know who or
what to believe, or where to begin figuring it all out
anymore. Everything made sense, yet none of it did.
If the Dark creature that had followed her for days
was what she suspected, and if the spirit of Lennet
was truly about, then either spell might be the wish
of either!

Did Lennet want her to banish the Dark, then give
him life again? Or did he truly wish banishment, but
not without showing Alluen a means, perhaps, to protect herself from his own unfortunate fate? It might
be possible to use the life-giving spell that way. . . .

Or had the Dark shown her the first spell, hoping
she would banish Lennet, only to have the wizard's
spirit turn the page to the second spell?

And was Lennet, indeed, Lennet? All creatures of
Darkness were well practiced in deception. The Dark
could have invented the dream, which meant that
Lennet—by some grace of god—had been the one to
court her these past few days. Neither presence

seemed a threat to her. Neither seemed capable of
evil. Yet neither could be trusted, for surely some of
what she sensed was the beast of Jon's warning—if
he was to be believed. And if Thella was to be
believed, Lennet was not to be trusted in any case!

The questions seemed endless!

Still, she could not just do nothing. Tomorrow night
would bring the Dark upon the village, and would
mark the one time when either spell might work. The
best thing to do was leave come first light. Go on to
the next village and never look back. Alluen shook her
head at this. "I will have to do the *next* best thing,"
she told herself, summoning her courage, finally settling on a plan, and a reason to believe such a fool's
gambit might even work.

She considered the idea as the rain was letting up,
as the sun began to rise. She was soaked, despite
spending half the night under the eaves of a stable.
Still, she waited out much of the day there, going
over her plans, and returned to the house only as the
shadows grew long again. As the day became Lammas Night.

Alluen stood in the circle she had redrawn upon
the floor boards of the wizard's house, still not certain
whether she was doing the right thing, or whether
she had a right to do anything at all. Someone, or
something, would surely die this night. She closed her
eyes now and recited the spell she had chosen, changing just one more word on her own. Where the spell
called for one name, she uttered two.

Instantly before her, two figures took shape, side
by side, one forming into a man perhaps a head taller
than Alluen, then the other, a man only slightly taller
than the first. They were both young and rather pleasant to look at, both quite naked. For an instant both

stared straight at her. Then they looked askance at one another, and lunged at each other. They fell struggling to the floor.

"Help me!" one of them shouted.

"Run!" the second cried.

Alluen drew her father's dagger, held it by the point, and threw. The man who had spoken first fell away from the second, clutching at the carved bone handle of the dagger, its blade buried in his side. Thick, black blood ran from the wound. Alluen waited until the body stopped moving, until she felt the Darkness leave the house, then she bent and worked the dagger free.

"Lennet," she said to the one remaining. The man beside her stood perfectly still but for a nod.

"You were both mage-born," she said, holding the knife up, practically shaking it in his face. "You by nature, and the Dark by that old fool, Kimall."

Lennet nodded again, his expression one of amazement.

"It was you followed me through the house, and left the blossom on my plate," she went on. "You tried to banish the Dark thing, and failed."

"I nearly succeeded," he said, his voice low and tenuous. "It might have worked, tried once more. But when the Dark came to you in your dreams, I thought he had convinced you to use the spell on me."

"That was when you turned the page," Alluen said with a grin. He was all gooseflesh. She went into the bedroom and brought back a blanket, which Lennet wrapped around himself.

"What I didn't know was whether I could trust you," Alluen told him. "Jon the mayor might have, I think, yet his wife thought you a louse." Alluen's grin widened. "But I rather like poor old Jon. When the

voice in my dream warned me to believe nothing any
of the villagers said, I took that only one way."

"Ah," Lennet said, coming close to her now, showing her eyes she had felt for days, eyes now filled with
her own reflection. "But how did you know which of
us was me?"

"I've known only one man who truly loved me. Had
he been one of you, no matter how desperate the
struggle, he would have told me to run to safety."

"I . . . wasn't sure of what might happen."

Alluen smiled. "Neither was I."

"We should go, and tell the villagers," Lennet suggested. "Did you find any of my clothes about?"

"For now, we are not going anywhere," Alluen
informed him. "Trust in that."

The Captive Song

JOSEPHA SHERMAN

After the War had ended and our side had won—at least as far as royalty and generals were concerned—I could have had my pick of positions, maybe even have taken some noble title and settled down at court, though such vanities are rare among the wizard-kind. But I had seen enough of crowds by then, enough of armies and men torn and bloody or dying warped out of all humanity by war-spells; I could not bear the burden of city or court.

So one night I set out by myself, on foot as is traditional of wizard wanderers.

And wander I did, one woman alone, traveling restlessly by day, sleeping restlessly by night, my dreams still touched with horror. The War had been meant, as all of them seem to be, to bring peace. It had, in a way; there were regions blasted to peaceful ash by wizardry. I wandered on, trying to outpace memory and find some place where they'd never heard of the War save as a vague rumor.

At last I came to Woodedge, a well-named little village tucked in among the trees, just at the verge of true wilderness. *Clean trees*, I thought, standing on the crest of a small hill and sniffing the piney air, *clean wilderness*. Not a trace of anything to be sensed but the hundred little natural magics of a normal forest. I looked down the slope to Woodedge itself and found a nicely built place, shingled roofs, wooden walls. Each one- or two-storied house had its own small garden, bright right now with spring flowers, and the door frames and window shutters were cheerfully carved. The sound of children playing drifted up to my ears, and I realized, wondering, how long it had been since I'd heard open, honest laughter.

Of course no stranger is going to enter a village unnoted. Before I'd taken a dozen steps I was the center of a wondering crowd. I stared right back. Mostly blondes and redheads here, fair skin, light eyes: I must have looked very alien to them with my dark hair and eyes. The dresses of the women and shirts and breeches of the men were of simple weave but nicely embroidered and rich with herbal dyes; my own traveler's robe was unornamented, but its color—stark green such as no magicless folk dared wear—marked me, as it was meant to do, as wizard.

"I come in peace," I told them, inwardly wincing at the cliché.

The cliché didn't matter; they didn't understand me and began chattering among themselves. After a moment, I identified the language as a dialect of Rishan: I'd wandered far, indeed. But wizards are trained in many tongues, so I repeated in Rishan, "I come in peace."

That caused a new stir. They were calling for someone: Sashan? The man who worked his way through the crowd was no longer young, his skin rough and fair hair more gray than gold. But his eyes were shrewd, and I knew Sashan could only be the village headman.

"You must be weary, lady." The formal words sounded odd in this rustic dialect. "Will you rest and talk with me?"

In other words: Will you tell me who you are and why you're here and if you're any threat to my people? I dipped my head politely. "I will."

Their beer was cool and rich, soothing to the throat. I sipped carefully, aware of its strength, and told Sashan, "I am called Reilanan, and as you've already guessed, I am a wizard."

He gave a little "tsk" of wonder. "So young a woman!"

Young. After the War, I hardly considered myself young, no matter my actual age or what Sashan saw. "I am fully trained. And fully tested, for that matter," I added wryly.

"I'm not doubting you, never that!" To my surprise, Sashan was all at once fairly quivering with eagerness. "It's just . . . lady, we have no wizard. Or rather, we don't have one any more."

At my raised brow, he added, "His name was Tiern; he'd grown up near here and returned to us a full wizard—not much older than you, lady. But he kept us safe enough for all his youth."

I couldn't see why a village should need a wizard rather than some competent wise woman, but I guessed that living surrounded by all that natural forest magic made folks edgy. "What happened to him?"

"Ah. Um. We're not sure. Tiern was . . . well, he wasn't the friendliest of folks, kind of cold. He was always at his books, always studying and hunting new spells."

Not surprising; fierce curiosity was the wizard's boon and bane. "He found something too strong for him, eh?"

Sashan bit his lip. "You'd know more of that than me, lady. All I can tell you is this: he was up to *something* last Lammas Night. We found him in the morning, stark dead with not a mark on him." Sashan shivered. "Lady, since that dark day, there hasn't been anyone able to weave us any protective spells."

"You're offering me a job."

"Ah, yes. You can have Tiern's house—it's a fine one," he hurried on, "very comfortable, yes, and all his magic gear, too. Lots of books, scrolls, that sort of thing." Sashan stopped short. "Lady, I'll be blunt. We can't offer gold or much in the way of city pleasures. What we *can* give you is food and a nice, clean place to live. And our gratitude and, I hope, friendship."

I thought of what I'd seen so far, the attractive little village, the cheerful, rural folk. Folk who would have their quarrels, yes, their petty feuds, perhaps. But folk who had never seen the land turned to blazing mud, or their fellows melted into—

"I'll be honest with you," I said to cut off the memories. "I've come from the War." His blank stare was reassuring. "Never mind which war," I continued. "Let's just say it was a very ugly one involving war magics."

"And you're worn out," he said to my surprise. "Need healing."

"Sashan, I couldn't work a master spell right now to save my life."

"Your magic will return?"

"Yes. With time."

Sashan's smile was wide and warm. "Time we've got. We've waited this long for a wizard, we can wait a little longer. What say you? We'll give you our protection, you give us yours."

To my embarrassed horror, I almost burst into tears of sheer relief. Sanctuary. And hopefully healing. "Yes," I told him shakily. "Yes."

The late Tiern's house was just as I'd been promised: small, maybe, but well-made, with not a draft or a drip. It smelled sweetly of herbs; plainly the villagers hadn't been too afraid of Tiern's death to keep his house clean. The floor was earth, hard-packed to a sheen almost as smooth as glass, and covered with rugs of woven cloth. I found a mirror of precious glass lying on a table, caught a glimpse of my face (amazed to see how young it still looked, how unmarked; surely there should be something terrible marking the smooth skin, something besides weariness in the dark eyes). The bed bore a good feather mattress and the walls bore shelves crowded with jars and vials, books and scrolls. I took one book down, frowned at the title. Tiern had been truly ambitious! I gingerly returned "Demonic Summonings and Banishments of the Third Level" to its place beside "The Many Ways of Transformation" and "Ardenic's Key to Night-Altered Spells." An intriguing collection that would bear careful investigation.

Later. Right now, the bed was just too inviting. I pulled off my clothes and was asleep almost literally before my head hit the herb-stuffed pillow.

How long has it been? How long have I been bound to this place, unable to speak, unable to free myself, unable to do more than wait? Time means little to one in my sorry condition, not-alive, not-dead, and yet I am still aware that the seasons turn, still aware that every day brings me closer to perilous Lammas Night. The night when, if none aid, I will cease to be. There is no one in the village to guess the truth, none who bear even the smallest trace of magic. (None save that dimly sensed Other who'd brought us both to such a sorry pass, and that one would never be of aid to me, oh never.)

I know despair.

*   *   *

I woke blinking and bewildered, the morning sun blazing into my eyes from the window I'd forgotten to shutter. Where was this place . . . ? A house . . . Tiern's house . . . Woodedge . . .

Ah. Yes. Woodedge, and I was their new wizard. I sat up, brushing wild strands of hair out of my eyes. What an odd dream! But it had been a most welcome change from the usual nightmares of war and death.

In the days that followed, I found something wonderfully soothing in healing small harms, a child's wrenched ankle or a baker's scorched hand, in listening to the daily babble of small matters, in knowing that folk here respected but never feared me or my slowly recovering powers.

But my dreams were another matter. Not truly frightening. Merely . . . odd.

Her name, I've learned, is Reilanan. She is—I guess—young (though I can be no judge of age), a slender woman, hair and eyes dark. But these things are hardly worth the note. For magic hangs about her like a shimmering in the air. For the first time in so long, I dare to hope. (And that Other stirs as well, whispering, magic, at last, magic, that Other hopes as well.)

I think Reilanan is content here, at least for now. But I . . . I fight an endless battle with the Other, fight to let Reilanan hear me, only me, see only me, know only me. But how does one lure a wizard? A woman? I can only guess. Yet of course I try, by touch and whisper, hope and dream.

Was I haunted? Was there the occasional touch, softer than a wisp of wind, on my arm, the faintest, less-than-a-shadow sense of someone beside me? Wizard I am, ghost-sensitive I never was, and with my

Powers still so weary and my nerves so shaken, I couldn't be sure that what I felt wasn't mere fancy. After all, a true ghost, or so all the stories agreed, could never be more than a hint of mist or chill air. It could never reach, no matter how slightly, through into the tangible world.

And yet, and yet . . . I am woman as well as wizard, and even though wizards aren't likely to fall to temptation, I'd had my share of flirtations. Now . . . if my not-quite-ghost was doing anything, it was courting me.

Ach, nonsense. What I should do was find myself one of the stocky, good-looking village men and have some good, physical, no-thinking-about-it fun.

No. The wizard-kind don't swear vows of celibacy, but we all know how games of the flesh can weaken magical focus. The last thing I wanted to lose was what only now was returning to full strength.

Ah well.

What use is all this effort? Not even a wizard's skill, I realize now, can hear or see one barely on the mortal plane. Yes, she might raise her head with a frown or turn suddenly as though almost feeling a touch on her arm. She knows someone, something, courts her, I think. But more than this, I can not do, nor can the Other best me; we can give her no clue as to who or what her secret shadow is.

This was growing very strange. But when I tried what spells of banishment would work for me, the not-quite shadow remained. When I tried those spells intended to force a spirit into speech, I found I still didn't have sufficient strength. Instead, trying my best to be casual, I asked the villagers about my predecessor.

"What was he like?"

Sashan had mentioned remote, even cold. The others backed him up on that. Tiern had healed their wounds, cast spells to protect them, but he'd seemed to begrudge them the time away from his studies. He'd never befriended anyone.

In short, I thought, Tiern must have been a thoroughly obnoxious fellow, as totally obsessed a wizard as ever was warned by his elders. Warnings he plainly hadn't heeded.

Was Tiern haunting me? I tried calling to him, mentally and aloud, but felt not even the slightest stirring of air.

And the springtime passed into summer.

And the summer turns implacably towards Lammas Night, most magical of the year—most perilous to me. The Other and I both haunt Reilanan now more desperately than before, I at the same time too well aware of how the Other would gladly banish me to the endless dark. I own no hatred towards that one, though; I wish only to be free, one way or another. We stir close by Reilanan's side at every dawn, brush at her dreams every night.

To no effect. I watch the days slip by, another gone, another. Driven by a pure frenzy of panicked will, I remember one small shard of lore, a simple thing— for one of flesh and blood. How can I work it?

Desperation drives me to a strength that seems impossible: yes, yes, I reach for one small moment from non-life to life. Aching with strain, I break a rose from the twig, leave it for Reilanan—a rose with my will encircling it. In the next moment, I fall back into emptiness, so drained that if the Other had the strength to act, I would be dead in truth.

* * *

I woke with a start—and found myself clutching a rose. It was real, no dream, and I heard myself say foolishly, "He's here."

Bah, foolish, indeed. How else could the rose have gotten into this sealed room without a touch of Otherness?

"Impressive, ghost." Thinking my way through the weirdness, I continued, "But you must be pretty desperate by now, Tiern, or whoever you are. You didn't get a chance to cast whatever spell killed you, and so the unfinished thing is binding you here."

My hand stung. I looked down to see that the thorny stem of the rose was stained with my blood. I threw the thing from me with a gasp, but of course it was already too late. "Clever!" I snapped. "You've bound me, as well! Can you hear me, wizard?" To my disgust, my voice was trembling slightly. "Do you realize what you've done?"

Oh yes, the ghost knew. I heard, or thought I heard, the softest, softest whisper telling me, *Be not afraid. I need your help, I beg for it. Let me be free. One way or another, let me be free!* And the Other? I wondered. If the ghost was real, was the Other real as well? Did it beg, too?

I'd gone through the War. Nothing as small as a ghost, even a wizard's ghost, could frighten me. Besides, I am no more free of curiosity than any other wizard. Tiern's magical library must hold the clue, I told myself, and poured over all the scrolls, all the books he'd left behind.

Ach, useless. Nothing in here told me anything about a wizard's ghost or a nameless Other, nothing showed me a way to free him or them or whatever.

Hurry, the whisper told me, *hurry.*

"If you're in such a hurry," I snapped, "help me!" There was only one book left, a heavy, bulky thing.

I wrested it down from its place and set it on the table, hearing the stiff parchment pages crinkle as I turned them. Nothing special in here, either . . . ordinary spells, none I didn't already know.

The pages stirred. I sat back, knowing this was never the wind's work, and watched them turn slowly, one by one, then stop.

"Let's see what we have here." I read, and felt a pang of pity stab through me. "Is this what you want? A spell to set a spirit free—do you wish to truly die?"

Something touched my hand with the faintest chill, as though too weary to do more. Taking the hint, I turned the page and read the next spell. I blinked, stopped, read it again. And again. No matter; the words and their meaning were clear.

"Can *this* be what you want?" I looked up uneasily, though of course there was nothing to be seen. "These are two very similar spells. One word changed in each, only one—but with that single change comes a whole world of difference."

Dangerous stuff, too: the first spell brought true death to any ghost born of magic, but the second, barely altered spell let the ghostly magic-born live anew in a newly formed body. I heard the soft, soft whisper:

One spell, one little spell and then I live again.

But I could have sworn a second whisper echoed mockingly, *There can be only one choosing, only one body.*

So there could, from what I saw in these pages. "It's not an easy thing you're asking of me, ghost or ghosts or whatever you are. You must be aware of that if you're really of wizard-kind." Curse it, I was starting to babble. Taking a deep breath, I continued, "This spell, the other . . . both look as though they'll take the same amount of will and strength—the same amount of risk, for that matter. And," I added, glancing down at the spells again, "they can only be cast on Lammas Night, that time of primal power. You really *aren't* asking an easy thing of me."

Please, the whisper pleaded. *Please.*

I got to my feet, wrapping my arms about me. No way to avoid this, thanks to the rose that had shed my blood and created that link. But what a terrifying choice! To slay someone (I would not think of all the others I had slain; that had been warfare and no choice about it). To let someone live anew—ha, and I didn't even know for sure who that "someone" was, or even if there *was* only one! Besides, restoring a ghost to life . . . well, what right had I to go tampering in the affairs of gods?

If deities had anything at all to do with this. Maybe if I acted, I'd be righting a wrong, or rather, correcting nearly fatal stupidity?

Damn all wizardly nosiness. I knew the spells were perilous, I knew that dealing with the unknown was more so—and yet I couldn't fight the surge of curiosity, the one that forces every wizard to wonder *what if?* and never think of consequences.

Right. This carelessness had doomed Tiern.

And I might be able to save him.

"Lammas Night," I murmured, knowing that, no matter how foolish it might be, my decision was already made. "Lammas Night." And then, because I didn't want to sound too eager, "We shall see."

I wasn't a total idiot. I wasn't going to cast the spell in the middle of Woodedge. If anyone got hurt, it wasn't going to be some innocent villager.

Besides, almost all spells involving the dead or the Otherworldly are best worked at a crossroads.

So there I stood in the middle of Lammas Night,

the moon casting its cold light over everything, my wizardly robe flapping about me, my loose hair tangling in the wind. Two spells lurked in my mind—and just then even I had no idea which I would cast. Life or death, death or life. . . .

Please, whispered the soft voice, and I sighed, once more wishing curiosity to the Pit. I couldn't banish an entity without first knowing what I banished! I had to see who—or what—had been hovering over me these many days. That meant, of course, that there was only one possible spell I could cast: the one that brought the ghost or ghosts back to tangible life.

Wonderful. And not a clue as to what might actually take shape. Being human (as even wizards are), I couldn't keep a flood of horrific "what ifs?" from my mind. But, being wizard as well, I managed to force away such distractions. Grimly I began the chosen spell. If the entity turned out to be something better left dead, I was going to cast the fiercest war-magic in my repertory and not worry about nightmares.

The spell was a musical progression to be sung (thank the Powers I could carry a tune!) over and over again, each time with the emphasis on a different note. As I chanted the monotonous phrase, I felt the familiar tingle run up my spine, the first hint that magic was building properly. The spell gathered itself almost frighteningly fast after that; trying to pull itself free of my control. The wind, with a fine sense of drama, rose to a scream, nearly staggering me; the air was sharp with unspent Power. This was where Tiern had fallen, this moment when the magic was screaming, that it would be—no, no, it *must* be released, and I screamed with it, shouting out what could no longer even remotely be called a song. The wind shrilled, clouds raced across the moon, and in the wildness and the uncertain light I saw swirls of mist and in that mist not one but two figures, alike—or so I guessed in the dimness—as brothers of one birth. But the sight was unstable, the spell was unstable, and I must choose only one or both would be lost and myself with them. Yet choose *which?* All I could do was shout out a frantic, inane:

"Who are you?"

"Tiern!" cried one, voice thin against the wind. "Let me live!"

But: "Let me live!" cried the other as well.

"*I* am Tiern!" the first screamed. "That is no one, that is demon!"

The wind roared, drowning out the other's words. "True?" I asked, shouting over the roar. "Demon?"

"Yes!" That was the one who claimed to be Tiern.

"Yes," said the other.

I couldn't let a demon live; even if Tiern's life hadn't been at stake, I'd seen demons' work in the War. And yet—

"If I choose you," I shouted over the wind, "what will you do?"

"What do you think?" That was surely the one who named himself Tiern. "Continue my studies, of course. Hurry, the spell's tearing itself apart! Let me live!"

"And you?" I asked the demon. "What will you do?"

"Learn," it—he?—said, so softly I almost failed to hear.

"Learn what?"

A long pause, while I fought with the wind and the spell and wondered if they were going to tear me apart between them. "Learn what?" I repeated, gasping.

"Peace," the demon said.

"Nonsense!" Tiern shrilled. "It will destroy us!"

The smallest warning rang in my mind. "You can't know that."

"I know!" It was a frantic shout. "I summoned the thing!"

"Live," I said, and closed the spell. The wind whirled me off my feet, and slammed me against the ground, and that was it for me for a time.

My mind slowly cleared. I was lying face down at the edge of the road, chilled to the bone, and a blade of grass was tickling my nose. Muscles complaining, I pushed myself up to my knees, shivering. I'd been unconscious for quite some time, it seemed, for the storm and the night both had passed, and the sky held that dull gray glow that presages morning.

Wait, now! Where—

Ah. A man, clad in clothing such as they wear in Woodedge but blatantly never from that place, was sitting quietly, watching me. His face was olive-skinned, his hair dark as my own; I must have unconsciously shaped him like one of my own race. His eyes were dark, too, and deep with shadows. "Why save *me?*"

"Of the two, you mean?" I sat back on the grass with a grunt. "Good question, demon. You *are* the demon, aren't you?"

"I . . . was."

It was the sort of statement I had been hoping to hear. "But aren't any longer?" I prodded; gods, if I'd made a mistake . . .

"I hope not, no."

I shook my head, then winced: not wise to move suddenly just yet. "There's your answer."

"I don't understand."

"You could have claimed to be Tiern, claimed that he, not you, was the demon; you two looked exactly alike in the mist. Yet you didn't even try to lie. Tiern pleaded with me—ha, no, he ordered me to save him; you could have done the same. Yet you said nothing. Ach, don't look at me like that! I'm not a sentimental little girl! Tiern admitted conjuring you. Yes, yes, I know you don't mean any harm; you already had a good chance to kill me while I was unconscious, yet didn't take it, and there's not the slightest aura of evil about you. But Tiern couldn't have known he was going to get a . . . well, what are you? A pacifistic demon?"

He almost choked on what must surely have been his first true laugh. "Something like that."

"Your . . . ah . . . people aren't going to be coming after you, are they?"

"No. I am human now." He paused, considering that with a slight frown, then added, "Mortal. They cannot."

Amen to that. "So. A village has no possible need for demonic powers. Tiern had to have known it. Yet he had already risked Woodedge once and would have gone right on putting it in peril."

The demon blinked. "Why?"

"Why?" I let out my breath in a great sigh. "Look you, I've seen the type again and again during the War: the mage so lost in the pure lust of magical invention that he can't see the horror he's unleashing." I'd been there myself. "But you . . ." I shook my head. "You remind me of something else."

"What?"

"Why did you want to be human?" I countered.

The demon—or former demon—shuddered, as human a movement as anyone could want. "What can I tell you?" he asked softly. "I grew weary, so very totally weary, of evil. I had made my escape, or thought I had, and was nearly in this mortal realm when I was snared. Until now."

His gaze met mine. And in it I saw the same thing I'd seen often enough in my own reflection: not bitterness or even regret. Ah no, the emotion goes too deep for that. What I saw reflected in his eyes was nothing but utter, soul-aching weariness.

And I forced a smile. "I made the right choice. I only hope you like being mortal."

"I do." It was said with utmost certainty. "I will."

"Say that again in about fifty years or so." I scrambled to my feet, trying to brush out my wrinkled, grass-stained robe. He rose more slowly, plainly absorbed in the novelty of a new, tangible body. I looked him up and down and felt a grin forming. "I do good work."

That caused his second laugh, more convincingly human than the first. "For which I am truly grateful." He paused. "I wasn't sure how to court a mortal woman. Did you like the rose?"

"Till the cursed thing stuck me, yes."

"Ah."

"Just what does *that* mean? No, never mind. We have time to work on . . . whatever. But first we need a name for you. I don't suppose you have one that—"

"No."

"Right. You wouldn't." After a moment's thought I said, "Seirach. A good, solid name owned by so many men in my own land that it won't rouse suspicion."

"Seirach," he echoed, plainly startled at the idea of actually owning a name. "Yes."

"But how *am* I to explain you to the good folk of Woodedge? A wanderer, perhaps."

"I don't want to lie," the newly named Seirach said firmly. "I've had enough of lying."

"Not a lie. Just a slight . . . exaggeration. Ah well, we'll see."

I raised my arm. Seirach, puzzled, raised his own, and I let my hand rest on it, feeling it warm and solid and, yes, human. The first rays of the morning sun dazzling us, we went together back to Woodedge.

Midsummer Folly

ELISABETH WATERS

Amber awoke with a start, her heart pounding. She had fallen asleep over a spell book and dreamed the same dream again. And even though she was awake now, she could still feel the presence of the spirit who had been lurking in her dreams for more than two weeks. It was getting harder to convince herself that they were only dreams and that the feeling of not being alone in the house was only her overactive imagination.

She sat up, stretching cramped muscles and forcing herself to breathe deeply and slowly in an attempt to calm her rattled nerves. The sun shone brightly through the window she had left unshuttered the night before, highlighting the supper dishes she had pushed to one side when she started reading. A flower lay on the plate: a single blossom that had not been there the night before. One forget-me-not.

Her breath came quickly again as she lifted the flower with a shaking hand. "So now I know," she said aloud. "He *is* still here."

As she automatically gathered up and washed the dishes, a task she had always found calming—if not mind-numbingly boring—she thought back on the events of the past few weeks. She had been traveling for the better part of a year before she had come

here; her magic school required a year of wandering
from each journeyman mage. After that, they could
settle down anywhere they wished or return to the
school for more study.

Amber planned to return to the school as soon as
was permitted. Not only did she have a passion for the
study of magic, but Sammel, her betrothed, waited for
her there. He had done his year of wandering during
her last year of apprenticeship, and they planned to
marry when she returned from hers. She had been
slowly heading back towards the school when she
entered this village.

It was not unusual for the entrance of a mage into
a small village to attract attention, but it seemed to
Amber that the entire village came to stare at her.
The headman approached her as rapidly as his dignity
allowed and gave her a bow much deeper than her
journeyman status warranted. This was strange
enough to arouse Amber's curiosity, her strongest
character flaw—or strength, depending upon who was
describing her and what her curiosity had led her
into lately.

The first part of the mystery was explained easily
enough when the headman told her that their mage
had died recently—he even admitted that they didn't
know how or why—and begged her to stay. The villagers all seemed to feel strongly that they needed a
wizard. Amber knew that a mage could be useful, but
she didn't suffer from such self-importance as to
believe that a village could not survive perfectly well
without one. These people were clearly terrified of
something, but what?

Then the headman told her that the former mage's
house and books were hers if she would agree to
remain. The house was a simple cottage, although it
had a very nice herb garden, but when Amber saw

the books, she accepted his offer on the spot. There were enough volumes to keep her occupied for several months, there was a mystery to solve, and she would not willingly leave anyone to face the terror these people so obviously felt. She still had almost two months before her year was up, and if she were delayed, which she hoped she wouldn't be—well, Sammel shared her love for books and would understand. So she settled in, determined to find out what was going on before her journeyman year was up.

The dreams had started the first night, but she had thought they came merely because she missed Sammel and was thinking of him. There was nothing particularly frightening in the early dreams, just a sense of someone watching her and finding her beautiful, and the touch of a hand on her hair. As the nights went on, the dream lover grew bolder; Amber was fairly certain that he had been kissing her throat before she woke up this morning. This was outrageous and not something she was prepared to tolerate.

This was no simple dream; this was an earthbound spirit, trying to get her attention. *Well, he has it now,* she thought grimly, *and I will deal with him.* The first step was to determine who was haunting her—and why. She had her suspicions, and they would be easy enough to check.

She looked out the window. In the herb garden outside the cottage, Ysetta knelt in the dirt, carefully pulling weeds from around the herbs.

Ysetta was the headman's youngest daughter, sixteen years old, and very much indulged. She was interested in herb lore, so her father had allowed her to work in the wizard's garden and learn what he was willing to teach her. He had been happy that Amber agreed to keep the girl on—and even happier that Amber was a woman. Probably he suspected that

Marius, the former wizard, had taken advantage of Ysetta's youth and innocence. Amber, whose specialty was healing magic and who had the sight that went with it, could tell that someone had. Ysetta was almost three months pregnant. She wasn't showing yet, but in another two months, it would be obvious, even to those without the mage Gift.

Amber sighed, picked up the forget-me-not, and went outside.

"Good morning, Ysetta. How are you feeling today?"

"Well, thank you, lady," Ysetta replied cautiously, casting a sidelong glance at Amber as if she suspected the reason behind the question. Then she saw the flower in Amber's hand and burst into tears. Amber hauled her to her feet and hurried her inside the house. *No sense in letting the neighbors see this.*

She passed Ysetta a handkerchief and let the girl cry herself out. When she had reached the sniffling stage, Amber tried again.

"Did this flower come from the garden here?"

Ysetta nodded. "Marius used to give them to me. Where did you find it?"

"On the table, when I woke up this morning." Amber shrugged. "But I fell asleep while reading last night and didn't even shutter the windows. Anyone could have put it here."

"Oh, no, lady." Ysetta shook her head decisively. "No one from the village would dare to disturb you or your things. It had to be Marius. He said he would come back."

"Is it his child you carry?" Amber asked. Ysetta looked at her in horror; obviously she had thought this still a secret. "Conceived at Beltane?"

Ysetta nodded and started crying again. "We were betrothed," she said between sobs, "but he wanted to wait to tell my father until he had completed a great spell he was working on. He was almost done when he died—but he isn't really dead, is he?"

The girl was quick, Amber realized, at least about some things. *Too bad she doesn't have the mage Gift; she might be a good one.*

"Do you know what the spell was?" Amber asked. As she had expected, Ysetta shook her head. Marius wouldn't have told her directly, but Amber was sure that Ysetta knew more than she thought she did. She tried another tack. "Did he know you were with child?"

"Yes," Ysetta said. "I told him as soon as I was certain. He was happy about it!" she added defiantly. "He said he was going to make me a potion to take care of the baby as soon as he finished his spell."

Amber had enough experience with potions intended to "take care of" unborn babies to know that the phrase did not mean what Ysetta obviously thought it did. *So he needed her pregnant with his child for the spell and then planned to have her miscarry. . . . That narrows it down a bit. He was doing something that required an anchor, something to tie him to the physical world.*

"Who found his body?"

"I did," Ysetta said, her lip quivering. "It was Midsummer morning. He was lying on the rug in front of the hearth, and I thought he was asleep, but the fire had burned out, and I couldn't wake him, and—"

Amber cut off what was threatening to become an attack of hysteria. "So there were no marks on his body or signs of disturbance in the house."

"No."

"Were there any books lying open anywhere?"

Ysetta frowned in thought. "Yes, there was a book on the table and a flask with a potion next to it." She bit down on her lower lip to keep from crying. "I thought the potion might be the one he promised me, but it wasn't. It had pennyroyal in it, and that's bad for babies, isn't it?"

Amber nodded. "Very bad. If you had drunk it, you would have lost the baby."

"So it must have been something Marius was using for the spell. Perhaps a restorative for afterwards."

Amber shrugged, careful to keep the distaste she felt from showing in her face. *Marius ought not to be earthbound,* she thought angrily. *He should be in the deepest hell, with demons tormenting him!* Aloud she said only, "Can you find me the book that was out that morning?"

Ysetta rose and went to the bookshelf, dragging the stool she had been sitting on. Standing carefully on it, she removed a book from the far side of the top row. "I put it up here," she explained, returning to the table with it, "in case it was something dangerous."

"That was well thought of," Amber said approvingly. "You would have made a good mage."

Ysetta looked startled. "Marius said I hadn't the Gift."

"You don't," Amber agreed, suddenly realizing what she had been seeing every time she looked at Ysetta lately, "but your daughter does."

Ysetta sat down suddenly on the stool, her hands going to her belly in a protective gesture. She smiled, and Amber realized it was the first time she had seen the girl smile. It transformed her from a pretty girl into a radiantly beautiful young woman. No doubt this was what Marius had seen in her.

If her father casts her out when he finds out about the baby, Amber thought, *I'll take her home with me. She can study herbs at the school, and we can probably find her a suitable husband. Or if she doesn't wish to marry, she can stay at school and raise her daughter there. The masters will allow it; that child is going to be a strong mage.*

Amber drew the book to her. It was an old grimoire, a motley group of spells some doubtless long-dead mage had collected for his personal use. "I don't suppose you remember what page this was open to when you found it."

Ysetta, still staring in wonderment at her unborn child, absently shook her head.

Amber balanced the book on its spine and allowed it to fall open where it would. Luck was with her; it fell open precisely, like a cookbook falling open to the recipe most often used. She repeated the process three times, getting the same page each time. "I think this is it," she said, shoving it toward Ysetta. "Does this look like the page it was open to when you found it?"

"I think so," Ysetta said. "I didn't look closely, but it certainly could be that page."

Amber nodded, pulled the book to her, and began to read the spell silently, taking care not to move her lips. Some spells required very little to activate them. But as she read on, she relaxed on that point. This was indeed a major spell and, as she had suspected, it required a strong anchor to the mundane world. For some spells it was enough to have lain with a woman; that link would suffice. For this one, the union must produce offspring in order for the link to be strong enough to draw the traveler back to earth. For this was a spell that allowed a mage to travel on the higher planes. Amber had never tried such a journey, but the subject had been covered in her lessons. The higher planes branched away from the earth quickly and were notorious for their lack of landmarks. A magician with nothing to draw him back to earth could easily become lost there, unable to return to his body, which would then perish, leaving the mage drifting aimlessly.

But Marius had Ysetta and his daughter, so what happened to him?

"Ysetta? Did you save the potion that was next to the book?"

"It's in the blue flask on the top shelf of the cupboard." Ysetta stood up and put a hand on the stool. "I'll get it for you."

"Sit down," Amber said. "You shouldn't be balancing precariously on anything in your condition. You want to take good care of your baby, don't you?"

Ysetta subsided, and Amber dragged her stool over to the cupboard and carefully removed the blue flask. Its contents were precisely what she had suspected: an abortifacient. *Damn that man! He'd have given this to her, made sympathetic noises when she miscarried, and then, no doubt, cried off from the betrothal on the grounds that he didn't want a barren wife.*

And that's why he never made it back to his body, she realized. *He had the physical link, but he had dissolved it on the non-physical level. When he made this potion for Ysetta, he broke the link between himself and her and the child. "Magic is a matter of symbolism and intent"—and his intent was wrong. But since the physical link still existed, he could find this place again, even if it was too late to save his body. If he wasn't back here before I came and started working magic in his old house, he's certainly back now.*

Well, there's no help for it now, I'll simply have to banish him. And may the gods deal with him as he deserves.

Amber flipped through the grimoire, looking for a spell to free an earthbound spirit. "Here we are!" she said with satisfaction, finding one she was familiar with.

"What have you found?" Ysetta asked.

"A banishing spell," Amber said.

"What?" Ysetta looked horrified.

I may as well tell her, Amber thought ruefully. *With a Gifted child, she's likely to need the knowledge someday.*

"Marius was using a spell to travel in magical realms, separated from earth," Amber explained. "He couldn't get back to his body, so it died, but his spirit is still trapped nearby. This spell," she tapped the page lightly with her fingertip, "will free his spirit to go on to the afterlife."

A page fell against her fingertip, and Amber pulled her hand back in startled reflex. Several pages of the book turned, apparently of their own accord, then the book lay open to a new page. Amber reached to turn them back, but Ysetta's hand shot out to hold the book open at the new page. She turned the book to her and looked at it. "Amber," she said excitedly, "look at this!"

Amber crossed to Ysetta's side of the table. "Ysetta, just because the wind turns a few pages doesn't mean it's significant."

"There's no wind this morning," Ysetta replied promptly. "I noticed that when I was weeding. And if you look at this spell you'll see that it *is* significant."

Amber looked, and a chill slid down her spine. This spell was very similar in form to the banishment spell, but the end result was different. Instead of sending the spirit away, this spell called a mage's spirit back into the world, to take flesh and live again.

"Do you realize what this means?" Ysetta was elated. "You can bring him back, and he and I can be married, and I won't have to raise our child alone—"

"You don't have to do that in any case," Amber said. "If you wish, you can come with me and raise your daughter at my magic school. You would both be welcome there. Are you certain that you want Marius back? After all, he has been dead for nearly six weeks."

"Yes, I *am* sure," Ysetta snapped. "Are you unwilling to bring him back because then you wouldn't be needed here? If you were betrothed, you'd understand how I feel!"

Amber sighed. "I am betrothed; he's waiting for me back at school, so I'd be more than happy to leave here. It's just that the mess he got himself into does not give me a high opinion of Marius's intelligence. And the spell *is* dangerous, to him as well as to me."

"I'll help you, if you're scared," Ysetta said.

Amber sighed. "If you knew what this involved, you'd be scared too."

Ysetta's lips set in a determined line. "I'm still willing to help."

"I'll think about it," Amber said. "In the meantime, why don't you get back to the garden. That has to be taken care of whatever happens."

Amber spent the next two days studying the spells. Both of them had to be done on Lammas Night, which gave her only a few days to make a decision and prepare for whichever spell she chose to use. Ysetta came every day, but didn't nag her, which made Amber wonder what sort of temper Marius had and how he had treated Ysetta when he was alive— aside from the way he had seduced her and planned to cast her aside when she had served his purposes.

It would serve him right if I did *banish him. And would I be doing Ysetta any favors if I did bring him back? Only if he could be persuaded to marry her and treat her well . . . Persuaded—or forced?*

She even went so far as to start looking for a geas—

a spell that limited the subject's free will. If there was one thing she didn't trust at all, it was Marius's free will. Of course, putting a geas on someone without his consent wasn't exactly white magic. She shouldn't do it; she knew that. She wasn't sure she could make herself do it, no matter how annoyed she was at Marius and how much she liked Ysetta.

But maybe I don't need a geas; maybe I can do something with the link. After all, he was the one who set it up, so using that would not be against his will—his expectations, perhaps—but not his will. It wouldn't be black magic.

By Lammas Night she was ready. She took Ysetta up on her offer of help, putting her in a separate circle where no harm would come to her or the baby. Then she cast the main circle and started the spell that Ysetta had asked for. Come to think of it, this was the spell Marius had wanted as well. *Be careful what you wish for, Marius . . .*

The spell was tiring—and dangerous if one got careless, but Amber was not careless, and she had studied it thoroughly for days, trying to anticipate every place where something could go wrong. Even so, she proceeded slowly and carefully. But the spell worked just as it was supposed to, and eventually Marius lay on the floor at her feet, alive and breathing. Exhausted, she sank to her knees beside him, shielding him momentarily from Ysetta's sight.

His eyes flickered open and he smiled up at her. "My love," he whispered, "I knew you would save me."

Amber frowned at him, pressed her hand over his mouth to silence him, and shifted so he could see Ysetta. "Your promised wife saved you," she informed him softly, "with the help of your daughter. I merely reformed the link you inadvertently broke." She lowered her voice further to continue, "And I didn't tell Ysetta *how* you broke it. She thinks you love her and the baby, and if you wish to remain alive, you had better. *They* are your tie to this world; lose either of them and you die again."

Marius glared up at her. "You've trapped me," he whispered angrily, too softly for Ysetta to hear.

"You trapped yourself," Amber whispered back. "As you may remember from your attempt at the travel spell, breaking your link to them breaks your link to this world. All I did was correct your error."

She raised her voice, turning to Ysetta. "I'll stay long enough to dance at your wedding, if your father will give me house room—I certainly can't stay here unchaperoned—and then I can go home."

Taking her dagger she cut a break where the two circles touched so that Ysetta could join them. As Ysetta held Marius in her arms and showered kisses on his face, he did seem to become a bit more resigned to his fate.

"It was a lovely wedding," she told Sammel when she finally reached the school. "Everyone was delighted—with the possible exception of the groom."

Sammel looked concerned. "I wouldn't have felt safe leaving that grimoire in his possession."

"I didn't either," Amber grinned at him. "I took it in payment for my services to him. It will be a nice addition to the school library."

Sammel laughed in delight and hugged her. "It will indeed."

Amber hugged him back with enthusiasm. It was good to be home.

The Mage, The Maiden and The Hag

S.M. & JAN STIRLING

A premonition of death touched Narvik the Sorcerer as he walked through the fair, the feather-light brush of a dark wing across his eyes. He turned and followed as the feeling drew him across the fairground; it was never wise to neglect the unsought omen.

He tossed long blond hair from his face as he walked, intent on the inner vision, blue eyes thoughtful and slitted against the sun, heedless of those who stepped warily aside from his passage.

The vision drew him to a fortune teller's booth; he stood surprised and a little at a loss. A woman dressed in gaudy rags hunched over her rune sticks like an arthritic crone, casting the carved wood and mumbling. Two boys crouched before her, listening avidly. Suddenly the chubby boy turned cherry pink and his friend stark white. She leaned towards them and they recoiled a little, like dogs before a snake.

A charlatan, he thought. *And yet* ... Reluctantly, he dropped into a light trance and probed gently; with a shock of surprise he felt himself skillfully blocked.

The woman turned her head slowly, unerringly, towards him. Her customers fled as soon as her gaze released them.

Younger than I! he thought in surprise. But very homely. Her nose resembled a generous wedge of cheese, below was a mouth like a slit cut into raw dough, deep-set brown eyes burned beneath wiry brows under a high, narrow forehead. Her hair, under a brown hood, was a frizz of black curls, but clean. The dark eyes watched him coldly, above a smile sly with malice.

Surprise turned to an icy prickle of alarm. *She's dangerous.*

Suddenly she grinned; a row of big, yellow teeth split her sallow face. Some cold emptiness poured itself into a hidden well behind her eyes, leaving only curiosity and humor.

Yes, she could *be dangerous,* Narvik thought with relief. *She has skill enough to sense my probe.* But she'd also apparently decided not to be offended. *No duel arcane in a marketplace!*

"Hello," she called out as he approached, her voice low and mellow as a wood flute.

"I've no wish to pry, mistress, but I sensed . . . something amiss."

Some of the cold returned to her eyes. "Never fear," she said, "my wards are strong, I took no harm from your attack."

"I meant no offense," he insisted, offended himself, resisting the urge to defend his actions. "I came to offer aid if needed."

The shadow stroked down his spine, held him leaning on his staff when reason told him to leave.

"You meant to be kind," she murmured. "Perhaps kindness comes easier, when you've a roof of your own." She jerked a chin towards her rags. "I truly dread the winter; like a cat, I hate the cold."

"You've power," he said cautiously. "And skill as well . . . in more than telling fortunes."

"I'm a sorcerer," she admitted. "Yet, no town has

invited me to stay." She lowered her eyes, her lips quivered with some emotion.

Disappointment? Anger? Narvik frowned behind a motionless face. It wouldn't take a sorcerer of his skill to see the strangeness in her; not an attribute endearing to town councilors.

"Where are my manners?" the sorceress said. "I'm Wythen, I apprenticed under Navila the Yellow."

"I'm Narvik, son of Phocon, apprenticed under Fahon of Kint."

"Ah," she said, looking down to scoop up the coins her young customers had thrown her. A pupil of the famed Fahon would never tell fortunes in rags. "Where's your town?"

"Parney's twenty miles south of here," he replied. "Just below the foothills of the Leton Mountains."

She shook her head, smiling up at him.

"I don't know it."

"A beautiful place. If ever your wanderings take you there you must be my guest," he offered politely.

He froze. The words left his mouth like syllables of burning ash; the deadly shadow of things that were not, things that might be, a fate settling into the groove his act had chosen. He probed the pathways of the future and met only swirling mist. *No mage can read his own fate.*

"Wythen," he asked gently, "*is* anything wrong? Are you in trouble of some sort? Or ill? I'd help if I could."

Her eyes shuttered and she hunched forward, face stiff with pride. "Wrong?" she said. "Others of no greater skill have homes, and I none." She turned her head away. "A safe journey to you, Master Sorcerer."

Narvik frowned down at her and bowed, lifting his staff formally. *Too changeable by half,* he thought. *An illness of the mind . . . or spirit-ridden?* Instinct

warned against probing her wards to find out. *I
offered help, and hospitality. There is no more I
may do.*

"A good journey to you, Master Sorceress," he said,
and turned on his heel.

Wythen watched him go, then spat in the dust
beyond her blanket.

*Pah! How fine we are, how noble and good. Come
visit to see what you've none of. And when you've
filled your heart with longing for things you'll never
get—such as my handsome self—then it's "off with
you, you great ugly lump."*

She turned and dug through the canvas sack that
held her belongings, burrowing beneath leather-
strapped books and bags of herbs.

Her hand found the hammer of polished stone and
the long iron nail, moving without her will.

No! Wythen thought. *Not that!*

She placed the nail on the circle Narvik's heel had
left in the dirt.

Don't do this.

Her mouth made words, shaping the stuff of the
world. With a single hard blow she drove the nail into
the footprint. Her hand started forward to pluck it
out and undo the curse, then sank back quivering.

Death curse, she told herself. A low moan sounded
as she pressed her hands to her aching forehead.
Death.

Unless he could find his way to this one footprint
among millions and pull the nail out himself.

Forget! snapped a voice that only Wythen could
hear.

Memory faded into black mist and hungry yellow
eyes.

*   *   *

Wythen looked up at the mountain peaks south-
ward of Parney and shivered at the sight of the snow
already creeping down their flanks, turning her hood
up against the wind. It was a relief to come to Parney
town, past the dark bare-branched vineyards and in
among the houses, lights showing yellow and warm
through the windows against the gathering night. She
passed the houses of wealthy merchants and vintners
on the outskirts, set back amid walled gardens, passed
on to where brick and timber buildings leaned over
narrow streets of worn cobblestone. A sign creaked
over one, bearing a pictured mug and sheaf of wheat;
beside it was an entrance to an enclosed courtyard
rimmed with stables.

"Innkeeper?" she called, pushing through the
doors.

Warmth greeted her, and tantalizing cooking smells
from beyond the common room. There was a big
brick hearth on one side, with a pot of mulled wine
rich with cinnamon hanging over the coal fire. Booths
and tables lined the other walls, save for a counter
with barrels behind it.

"Innkeeper?" The man behind the counter looked
up. "Could you tell me the way to the house of Narvik, son of Phocon, the sorcerer?"

He started. "Would you be a friend of his? A col-
league, perhaps?" His eyes went to her staff and
pouch, both carved with the markings of her trade.

"I'm a sorceress, if that's what you mean," she said
with an uneasy smile.

"Please," he said, suddenly at her side. "Sit. You
honor this house with your presence."

He urged her to a table, pushing a cup of the hot
wine into her cold hands. A plate appeared as if by
Art, heaped with slices of roast mutton and roots in

cream sauce, with a fresh loaf and butter and a wedge of cheese. The innkeeper waved aside her protests.

"No, no payment—an honor, as I said."

Wythen closed her mouth, except for eating. Chances like this didn't come very often; the server refilled her plate, replacing it with a fruit pie and a cup of wine better than she could afford. As she ate a half-dozen men and women slipped into the room, standing and talking quietly among themselves. Prosperous-looking folk, in coats of fine dyed wool and shoes with upturned toes, holding their floppy hats in their hands, casting an occasional glance her way. When she pushed away her plate with a sigh, one came over to her with a courteous bow.

He was the smallest among them, an older gentleman with a neatly pointed beard.

"I'm Cafrym, good sorceress, Syndic of the Corporation of Parney. I wonder, would you be so good as to allow us to discuss a business proposal with you?"

Wythen gestured wordless invitation at the seats across from her. The others gathered, clearing their throats.

Business? she thought. *How curious. What about Narvik?*

"We've sent out numerous messengers," Cafrym said, "Are you here because of them?"

"No." *News?*

"Are you, uh, great friends with Narvik?"

Wythen shook her head again, this time frowning.

"No. We met at a fair last autumn. He invited me to visit if I was ever in the area."

"Ah. Well. I'm sorry . . . Narvik, son of Phocon, took ill and died in the early summer. Just . . ." Cafrym grimaced and spread his hands, "faded away, unable to help himself."

A tearing gasp broke from her. Something cold ran

through her body, like a wisp of icy mist. Tears filled her eyes. *My fault!* her mind accused.

She'd forgotten. She always forgot when she did something truly evil. Only to remember when, as now, someone told her the results of her wickedness. Despair crashed down upon her like an avalanche. She wanted to destroy herself.

No use. She'd tried before. Once she'd placed a noose round her neck and tightened it, and once she'd a flagon of poison actually at her lips. Both times Wythen suddenly found herself trudging the road, footsore and far from where she'd been, all her possessions on her back, with a headache like a spike driven into her brow.

Why? Her heart was beating so fast she feared it would burst. *Why would I hurt him? He was kind to me.*

Cafrym reached out as though to take her hand and one of the councilwomen offered brandy. Wythen took it and gulped, gasping again as the fire burned its way down her throat.

"I'm sorry," Cafrym said. "He was a friend to us all."

Wythen nodded, struggling to regain her composure.

"I'm sure . . ." Cafrym paused.

"That he'd want us to welcome you," the councilwoman supplied quickly. "I'm Radola. Narvik was a *great* friend to my family. I know he would have wished you to find—"

"A place with us," snapped Cafrym, reestablishing control. "Ah, assuming you don't already have a place of your own. You've the look of a, um, wandering scholar."

Wythen stroked her brow with trembling fingers.

"You need a replacement," she said. "Of course. I've . . . several testimonials you could look at."

She took a deep breath. *They're quick to replace the man who was their friend,* she thought, with a feeling of distaste.

Cafrym seemed to sense her doubt: "Winter's almost on us, sorceress. There's deep snow in the pass already; in two weeks the roads will be closed."

He leaned forward earnestly. "We're in danger here. There are ice demons in the winter and . . . other things. Who'll set the wards for us and keep them out of our houses and away from our stock? And we need a healer. Winters are hard here."

"Narvik warned us in the spring to seek a replacement," Radola said. "We've searched, but found no one. Surely your coming was fated; for without knowing our need, here you are. Please stay. There'll be deaths here this winter if you don't."

Radola's face matched her words, but not the eyes. Wythen stared until the older woman looked aside.

"You shall have the Sorcerer's cottage," said a tall thin fellow.

"And his books and instruments," added a woman.

"And thirty silver groala as well," put in a thickset, bushy bearded fellow. The whole crowd of councilors shifted in displeasure, but the fellow winked at Wythen. "And a winter indoors, into the bargain. If you hate us you can always leave in the spring," he added.

She grinned at him.

"And if you hate me, you can always ask me to leave," she said, smiling.

Wythen shook Cafrym's hand to seal the bargain.

The cottage was lovely, modest in size and cozy, with comfortable furnishings and a good-sized herb garden, now dying in the cold. Radola had ordered her servants to see to its upkeep, so it was clean and aired as well.

Best of all were the books. Wythen had never seen so many. *Fourteen* of them, huge leather-bound volumes with brass clasps or silver locks. Her hand shook as she reached out to touch them reverently.

"Oh, Narvik," she whispered, "I *will* take care of Parney! I swear it. I'll never hurt your people." Her heart was in the promise, but she didn't know if she could keep it. The evil she did came out of nowhere and vanished into the mist, only to be caught out by chance. But she would *try*, with all of her heart and mind and skill.

At first, it was difficult to settle in, the mood in the cottage was hostile, as though the very hearth rejected her. And her sleep was restless—with half-formed dreams laden with anger.

Narvik's anger.

Wythen dreamed.
She walked by a stream, through a meadow, searching for a bracelet lost by Radola's daughter. The meadow was bright with sun, water chuckled over polished brown rock . . . but the grass grew, clutching at her feet. She ran, falling as it snagged her ankles. The sun turned to Narvik's face, blazing down out of the sky in fiery wrath, and the stream heaved itself up in a wave to crush her, the rocks churning like a quern. . . .

Wythen sat bolt upright, her mouth wide as she gasped. She fumbled on the bedside table for her candle and willed it alight, looking around for the man whose presence she could feel.

"Oh, Narvik," she whispered, in a small tear-filled voice, "forgive me. I didn't know, I swear I meant—"

She stopped. *I meant you no harm.* It seemed obscene even to shape the thought.

She'd murdered him.

"I'll take care of your people," she said at last, "to the best of my ability. And I will *try* to do no harm here. And . . . if another comes to take your place I'll leave at once, whatever the season." She lay back in the bed and closed her eyes, leaving the candle burning. "Please, give me a chance."

Oh, easily said, Narvik thought. *How can I stop you, after all?*

His anger rose again—he wished he could throttle the figure in the bed. But he couldn't. His fiercest blow would feel like a caress to Wythen.

The darkness and the sleep had ended when she crossed his threshold. He heard the sound of her footsteps as she came in from fetching water from the well. When she opened the door he cried out: "You!"

She'd lifted her head, looking about herself mildly, not frightened, sensing something only because of what she was. He'd railed at her for hours, wasting strength. Nothing, not even another glance of curiosity. That was when he'd decided to stalk her dreams. Tonight was the first time she'd seen him.

Murder made a strong ghost, twice over when it was a sorcerer's. The mage-born were tenacious of life, and death did not take them in the same manner as other folk.

And it won't be the last dream, you murderess!

His people were in danger as long as she remained. The Syndics of Parney had let a madwoman into their midst; a madwoman with a sorcerer's powers. And he couldn't warn them. They couldn't even sense his presence as more than a vague unease.

He'd have to drive her away.

*   *   *

Wythen threw another scoop of coal on the fire and sat back, the book in her lap. Its pages glowed with a cool blue light; a small working, and well worth it for saving strain on the eyes. Outside the wind rattled at the shutters, but the cottage was warm and snug. There seemed to be a snicker of wicked laughter in the gale; she drew her robe tighter and frowned at the parchment page.

"Birthings, lung fever, ice demons. I can handle those. But rock imps . . ."

She'd never seen one, though she'd heard their maniacal cackling and seen the destruction they wreaked. One farmer in particular they loved to plague, tossing stones down his chimney and chasing three of his sheep to death in two weeks. The poor man and Wythen herself were at wits end.

She looked at the bed, over beyond the hearth and the oven built into the wall beside it. It was warm and soft, the bed she'd dreamed of when she lay huddled in cold haystacks or under hedges, but she felt a little catch of fear as she turned back the coverlet and laid herself down. Sleep meant Narvik . . .

Wythen closed her eyes and willed sleep to come. The dead sorcerer came with it, a being of anger and terror.

"I need your help."

His blue eyes widened. The nimbus died around his dream shape.

"Saymon, son of Daura, has rock imps on his farm! Nothing I've tried works!" she shouted in exasperation. "What should I do?"

Narvik glowered at her, then was gone. Real sleep claimed Wythen; for the first time since autumn she rested.

*   *   *

Narvik ground his . . . well, they were something like teeth. *Seeing her eat off my plates, sleep in my bed, use my books . . .*

It was more than he could bear; and there was nothing else to *do*, either. *I don't want to be dead!* He supposed few did, but a sorcerer's ghost had more ability to express it.

She will do my people some injury. Months so far and she'd been a model sorceress. Skilled, not grasping, generous with her time. The people of Parney liked her, and she'd earned that.

But there was an evil about her, and sooner or later it would break free. And he helpless to prevent it!

She was mage-born, and so he could walk in her dreams, stand always at her shoulder. Yet her wards protected her. . . .

Something dark clung to her, twisting around the roots of her soul like swamp fog, a flavor of pure evil. But whenever he approached for a better look it disappeared. The last time, he'd seen it grinning out of Wythen's dark eyes.

She's possessed! he thought grimly. Nothing else made sense; one who was evil of her own soul would have shown it in a thousand petty ways. Couldn't help but show it. No, she was possessed by another.

Even dead he was in danger from it. The spirit had only to take over her body, perform a rite of exorcism and he'd be back in his grave. Or worse. It probably had a vile sense of humor.

Narvik sighed, then frowned. When he wasn't angry he was sighing. This wouldn't do. He was used to taking action when something troubled him. *There must be some way to help her,* he thought. Something niggled at his memory, but he couldn't catch it.

Ah, well, about those rock imps.

*   *   *

When she opened her eyes to the pale gray light of a winter's morning, Wythen leapt out of bed heedless of the cold flagstone floor. A book lay on the kitchen table, a key in its silver lock. In the place marked with a clean straw she found what she was looking for.

"Of course!" The red granite in the walls of Saymon's farmhouse. That must have come from the imp's home boulder; if she exorcised it . . .

"Oh, Narvik! Thank you." Tears filled her eyes. "Thank you so much."

Tension drained suddenly from the air of the cottage, like a pain endured so long one was only conscious of it when it left. Yet the air didn't feel empty or solitary; it was as if someone listened, smiling.

"She's better," Councilwoman Radola said with relief.

Wythen nodded and sighed, feeling the child's forehead. The girl stirred in her sleep, but the simple rest-spell held. The room was warm, slightly damp and fragrant with the herbs boiling over a brazier in one corner. A stuffed dragon peeped out from the coverlets.

"Lung fever's dangerous at her age," Wythen said. "But the crisis is past. Once spring sets in fair, we ought to be over the worst."

Narvik relaxed his hold and his consciousness snapped back to its psychic anchorage in the cottage. Water dripped from melting icicles around the eaves. He turned to the flower boxes beneath the windows, where the translucent silver sheen of ice lilies showed, peeking through crusty, melting snow. He extended his hands—they felt like hands—and strained. It was harder than the straws, heavier, not spell-sensitized to his command like the books and instruments.

A ghost could not gasp, but he felt himself *thin* as he pulled, as if the effort were draining the strength that let him remain near the land of the living. At last the flower parted and came free in his hand. He laid it on her plate before her chair.

A few seconds later Wythen bustled in; laden with a full basket from the councilwoman's house, her face flushed with the raw chill of early spring. She unwound the scarf from her head, fumbling with the bone clasps of her long sheepskin coat. The basket of food almost went down on the lily, but she snatched the wickerwork aside and stood staring for a long moment.

When she raised her head there were tears running down the frost-reddened cheeks. Wythen would never be anything but homely, but Narvik forgot that as he watched.

"Nobody . . . *nobody* ever gave me a flower before," she whispered. "Thank you."

She slid the frail stem into a small vase and set it in the center of the table, blushing and smiling.

Wythen woke in blue, predawn light and crawled reluctantly out of bed, shivering as she drew her robe around her shoulders and stooped to stoke the banked fire. She lit a splinter of wood at the cheerful flames, using it to light the oil lantern on the mantlepiece— and froze, as she saw a book on the table.

"What is it, Narvik?" she whispered. "Is trouble coming?"

As before, a clean straw marked a place and she opened the book to the page indicated. Leaning close she read: "To Lay a Troubled Spirit."

Wythen closed her eyes and bit her lip, as grief

shot through her. *Rest,* she thought. *He wants to rest.* Her fingers curled to slam the book shut in denial. *No. I killed him. I cannot wrong him again.*

"I'm sorry," she said, and began to read.

"I-I've never done anything so complex," she stammered. This time it was fear that made her fingers itch to close the book. The diagrams alone . . . and the *danger*, if only one thing went wrong.

A feeling passed by her eyes as she sat; warmth, comfort, the touch of a hand on her shoulder. "Every time I think of you, my heart breaks," she said. Then she sat a little straighter. "But if this is what you want, I will try."

Slowly and deliberately, the page before her turned . . . in still, cold air that didn't even ruffle the wisp of hair at the back of her neck. That rose on its own. To find the results of Narvik's actions was one thing; to see them in the waking day, another.

She read, "To Bring the Mage-Born Back to Life When Untimely Slain." Her heart gave a kick. *This is what he wants!* It was what she wanted too. Of course she'd have to leave then, but still . . .

She read the spell and frowned. But for one word, they were identical.

She sighed and rubbed her forehead. *He was so fair,* she thought, *to show me both.* Leaving the decision up to her.

I must give up Parney, she thought bleakly. *Friends. Respect. Home.* The road again, the loneliness and the cold rain.

Or . . . he might turn her over to the Syndic for trial. He'd seemed to forgive her, but . . . *trust no one,* her teacher Navila had warned, cackling, *not even me.*

She sighed. Either spell must be worked on Lammas Night, two months away. She'd plenty of time to think about it.

Carefully, she closed the book. "I will," she promised. "Narvik, I will."

In a place that had neither dark, nor any hint of light, Navila the Yellow chuckled. *I shall live!* she sang.

No more clinging to her former apprentice, feeding from her energy like a bloated tick. No more having to store up that energy until she was strong enough to claim the use of Wythen's body. Nor of being forced out when that power was gone.

I know her, Navila thought. *Little fool!* Wythen would choose to bring the handsome sorcerer back to life. All she need do was wait for the precise moment, seize Wythen's voice and say Navila instead of Narvik. *Then I shall live!*

Whether the fool noticed or not, the spell must be completed or the magician would die. And Wythen was tenacious of life, as she had cause to know. Then Navila would make her a slave again. The chains forged when Wythen was a child were still there, requiring little effort to take them in hand again.

And then we'll have some fun with the good people of Parney, eh? Beginning with Narvik. There were most entertaining things one could do to a ghost.

*   *   *

Narvik's tomb stood in Radola's family vault; plain limestone among the marble and porphyry. The lock turned with a snapping *click*, and the door shrieked as Wythen pushed it to. It was both chilly and a little damp, half an hour short of midnight.

She stepped to the center of the floor and extended her staff, chanting. And chanting she turned, the bronze ferule tracing a circle on the stone precisely as a geometer could have graven with a compass. Blue-green light sprang up behind it.

"*Aleph,*" she said, when the circle was complete, and grounded the staff with a *thump* in the center of the ring.

It stood rigid when she removed her hand, as if sunken half its length in the living rock.

Wythen began to trace the outer edge of the circle, trickling a precise handful of sea salt.

> *Arlin's bigghes have mickle might*
> *Strong to daunt and strong to bind;*
> *None may dare the sun-strong line,*
> *None may cross the salt-drawn cord—*"

When the last glyph was drawn she forced a word through lips already numb with fatigue: "*Gimel.*" They shone around her, silver and green and blood-red, living shapes of power.

Navila watched Wythen work, with critical attention. *Taught her better than I knew,* she thought, surprised, feeling the tension in the young woman's body.

She stretched her senses, *seeking* Narvik, finding no sign of the ghost. Odd. Suspicious. It worried her until the circle was completed. Now the ghost was locked out and couldn't interfere with her plans.

Fool! she thought cheerfully. *So stupid he deserves to suffer.* And he would, oh, yes, he would. Forever, to begin with.

Navila wondered if she'd come back young. *Oh, glorious, to have my beauty back,* she thought longingly. *To be free of this horse-faced slut.* Men had noticed the young Navila. When Wythen came in sight they turned away, or laughed outright.

Ah. The moment was upon her. Navila slid into Wythen's body with practiced ease, so smoothly that the girl's speech was not interrupted.

". . . and call forth the one known as *Navila* that they . . ."

Navila slipped free. Bonds stronger than mortal steel tugged at her, she screamed in joyful pain as they wrenched free—the hooks of soul and spirit that linked her to her apprentice. *Now! Now!*

Wythen chanted on; there was no stopping, except for death. *I blacked out!* An instant with no sight, no sound. Panic dragged at her concentration. Tension gathered in the tomb, the air itself felt *stretched* with the power drawing down into the focus, like water spiralling into a hole that reached through creation.

"Wythen," a voice whispered softly in her ear. "Do you trust me?"

Narvik? How could she answer him? She could speak no word, make no gesture that was not part of the ritual.

She could feel something sinking into her. Her skin went numb. Her heart beat so that she could hear the pounding of the red drum in her ears, and still voice and hands made their ancient, precise additions to the structure of energies towering above her like a frozen avalanche.

Think your answers, Narvik said. *I'll hear them.*

What are you doing? she demanded frantically. *Why are you in my mind?* Sweat ran into her eyes, trickled coldly down her spine. Her knees trembled and her mouth was dry as crumbling parchment.

Do you trust me?

Yes. No. I . . . don't know. Her thoughts scattered like beads from a broken necklace. What was he doing? He didn't trust her.

I do trust you, Wythen. And I need for you to trust me. I want you to recite the spell that lays a spirit to rest.

No! she thought wildly.

Please. I don't ask this lightly, Wythen. It's what I truly, desperately want.

Narvik sensed her sad acceptance. The moment approached and he could feel Wythen's resolve wavering. *Please!* he said. And with a sense of utter desolation, Wythen complied.

The *thing* danced around him. It had the form of an old woman, but the eyes could never have been human; they were like windows into nothingness, an oblivion that *pulled* into a bottomless hunger.

Navila stopped her capering and stood before Wythen, her arms reaching for her.

Give it to me, she demanded. *Give me life!*

But wait. The girl was weak-willed, never knowing her own mind from day to day. She might decide to lay Narvik to rest. That wouldn't do at all, now would it? Navila decided to make sure. She reached for Wythen. And was blocked!

What's this? She probed the solid barrier that stopped her. *You!*

Narvik! In her servant's body.

How dare you? she screamed.

Navila reached out and to Narvik's utter shock yanked him from Wythen's body as easily as pulling the skin off a boiled root, flinging him hard against the edge of the circle.

Narvik cringed back from it, burnt with an icy draining.

Wythen staggered as she felt his pain. Her mouth shocked open in an O of agony, but her hands went up in the last gesture and she breathed the words that would lay her love to rest.

Navila felt herself fading, drawn beyond the living

world. She knew what waited for her; knew very well, and how it would greet her after the long, long wait past the appointed hour. With a shriek of hatred she turned and launched herself at Wythen. Reaching out with the last of her strength, she caught hold of Wythen's heart.

Narvik heard the last word of the spell. Blood burst from Wythen's eyes and mouth and fingernails. Her heart beat once, and stopped.

Wythen opened her eyes on darkness; the pain was gone, and she felt so calm that her wonder at it was mild. In the distance was a light; a swelling star casting flickering curls of gold around it. She started walking towards it, faster and faster; her calmness blossomed into joy, joy that was also deep contentment.

"Wait!" a voice called.

She ignored it. There were others calling to her from ahead now.

"Come back."

"I don't want to come back," she said. Reluctantly, she slowed, turning to look over her shoulder.

"There's so much you have left to do. So much life has to offer you."

"No," she said, frowning. "I've done terrible things. I don't want to hurt people anymore. It's best I don't go back. Leave me alone."

"You've never hurt anyone, Wythen. It was the old woman. You don't deserve to die for her crimes. Please, come back."

"But it was I who killed you, my hands, I saw them . . ."

My hands, but not my will within the hands.

"Thank you," she whispered, stepping forward, moving quickly again.

"Don't leave me!" Narvik begged. "You can't leave me like this."

Wythen stopped. He was right.

There seemed to be no space between decision and action here, no hesitation—as if to recognize the right was to do it. The light receded from her, growing smaller and smaller.

Darkness fell.

When she opened her eyes, Narvik was seated beside her, transparent as a reflection on still water. He smiled and took his hand from her brow; a touch so faint she was only conscious of it when it was removed, like a whisper of wind on a calm day.

Wythen licked dry lips and tried to rise. She came to one elbow with an effort that made her moan in pain. One look around and she let herself collapse again.

"The lines are ruined," she said in despair. Darkened, blurred.

Narvik laughed.

"Wythen," he said, leaning over her. "You couldn't feed a kitten milk now, much less raise the dead." He smiled with amusement and tenderness. "Go home. Sleep."

"Oh. But you'll have to wait for . . ."

"Next year?" He shrugged. "What's a year, to a ghost?"

"I'll take good care of Parney," she promised weakly. "And when the time comes I'll leave without a fuss."

"When the time comes," he said leaning over her, "I shall bind you to me with the strongest bonds I can weave." He kissed her on the lips.

I felt that! she thought. Then realized what he'd said, and stared.

He laughed.

"You shall have a place, and friends all around you, and a warm hearth in winter."

"And . . . you?" she asked.

Narvik stroked the curls back from her high forehead.

"And me most of all," he promised.

The Road Taken

LAURA ANNE GILMAN

She closed the spellbook carefully in the faint glow of dawn, letting her body slump until her head rested on the book itself, her pale brown hair spilling over the book's leather binding and across the scarred and pitted worktable. It was done. She had worked her magic, for good or ill, and it was done. The presence which had so haunted her was dispersed, the cottage free from any influence save her own. It had taken all of her strength to complete this night's work. All she wanted to do, all she could do now, was sleep.

"Marise."

The sound was a barest whisper, a voice harsh from disuse, but it jerked her out of her doze, knocking aside the stool she was sitting on, forcing her to her feet and turning her towards the door. A tall figure stood there, his face, indeed all details of him, in shadow. Marise squinted, trying to see who it was. She hoped, as she passed a hand over her eyes, that he did not come to her with an emergency. At this moment, she could not have mustered a spell to save her own life. And with that thought came another— was he a danger to her? She could not think of any who would wish her ill, and yet . . .

Her body failed her, and she swayed with exhaustion. The stranger was at her side, capable hands lifting her at knee and shoulder, bearing her to the wide rush bed shoved against the far wall.

"You must rest. Then we will talk," he said, settling her on the bed and adjusting the quilted coverlet under her chin. She reached up to touch the side of his face, and gasped as sudden familiarity washed over—through—her.

"You!"

She struggled to rise, but he passed one cool hand over her forehead and she fell back against the bed, close to passing out. As she drifted into the darkness, she heard him say, "There will be time enough for questions, my lady. Questions, and perhaps even answers."

There were sounds in her cottage. Marise lay still and tried to identify them. The scritch of the broom against bare wood floor. The hissing of a fire. The rolling bubble of water boiling. The low rumble of a deep voice. Humming. Someone—a male—was sweeping her floor. Humming. How odd. She laughed at the absurdity of it, and the humming stopped.

Sitting up in her bed, Marise looked at the man she had called from death as he leaned on the broom and looked back at her. He was slender without being thin, tall, older than she, yet with the carriage of a younger man. His eyes and hair were brown against pale skin, but somehow when she looked left rather than right his eyes seemed more green than brown; his hair showed red highlights.

"It worked," she said to the room. She hadn't been sure. The first spell had been simple, something she had performed many times—murder victims still angry, young people unwilling to accept their fate. It wasn't easy, but the result was never in doubt. But the second spell had frightened her. The original receipt called for putting a lost spirit into a body, his or another's. But Marise could obtain no body, and so had improvised. Casting an appraising glance over her guest, she nodded in satisfaction. Perhaps she should improvise more often!

"What is your name?" she asked, swinging her feet over the side of the bed and standing up. She did not miss the slight hesitation, or the frown that crossed his brow before he replied, "I don't know."

One narrow eyebrow rose, and she shrugged. Perhaps the shock of returning to flesh had wiped his memory. That would be a disappointment. Marise had hoped to discover who he was, and what his spirit had been doing here in the wizard's cottage.

Perhaps the wizard had killed him? No. From all she had heard from her neighbors, Aginard had been a gentle soul, stubborn but kind, with a passive nature. Not one to be a murderer. And this stranger in front of her wasn't, she thought with not a little regret, the wizard himself. Even a created body would bear the impression of the soul's former housing. Aginard had been an older man, full of gray hairs and creases. This man in front of her had neither, although there was a certain tenseness about his narrow face that indicated years lived in hard places.

"Well, don't worry yourself over it." She kept her voice calm. "It may come back, and it may not. Do you remember anything else?"

He frowned again in thought, as though the action disturbed him. "I remember being here, eating a meal. Only the table was over there," he pointed, "and the bed was there."

Marise nodded. Those were changes she had made upon moving in. "Anything else?"

He made a face, more at himself than at her. "You're asking if I remember how I died."

She shrugged, crossing in front of him to take the water off the fire and pour it into an earthenware mug, adding a spoon of lemongrass to it and putting it aside to steep. Sitting on the bench, she studied him. "And do you?"

He sighed, resuming his sweeping more as a way to occupy his body than to clean the stained floor. "I remember an argument. Fighting. Shouting. I was very angry, then I was in pain. Then ... there was more pain, and it was over. Then nothing until you came."

"And last night?"

"More pain. Almost unbearable. An intense heat overwhelming me. And then I was here, and I knew your name but not my own." He looked at her from under dark lashes, his expression shy. "I thought you might be able to help me remember."

Marise made a decision as she made all of her decisions, with the rueful knowledge that she might regret it later. "I will. You will stay with me, and we will discover your past. But you need a name. People would wonder, and ask questions you cannot answer yet." She stopped to think a moment. "I will call you Efeon, if that sits well with you."

"Efeon." He tested the name out on his lips, tasting it like a new spice. "What does it mean?"

"River fox," she told him shortly, not adding the rest of it, that the river fox was known to be a changeable beast, full of magic and mischief, and utterly unpredictable. It was also said that should a person be so foolhardy as to catch a river fox, three strands from its red tail bound into a charm would bring the bearer his—or her—deepest desire.

Several weeks passed peacefully. Efeon found that he was skilled in writing, and began to scribe letters and agreements for the villagers. Always with a quick joke or a tiny sketch to delight the children, he seemed content. But at night, as he paced the walls of her cottage, Marise saw another side to him.

"There must be something you can do, some magic you can cast, that will solve this damnable mystery!" he raged at her after a particularly bad day. "I know I've a mage's training—I can feel it running in my bones. And how else could I have come to you, asking to be released?"

Marise turned a page in the spellbook carefully, smoothing the vellum so that it lay flat against the other pages. "We've discussed this before, Efeon. The spell was a powerful one. It is probable that, in exchange for breath, the spell consumed your talent. Would you have preferred to remain a spirit, aware yet apart?"

He turned on her, one clenched fist slamming down on the table so that her clay dishes rattled. "I want both!"

Marise stifled her instinctive start of fear. He had these bursts of temper often, and although she understood, and sympathized, they frightened her as well. He was a strong man, and without a spell at hand she was vulnerable should he rage out at her.

"Sit down, Efeon," she commanded, but he had already dropped onto the hardwood bench across from her.

"I'm sorry," he said in a harsh whisper. "I swear, I never mean to do that. I would never hurt you, I *could* never hurt you. You know that, don't you? All that I have, all that damnable spell left me, is you."

His head sunk onto his chest, Efeon looked so defeated that Marise once again forgot her plan to scold him, instead kneeling beside him, one arm curved across his knees. "It will come back to you," she said soothingly. "You simply mustn't push it. You were dead, if you care to remember! It takes some time to heal from that, even for wizards."

In the morning, Efeon seemed to have come to terms with his situation. Marise, on her way back from walking the borders of the village to reinforce the warders, stopped to watch him go over the details of a marriage contract with Mika and her intended's parents. The wizard smiled, soaking in the sight of such a normal activity. This would be the third marriage to be contracted since she came to stay. It was a good sign, meaning that the people had faith in her ability to keep them and their village safe. She hoped that she could live up to such expectations.

Efeon looked up just then, his solemn face breaking into one of his rare smiles at the sight of her. The smile was fleeting, but Marise could feel the warmth it engendered still within her. She smiled back at him, and continued on her way. Peddlers had arrived the night before, and Cheon wanted her to handle their goods, ensure that nothing was bespelled.

She smiled again, amused at the level of contentment she had found in this simple village. After all those years of wandering. All those mornings of being convinced that your fate lay over the next hill, and then the next, to come home in a ragged village half the size of the home you left in such a hurry. She thought of Efeon, and her smile grew warmer. Home, indeed. And someone to share it with, perhaps?

"I think it would be a good idea, m'boy. You've not stirred from this place since your arrival. Now, you've seen more of the world than I, that's obvious, but even a place so charming as this must wear on the senses after a bit. Even Marise gets out and about every day. You just sit here, never so much as leaving sight o' this cottage. That can't be healthy, now, can it?"

Marise stopped outside the door and eavesdropped shamelessly. Betin had been after Efeon for weeks now, trying to convince the younger man to go with him on his rounds. The only healer within five villages, he spent much of his time traveling. He had asked her, but Marise didn't like to leave the village unprotected for longer than a day. That was all it would take for bandits to ride in and torch everything. So now he was turning his old man wiles on Efeon, who so far seemed immune.

"I told you already, Betin. I have no desire to go anywhere. This place suits me."

"Eh, sure it does. And the view suits you fine too, I'm sure. Well, that's all well and fine between you and Marise. No shame there, she's a fine woman, and a fine wizard too. But a man shouldn't be too settled, not at your young age. Plenty of pretty girls to wink at, where I'm going. And Marise none the wiser, eh?"

"Thinking to hide something from a wizard, old man?" she said, choosing that moment to enter the cottage, her arms laden with the first produce from the glass-enclosed garden she had helped build for Eiline over the winter.

Betin rose to help her, his customary grin telling her plainly that he knew she was not upset with him. Taking the pale roots from her arms and carrying them into the tiny storeroom, he said over his shoulder, "Ye may think I can't, but ye'd never know it if I could, now would you, child?"

Marise made a fond face at the old man's back, then turned to greet her houseguest. Efeon sat at the worktable, watching her with those brown-green eyes, his face smooth, as though he had never had an angry moment in his life. Marise smiled at him, trying to coax some spark to his eyes, then sighed, giving up. He was in a mood, then. She damned Betin, then retracted the thought. It wasn't the healer's fault that Efeon could range from laughter to scowls faster than a person could track.

"What is it, my river fox?" she asked gently, moving to stand in front of him, her hand tilting his chin up so as to look into his eyes. "Tell me what bothers you."

Efeon took his chin out of her hands with a jerk, not meeting her eyes. "That man. He comes in here, without so much as a by-your-leave, and starts harassing me to travel with him. As though it would be some honor to be chained to the prattling fool for days on end!"

Marise looked to the roof as if patience might be there, waiting to be found. "He is a good man," she began, "and wants only—"

Betin returned then, wiping his hands on his dun-colored pants. "You should clean in there more often, wizard," he scolded her, seemingly oblivious to the tension in the room. "Do you think your skills will save you from rats? Or food turning because you left it out too long? It must be something in your training is all I can think. You're almost as much a fool as our last wizard."

Efeon slapped his hands down on the table, startling Betin into silence. Marise, having seen the warning signs, was less surprised.

"Efeon, no." If she remained calm, he would cool down. "He meant no harm, no disrespect."

This time it didn't work. Betin backed up as the younger man advanced on him. "You will not speak that way of wizards," Efeon warned him, his tone cold and even like thick lake ice. "You will have respect for those better than you."

"Efeon!" Marise said desperately. This was what she had feared, that his anger would turn against one of those she had sworn to protect. "Efeon, *no!*" She prayed that Betin would back away, let the stranger inhabiting Efeon's body win. But the old man, over-talkative and nosy, had never backed down from a fight, whether against illness or injury or the challenge of a bully.

"Better?" Betin spluttered. "Better? Why you insolent cur! We take you in, a stranger to our town, offer every chance to be as one of us—"

Efeon laughed, a sharp bark of sound that chilled Marise. "One of you? Protect me from the thought! I would sooner lie down with the swine than claim such kinship." The corner of his upper lip turned in a mockery of a smile. "Or do you truly think yourself my equal? Come here, old man, and show me how equal we are." His hands, those long-fingered, graceful hands Marise so admired, called to the healer, inviting him to attack.

Had Efeon's opponent been a younger man, one who had not spent his entire adult life healing wounds rather than causing them, his taunt would have worked. But Betin hesitated a breath's pause before attacking. Into that hesitation Marise threw a hasty spell, taking control of their leg muscles. Efeon lurched forward one step, then wobbled, his fists open and dangerous-looking.

"You will apologize to Betin." Her voice was very soft, very even, and impossible to resist. Please, she thought, please let this work!

"I . . . apologize." Efeon's face clenched, then smoothed out as though someone had drawn a wet cloth over sand. "I am truly sorry," he said in a quieter voice. "I have a quick temper, as Marise can attest, and often speak words I do not intend."

Betin harrumphed, unimpressed. "Maybe so, maybe not. But I think I'll be watching you, young Efeon. Indeed I will." He stalked to the door, legs still stiff from the spell. One hand on the doorlatch, he turned. "And don't think that invitation to journey with me still stands, neither!"

In the morning, staring at the age-worn planks of the cottage's ceiling, Marise listened to the sounds that accompanied sunrise and thought about Efeon. He still remembered few details of his previous life, growing irritable when she pressed him on it. Whatever had killed him left him a restless spirit; those secrets he was holding dear to him, hoarding the not-knowing as one might an unknown inheritance. There might be jewels—there might be dust. But once opened, the precious moment of uncertainty would be gone forever, leaving him to deal with the results.

Marise could understand his reluctance, empathize with it. If it were only that she would encourage him to let go those secrets, wipe the past and start a new life in fact as Efeon. But another, darker shadow lay under his eyes when they spoke of who he might have been, and what might have happened to him-who-was. And that shadow frightened Marise. It frightened her both as a wizard and as a woman.

The day passed, Efeon never once out of her sight, never once anything other than the affable, caring man she knew, and yet the fear grew.

That night, after Efeon had finally dropped off into a restless sleep, Marise sat at the worktable, nursing a mug of tea, and poring over her journal, a slender book of remedies and spells she had brought with her rather than the massive tomes of lore she had inherited along with the cottage. One page in particular had her attention in the middle of that chill night. The Riding Folk had a charm to discern intent. It was a mild sort of magic, along the lines of love potions and see-clears. Most wizards scorned such cantrips as toys for the unskilled. But in this instance, such a charm had a powerful allure: it could neither be detected nor defended against.

She didn't want to cast it, had in fact talked herself out of it several times already. To doubt him seemed as great a betrayal as anything she might suspect of him. But his fits of violence were increasing, frightening her both for herself and for the villagers she had vowed to protect, and she had to do *something*.

Drawing the journal closer, she rehearsed the words in her head. As with most of the Riding Folk's magics, the spell required no physical components, simply the words and the wish. Twisting about to stare at Efeon in the dim firelight, Marise mouthed the words, barely vocalizing them for fear of waking him. He thrashed once as the spell took effect, and she held her breath, but he lay still thereafter. The cottage looked as before, the shadows no more threatening, the sounds from outside no less familiar. Taking a deep breath for courage, Marise closed her eyes, and *looked* at Efeon.

And there, in the flickering of her *sight*, lay the explanation for her love's tormented behavior. Marise opened her eyes, tears filling and overflowing. She had brought back not one man, but two.

In the morning light, Marise sat on the floor watching Efeon sleep as one would a wild cat, in awe and in fear. She wanted to wake him, to hold him against the truth, and at the same time she half-wished him gone, back to the ether from which she had called him.

Him. Them. Marise shook her head. She could not think of him as other than Efeon, anything but one man, despite the battle warring within him. But no body could hold two souls within it. They would never meld, not without magic far beyond her abilities. And his as well, if she was correct and half of him was Aginard, the wizard from whom she had inherited the cottage. It made sense, his being here, being familiar with the location and the people, having some memory of working magic here. But that left one very important question:

Who was the other half?

A squirrel chittered loudly outside and Efeon awoke with a smile, stretching his arms over his head in a graceful motion that made her heart break. Surely no evil could come of this man. And yet the warning of her *sight* stayed with her, putting a chill into the early spring air.

Efeon saw her staring at him, and his sleepy smile turned into a frown. "What?"

She started to make some excuse, then stopped herself. If she was right, if her *sight* showed true, then he had every right to know. In truth, he *needed* to know. But the words came to her with difficulty, the explanations sticking in her throat.

Throughout, he sat there on the woven frame he had built himself, one hand clenched in the square-patterned quilt Alyone had sewn for him in exchange for a letter to her son in Aldersvale.

"You're certain?" he asked finally, his voice weary and beaten. She nodded silently.

"I remember . . . I remember an argument. I—the two—they must have killed each other. The wizard, and another."

"He had a visitor the week before he died," Marise

said slowly. "But the villagers said he left on easy terms with Aginard."

"Was that other a wizard as well?"

Marise shook her head. "I don't know. No one did. I suppose he must have been, to take Aginard by surprise."

Efeon leaned forward, elbows on knees, forehead sunk into palms. "Two wizards battling, one destroying the other so that no trace is left."

"And the other taking revenge as he died," Marise finished. "Murdering the survivor. Both souls left to wander the place of their death."

"Until you came along." Efeon raised his head to look at her, his lips twisted in a smile that had no humor in it. "Both souls speaking to you, cajoling you—and you heeded them both. Oh, my lady, why didn't you just let us wander?"

Marise closed her eyes against the prickling of tears. He had not called her that since Lammas Night. It was an old-fashioned endearment, one a man of Aginard's age might use—for a woman his own age.

The gentleness, the courtesy of which Efeon was so capable. That had to be his legacy from Aginard. But the old wizard had been dour as well, folks told her, and no more capable of a joke than the planks of the floor. Efeon's ready wit, the pleasure he took out of a well-played prank or a bawdy tale—could those have come from the stranger who murdered her predecessor? Or was it Efeon's own self, called up out of magic and dust, that found such pleasure in a sunrise, and the smell of her herbal garden? So many conflicting signs, so much she had refused to see!

Marise groaned. What were they to do? It hurt her to look at him, to see that familiar face, and know that he was a stranger—two strangers—capable of cold-blooded murder.

"I don't suppose we could . . . ." He paused, uncertain. "No. Releasing one half would destroy the whole. I know that much, somehow."

Marise nodded unhappily. "We have to find someone who can bind your halves into one." And the only way to do that, she realized, was to return to where she had been trained. Where both—all three of them—had been trained. The Library.

There was only one flaw in that plan, which Efeon pointed out reluctantly but firmly. The Library was easily a two-week journey. Two weeks in good weather, barring unforeseen incidents. Two weeks when Marise would be away from the village.

"We swore an oath," he reminded her. "Or at least, half of me did. To protect the village. You can't do that if you're not here."

Marise refused to hear it. "They survived after Aginard died, before I came. They can do it again. There are villages that have nothing more than herbalry to ward off bandits, and they've done fine. But if you were to go to the Library alone—Efeon, *think!* You have no proof of yourself, no real memories to bring forth. Without me, they might as easily return you to ash as search for a solution!"

For the first time since that first dawn when he had carried her to bed, Efeon touched her, bending to his knees to look into her tear-filled eyes. He must have seen stubbornness there, because he simply sighed and sat back on his heels.

"You would return to the village the moment the Librarians were convinced?" He saw the mutiny in her expression, and his narrow lips firmed even more. "By the ether, Marise, you would turn a stone to water with your stubbornness!" He shook her, not gently. "You will heed me, damn it, or I will tie you to a post like a dog in need of whipping!"

She gasped, her brown eyes widening, and Efeon dropped her shoulders as though the flesh had burned him. Whirling away, he paced the length of the cottage, fingers running through his red-brown hair, leaving it standing on end.

"You can't go on like this," she said, forcing her breathing back under control. "You're dangerous. To yourself, to me." She used her sharpest weapon. "To the village."

Efeon stopped in his tracks, and Marise knew that her guess had been valid. The two halves making up the whole of Efeon had fought, had killed each other, over the village.

Perhaps the stranger had been a wandering wizard as she herself had been, finding this place to his liking. Perhaps he had been looking to use the village for evil means, or simply wanted to settle down in a bed already made comfortable by Aginard. It was impossible to know, with Efeon still blocking so many memories. But the village was the prize, and while those halves still fought, there was the potential for one or the other winning control. If it were Aginard, the village would have two wizards. An uncomfortable situation at best, but one they could possibly work around. But if it were the stranger—Marise shivered. She would have no choice but to complete the work begun by Aginard. She would have to destroy the person living within the shell of her beloved Efeon.

He moved to her side, his long-fingered hands playing in her hair. "What if I become violent?" he asked, echoing her thoughts. He bent to look at her, his brown-green eyes shadowed with pain. "Alone, on the road . . . Marise, what if I hurt you?"

"We have no other choice. You can't stay here, and you'll need me with you to face the Librarians." She put her arms around his neck, drawing his head to her chest as one would comfort a child. "You won't hurt me, my river fox. You're my magic wish, my good-luck charm, and you could never bring me ill."

He sighed, and she felt one warm tear drop onto her bare arm.

The morning crept into the cottage through the open door, the sunlight stretching across the plank floor to touch Marise gently against her eyelids. She jerked upright, shocked out of her slumber.

"Efeon, we're late."

There was only silence in the cottage.

Marise threw the light cover off and hurried to where Efeon slept, already knowing what she would find. The bedframe was bare, his blanket carefully folded. The worn leather pack she had given him the night before was nowhere to be seen. He was gone, gone without her, and Marise knew with a painful certainty that she would not catch up with him.

She might have birthed him, taken him from the ether and given him form and a name, but in the end he had made the decision of how he would live, and what he would live with. Could she blame him? Marise felt her lips twist in a wry smile. Of course she could. She could blame him for being a stubborn male, for wanting to protect her, for clinging to vows that only half of him had made—for being the man with whom she had fallen in love.

Retracing her steps, she stood over the worktable. Her hand shaking, she opened a small wooden box and withdrew three long strands of red-brown hair.

"My wish, river fox. That someday you find your way to wholeness. That one day you will find the road home again."

A Wanderer of Wizard-Kind

NINA KIRIKI HOFFMAN

Pigs could eat almost anything, but Sula wasn't sure about feeding her pig dragon bones. The time she had fed a nestling gryphon to her then-pig, Kara, the pig had given birth to kits instead of piglets, and had grown wings and learned to fly. Sula had brought the pig down out of the flower-nut tree with an arrow fletched with pegasi feathers, but oh, its meat had tasted strange, like storm sky, and not proper pig at all.

Sula had found the bones that morning while foraging farther afield than usual, in among fringes of the forest. Her now-pig, Kiki, was in the last month of pregnancy before farrowing, and needed bone meal. Sula brought the bones home before she noticed the red fire flecks in them that meant they were dragon bones.

If her Kiki should grow scales or a black heart from eating dragon bones, or farrow lizards, that was a loss Sula could ill afford so late in a gnawing cold winter. She had better burn the bones instead.

So it chanced that Sula was out in the weather, tending a blood-red fire of dragon bones and shifting away from the magic-tainted smoke on a morning when frost ferned the iron-hard ground and the chill wind froze the tears on a body's face. Everyone else

191

in the village was snug inside their hovels, sleeping perhaps and starving for certain, waiting for a break in winter's grip. Even the leafless trees shivered in the cold, shaking themselves out of dreams of spring.

Up along the path past the midden came a little bit of a man, begging tea or even water warmed over fire. What was Sula to do? She had a fire, never mind how mixed it might be with fallen bits of sky; and water she had aplenty—indeed, it seeped into her house when the rains were worst. So she fetched her dented pot and filled it with water, then put some dried kithi leaves in it and set it to simmer on the red dragon-bone fire, asking the man mite where he might be headed.

He curled thin fingers around the chipped mug she gave him, and he shivered inside his tattered cloak. He sniffed at the steam from the tea. His thin smile revealed teeth stained from chewing tanni leaves, so he'd been having a hard winter too—as if she couldn't tell that just from the size of him, with his bones too big for his skin to hold, almost. Not many in the northern reaches could find enough food to grow into their bones, but his skin was stretched tighter across his cheekbones than most.

He never said he was a wizard. He spun her a tale about heading south to the fief where his sister worked in the kitchens, where work waited for him with the hunting dogs. Had a way with animals, he did, or so he said.

"Chancy days to be on the road alone," Sula told him.

He showed her his little knife, a silver pricker shinier than many a metal she'd seen, even in the tinker wagons where many things shone bright whether they were worth a shine or not. When she admired it, he said he'd taken the metal from a god's turd, one of the flaming stones that fell shrieking from the sky on some summer nights.

That gave Sula pause. No one she knew would touch a god's turd. One never knew what sort of magic they might leak.

"So does it carve a treat?" she asked.

"Like a hot blade through ice," he said. He hid the knife under his cloak again and sipped his tea. "This has a fine flavor."

She smiled at him then. Much he might know about hounds, and perhaps about hawks and horses, but little he knew of herblore if he did not recognize the taste of kithi. "There's more if you want it," she said, edging away from the smoke again, with its smell like the hot red heart of a mountain. Some said smoke followed beauty, but she knew she had none. Smoke, she figured, followed wherever it pleased.

"More," said the little man, holding out the cup.

The kithi leaves had stained the hot water a warm and welcoming dark brown. The steam smelled like night-blooming flowers and late summer fruit. She poured him a cupful of tea that could have felled a fat priest, and he drank it and slid down smiling.

No, he had never told her he was a wizard, drat the little man. Or that he had locked his heart in a box and buried it in an ice wall up north where the sun never shone and the ice never melted.

Pigs could eat almost anything, but once Kiki had eaten the thin flesh from the wizard mite's bones, and the brain from its bone box, she turned canny and slippery. After Sula ground the wizard's bones and gave them to Kiki, the pig began to murmur.

Sula didn't notice right away, preoccupied as she was with scrounging enough leaves and roots and offal to feed Kiki through her farrowing. The wizard's sky

knife helped Sula slice the skin from trees, easily sliding between the outer and inner bark so that she had
fine fresh inner bark for Kiki; and when the weather
warmed a bit and Sula took Kiki to the forest to root,
the sky knife dug down through frozen earth wherever
Kiki pointed, seeking easily for the hidden treasures
beneath the frost: fat juicy roots, squirrel-cached nuts,
gryphon-buried kills. Never a thought did Sula give
to what the sky knife might be carving into the things
she and Kiki ate.

Sula and Kiki lived out the rest of the winter in
comfort, thanks to the leavings of the little man from
the north, and if Kiki's murmurs were more like
moans than grunts, her squeals more like screams, it
did not trouble Sula, who had weaving and knitting
to do in the long evenings so she would have something to market come summer.

When her farrowing time came upon her, Kiki took
rags and straw Sula offered her and made them into
a nest at the far end of the cave Sula had carved for
her out of the flank of the hill that nudged the house.
Sula woke one morning to discover that the man
mite's cloak was gone from where she had hung it on
a peg by the door. She held a candle into Kiki's cave
and peered toward the pig. The cloak had joined the
nest. For a little while Sula fretted about that—the
weave had been good and strong, and the cloak
strangely warm—but then she decided to respect the
pig's wisdom. Piglets would need all the warmth they
could find, and this nest was too far from the chimney.

Whenever Sula crept toward the nest, Kiki would
moan and grumble and mutter at her, shrieking
louder the closer Sula came, until the pig's cries
pierced the air and almost Sula's ears. Well, most pigs
would protect their lying-in place; this one was just a
little more protective than the others had been. She

left Kiki's food on the cave floor halfway between the
nest and the entrance to the house.

Six days after the winds changed direction and
spring started, Sula heard the cries of young and the
cooing purrs of a nursing mother from Kiki's nest,
and she smiled over her knitting. More than anything
she wished to count the babies so that she could make
her marketing calculations, but Kiki would not let her
near, even to clip the piglets' needle teeth.

She went out foraging instead and came back with
an apronful of early grasses. As she crept closer to
the nest she heard soft snores coming from the pig.
Ah. Just a glance she could take, if she could get close
enough before Kiki woke. Sula edged silently across
the cave floor, holding her candle up.

Tiny and pink, eight—no, nine—small creatures lay
snuggled against the pig's belly. Nine was a lovely
number.

Sula spilled the sprouts from her apron. She was
edging away when one of the babies woke, turned
nose to the air, and wailed.

It sounded wrong.

She glanced back. Its head was too round. Its ears
were too short. Its face showed in the flickering light
of her candle—ugly as hunger, human as a hand print.
It rolled over and pressed its mouth against a teat,
quieting.

Horrified, Sula studied the others. All their heads
were wrong. None of them had tails.

Well, this was a fine kettle of kithi. Not a one of
them would sell at market, not looking as they did.

She crept back to the house and sat on an upturned
bucket, staring into the embers. Her parents, who had
taught her piglore, had never had problems like these
with their pigs. What was she doing wrong? How was
she going to make it through next winter without the

supplies she had planned to barter the feeder pigs for? Had someone cursed her? Why?

Well, she thought, the little man had had reason enough, but he had gone down happy with the kithi tickling his brain, and she had killed him fast, with least hurt, and dressed him out immediately. He had not had time enough to cast a curse.

She glanced up at the yarn-tied bunch of dried kithi hanging from the rafters and wondered if she should make tea for herself. She was tired of scrounging and searching and scratching. She could do it if she knew that after marketing there would be a cone of crumbling brown sugar from the islands to the south, and a bag of coarse salt teased from the sea, and sacks of flour soft as feathers and finer than any earth to cook with all the coming winter; but now there would be none of that.

She sighed and looked up to see Kiki watching her from the cave entrance. The sow looked larger than ever. Firelight flickered in her small red eyes.

They had been friends ever since Sula had bought Kiki for a small silver nugget the previous spring. Sula had let Kiki choose among the village boars the one she wished to sire her farrow; Sula and Kiki had foraged together through summer and fall and winter. And now the sow was staring at her with the eyes of a stranger.

"What shall I do now?" she asked the air.

"Find me some taters," said the sow in a voice low and rough as rush matting.

"They're all gone, a fortnight ago," Sula said. Then she blinked. Kiki had never spoken to her before.

"I smell them," said Kiki. She lifted her snout. "And new-laid eggs, and just-open flowers. Get them for me."

"But I—but you—but—"

"Now," said the pig, lowering her snout and glaring at Sula. Sula noticed that Kiki had tusks now, long ones, and that her snout was shorter than it had been.

This was not the conversation Sula had imagined she might have with her pig if the pig could talk. Sula rose, took her gathering basket and the sky knife from pegs near the door, stepped into her clogs, and went out into the rain. She glanced toward the houses of the others, farther from the forest and the midden, closer to the square and the tavern. She had no friends among them. Should she choose to step out of her life and walk away from her house and everything in it, no door would open to her; no one would offer her so much as soup, not unless she brought them something they could use.

She turned into the forest instead and spent the afternoon robbing bird nests. The only taters she knew of were in other peoples' root cellars, where she let them stay, but she found some windflowers beside the stream and picked them to take home.

Kiki was waiting beside the fire for her when she came back. She set her finds on a wooden trencher on the floor and watched as the pig ate everything, carefully and delicately, spilling nothing. Its eyes watched her watching it. When she stooped to pick up the trencher, the pig whipped its head to the side, slashing her arm with its tusk. Sula was so surprised that she fell backward, and Kiki came at her where she sprawled on the rushes. She wondered if the pig would kill her now. She held her arms up to protect her face, and the pig licked the arm it had bloodied, then backed away from her, muttering and murmuring small sounds that resembled a song.

Sula's head swam. She sat up slowly and studied her arm. The slash burned, but it was not deep; it had scraped away skin to the blood beneath, but it had not sliced into muscle. The strange small song of the pig flowed into her ears, and she found her head weaving in time to it, and then her whole body swayed.

The pig finished singing and said, "You're mine now; do you understand?"

"No," said Sula.

"Body and soul you belong to me."

"No," whispered Sula.

"Yes. Say yes."

She tried to keep her mouth closed on the word, but she could not. "Yes."

"Remember," said the pig. "You gave yourself to me when you killed me. Nothing else binds two souls so strongly as murder. You gave yourself to me, and now I have accepted you."

Sula shook her head.

"Say yes," whispered the pig.

Though she tried not to say it, she whispered yes.

"You cannot kill me," said the pig, "for my heart is elsewhere."

Recalling how she had taken care of her last wayward pig, Sula glanced toward the place where she kept her bow and a quiver full of arrows. They were no longer there. She looked lower, and saw that her bow had been bitten in half, its braided hide string chewed to bits, and the arrows had fared no better; all that was left of them were fragments of snow-white feathers and the iron heads.

She unsheathed the sky knife and looked from its blade to the pig.

"You might cut me, but you cannot kill me." It glanced at the fire for a while, then turned back. "You will not cut me."

She sighed and put the knife away. "What are we going to do with the babies?"

"When they can walk, we will take them to my sister."

"Your sister?" she whispered.

"In the castle kitchens at Babiruse Fief, six days' march to the south."

In the darkness beyond the pig, faint cries sounded. "Sleep well," said the pig, and vanished.

As the days lengthened she spent more and more time in the forest, for she had ten mouths to feed now—eleven, if she counted her own. Every night she fell into bed exhausted, and every morning the pig sent her out again, sometimes with specific instructions.

Horses, hounds, and hawks he might know, she thought, but he had no herblore. When she went foraging she picked bitter herbs with the sweet, nightshade and gutburst, larkspur and amanita. She offered them all to the pig, mixed with grasses and nasturtiums and puffballs, when she went home. Sometimes the pig ate them and sometimes it didn't.

It never even got sick. Pigs could eat almost anything.

Circle of Ashes

STEPHANIE D. SHAVER

It had taken exactly two hundred and twenty-two steps to get up to Lord Benzamin's room. Maakus knew. He'd counted every . . . last . . . one.

"Maàkus, correct?"

"Indeed, Lord Benzamin," the bard replied, trying hard not to pant.

"Please, take a seat." The slightly gray-haired magus gestured toward a padded chair.

The bard sighed as he relaxed into the cushions, taking the time now to memorize the setup of the room he had entered, as was his duty. A comfortably sized rectangular room, the west and east walls—coincidentally, the longest—lined with books. The north wall had two beveled-glass doors that opened on to an impressive porch and a view of the City of Light. There were only two other doors in the room. One behind him in the south wall—the one he'd come through—and one in the west wall, which was shut at the moment.

Maakus turned his eyes now to the man he had come to visit. The *kioko* magus, Benzamin, one of the fifty High Lords of the City of Light. An unextraordinarily-looking, slightly pudgy and green-eyed man who commanded extraordinary power.

"Wine, sir madrigal?" the magus asked, and glanced

toward the door in the west wall. Maakus was surprised to see that it had opened without him hearing,
and a small child was looking in, her eyes flicking
from magus to bard, just far enough into the room to
show she was wearing the cream-and-silver of an initiate of the City of Light.

"That would be most fine," Maakus said. "White,
please."

Benzamin nodded and looked pointedly at the girl.
"You heard him," he said not unkindly, and she gig-
gled and darted out so quickly the golden curls on
her head bounced. The door shut behind her.

The magus waited until the girl had returned and
Maakus had had a few sips of the wine—which was
chilled and excellent—before saying, "So, sir madrigal. What brings you here?"

Maakus paused for a moment, then reached into
the satchel at his hip and withdrew a leather-bound
book. He set it on the magus' desk and pushed it
toward the man. Benzamin leaned forward, his face
now fallen into a mask of seriousness, and picked it
up gingerly. He flipped through a few pages, and his
face fell further, now toward sorrow.

"Aloren," he said, a soft pain in his voice.

Maakus nodded. "I . . . found this, sir. After she . . ."

Benzamin swallowed, his throat bobbing. "Thank
you, sir madrigal," he said. "I knew Aloren kept a
journal. I had wondered what had happened to it.
The retrieval of this is much appreciated. I can requi-
sition you a reward of—"

"No money," the bard said, and leaned forward.
"Sir . . ."

The magus raised a brow at him. "I have a feeling
you are about to ask for something I cannot give you."

"That might be, sir magus," Maakus said. "But I
have to know. What *happened?*"

The magus sat back slightly. "That depends," he said. "What do you know?"

"Just what is in that journal and what I got from speaking with her."

Benzamin nodded. "Then ... please, tell me."

Maakus smiled slightly. "Ah, Lord Magus, you truly know how to make a bard happy."

Benzamin chuckled, and Maakus began.

"I am haunted," she said, and I was inclined to believe her. The smudges beneath her eyes, the paleness of her skin, the slack fall of her ash-blonde hair. It was hard to look her in the eye for any length of time, and I never could remember her eye color. I had never met her before today, when she caught me coming into town and demanded to speak with me in private, but she was someone I instinctively knew to be honest.

"By what?" I asked. "And why did you ask me to meet you here and not in the house?" "Here" was the only inn the town of Waysedge had to offer. It was small and cramped, but it offered free room and board to any bard, so I couldn't complain. And the innkeep had accommodated us when we asked to be alone.

She frowned. "If we were at my house, *he* would be watching. He can't leave it, from what I understand. It's where he died. . . ."

"Who?" I asked, my hands flowing in intricate patterns in my lap. A silent spell of remembrance, so I would not forget what transpired between me and this young *kioko* magus.

Aloren sighed. "His name is Jesamen. He was the *kioko* magus here before me. Weaver of the Light, to keep the Dark at bay . . ."

I smiled slightly. Those words, *Weaver of the Light,*

to keep the Dark at bay, were almost ritual among the *kioko* magus of Sellgard; were, in fact, their credo. She said it with the unconscious ease of one who was used to reciting it.

"He died," she went on to say. "But he ... It was only a partial death. His body decayed, but his soul remained. . . ."

I blinked, a tiny ripple of chill crawling up my spine. I suppose such words from anyone else I would have called insane. But not from a magus. Not from one such as Aloren.

"Have you told anyone else?" I inquired.

"No. Just you."

"Why?"

"Because you can't do anything," she replied. "You can only watch. If I tell other magi they would try to set him free; if I told a villager, they would burn me for practicing Dark Arts and then touch fire to the house. You are a madrigal. Your job is to observe and listen. And that is all you will do." She caught my gaze again. "I know what you're thinking: 'But what if I tell a villager?' " She smiled. "I would refute your claims, and they would believe me over you. It is I, after all, who they have known for these last six months. It is I who has cast the spells that have turned aside the droughts, the hard rains, the locusts. I break their superstitions, and give them a sense of peace. And there is no other magus within a distance you could reach in time who could stop what I must do. I checked."

I stared at her openly now, wondering if she was mad. I'm still not quite sure that she wasn't.

"All right," I said after a moment. "I won't stop what you're going to do . . . whatever that may be."

"I . . . will tell you," she said.

"Why?" I asked, breaking the patterns now that the spell was complete and sustaining.

"Because someone needs to know."

I nodded. "All right."

"In five days is Lammas Night," she said. "The Darkest night."

I frowned. "I thought the darkest night was during winter or late fall—"

"No. You are not listening. I said the *Darkest* night, not the blackest night. Lammas Night is the night that a spirit—with the help of magic—may step through the shadowed veils of death's realm and enter into this one. Permanently. In the flesh.

"Lammas Night is the night Jesamen died, exactly one year ago."

I took another swallow of wine. "Go on," I said.

"The state Jesamen exists in now is a unnatural one. He stands on the border of the two lands, a denizen of shadow. He . . . has asked me to bring him back to life."

I absorbed this for a moment, then said, "How?"

"It is in a book that was his," she said, pushing a lock of hair behind her ear. "A grimoire of the dead. I had thought such books no longer existed, but . . ." She paused. "From it, if I perform the spells correctly, I can do one of two things. Set him free in the lands of the living, or set him free in the lands of the dead.

"And I do not know which I will choose."

I frowned. "Well, the choice is obvious—"

She laughed. "Is it? What would be your choice?"

"I would let him die. Obviously, the gods willed that he should be dead, and, through some unnatural means—perhaps even of his own making—he has lingered on."

"Ah, I see. So not only do *you* decide who lives

and who died, but you are also privy to the gods."
Her words were laced with a fierce sarcasm.

I sighed. "It would be unnatural to bring him back."

"It is also unnatural to linger in the shadow," she
said softly. "The power to return him to his original
state on this earth is within me. Why else would it be
there save to use?"

I went silent, thinking of this, then said, "Lady, I
do not envy your choice."

She smiled bitterly. "But it *is* my choice, as the
gods seem to have decreed. And, in the end, I would
have it no other way."

"And what do you wish me to do?"

"Stay," she said. "Until after Lammas Night. I will
make my decision that night. I have no other
alternative."

I blinked. "Why not?"

"Because after that night he departs whether I do
anything or not."

I frowned. "Shouldn't that answer all your questions
right there?"

She shook her head. "You don't understand. He
has . . . for whatever twisted reason of the gods,
become bound to my soul, like strings on a lute. Pluck
the strings, and the lute vibrates. Cut the strings yourself, and they snap, leaving the lute intact. But expose
both to wind and weather, and not only do the strings
corrode, but the lute will warp and crack."

The shiver of ice now grew claws, drawing ragged
lines of chill across my chest.

"So if he departs . . ." I said slowly.

Her voice went so quiet I could hardly hear her.
"I go with him."

Benzamin waited until Maakus' glass had been
refilled before talking.

"What else?" he asked.

"Other than that, I saw her but a few more times. All other knowledge I have acquired was from the book."

Benzamin nodded.

"The book is not accurate, though."

The High Lord raised a brow.

"It only holds passages of what occurred before Lammas Night. Nothing after it."

"And that is what you wish to know?"

"Indeed, High Lord."

Benzamin nodded and rubbed his chin.

The madrigal paused for a moment. "As she bid, I went to her home after Lammas Night and found the journal. There was a hand-written note pinned to it naming it mine. I found circles of chalk in the attic, some candles, ashes, and what appeared to be the burnt remains of a book ... probably the grimoire she spoke of."

Benzamin nodded. "But no sign of her?"

"None. No clothing, no stray strands of hair, no jewelry. She wore a locket of silver, I remember that."

The *kioko* magus nodded. "What do you think happened?"

Maakus furrowed his brow. "One of three things: she panicked, and allowed him to go on to the land of the dead. ..."

"And went along with him. Then there should have been a body left."

Maakus shrugged and nodded. "Or she miscast, and destroyed them both. Or ... brought him back ... and he destroyed her."

"You think he was evil?" Benzamin asked curiously.

The bard sighed. "I read her journal, sir. You do know how she fared ... in the war. ..."

Benzamin nodded. The war on the west border of

Sellgard had been raging for nearly two years, and Aloren had been on the front lines for almost as long as it had been running. Her journal had extended back to that time, and Maakus had not been blind to the slow eroding of her personality that had occurred over the course of the months she had spent fighting the *ni'ochi* magi who were the anathema of the *kioko*. Indeed, if one were to compare the entries at the beginning of the journal—when she was just entering the war—to the ones toward the end—after her honorable discharge and restation at the village—one would hardly be able to recognize them as having been written by the same person except by the handwriting.

"What about it?" Benzamin asked.

"He . . . played on this. I don't know if she realized it, but . . . many times, in my job, you will never get the truth. So you must learn to read between the lines, and come to conclusions of your own. . . . My conclusion is that he played on her loneliness. At one point, she said she thought she was in love with him. . . ."

The High Lord looked upset at this. "In love enough to go on with him into death, I imagine."

"*If* that was what he wanted. Which he didn't. He was *quite* adamant about that."

Benzamin nodded. "I see," he said.

The bard shrugged. "That's all I know, or have concluded. You?"

The magus shook his head, but said nothing. After the silence had continued longer than Maakus cared for, the bard reached into his satchel again and set a scroll on the High Lord's desk.

Benzamin raised a brow. "What is this?"

"A song I wrote. A song as yet uncompleted."

The High Lord nodded, and unrolled the scroll, his

eyes scanning rapidly over the words. After a moment he looked up. "Interesting ending," he commented.

"Quite the opposite. It *has* no ending, sir."

"Is that why you came?"

The bard nodded. "It's maddening to have questions with no answers."

"And what makes you think I have any answers?"

"You were her teacher. You are magus. You would know if she yet lives."

Benzamin smiled bleakly. "I might."

The madrigal wet his lips, reaching within himself for the next puzzle. "By Aloren's own hand," he began slowly, "*kioko* magic is not a definite thing. Even spells . . . are not definite."

Benzamin nodded.

"She also says that the magic . . . is alive. She called it the Light. She often referred to it as though it were a living thing."

Benzamin chuckled. "It can be."

"*Ni'ochi* magic is different, it *requires* spells, and it was probably a *ni'ochi* magus that wrote the grimoire."

Benzamin nodded. "Correct."

"Could it be possible . . . for a *kioko* magus to go corrupt and turn to the Dark magic rather than the Light?"

The High Lord flushed slightly. "If you are implying that she—"

"No." The madrigal's voice was firm. "I am implying that *he* was winding down that road."

Benzamin nodded. "That would make sense. But you must understand that the Light is rather vicious. It visits retribution on those who have spurned it."

Maakus smiled. "What better retribution than spending time as an earthbound soul?"

Benzamin blinked, and Maakus saw his glance dart

toward the door from which the child had come. "Of course. . . ." Benzamin said softly. "So that—" he stopped suddenly, looking at the bard again.

Something flashed in Maakus' mind, something he had noticed without noticing, something at the edge of his memory. . . .

Maakus shook his head. Whatever it was, it would come in its own time.

"All right," the bard said. "I've told you my part . . . now it's time for yours."

Benzamin chuckled. "Bards are such flatterers. Aye, there is something I know: the piece you do not."

"You know what happened to her?" Maakus breathed, sitting up.

Benzamin nodded. "And I shall show you."

The wind rattled against the windows, striking like a snake. I closed my eyes, calmed myself within, then opened them to stare at the circles I had drawn.

I reached within me to the well from which I drew the Light, and called it. It curled like woodsmoke from my hand and flowed into the outermost circle.

"Jesamen," I breathed, and a shadowy figure appeared in the circle, staring at me with ethereal green eyes.

"Aloren. . . ." he said softly, voice louder than it had ever been, but still a shade's voice. It had strengthened as Lammas Night grew closer. My body trembled at the sound of that voice. I wondered what his touch would feel like. . . .

The book lay open before me, pages worn nearly brown by time. I stared at them, wishing that I had had more time to look through it.

Two spells, both so similar. . . . Which strokes of the pen do you choose, magus?

"Midnight draws close!" the shade said. "You *must* bring me back, Aloren!"

The wind whistled, flailed against the window, and then suddenly broke through the constraining latches. The gale howled through the room, extinguishing the candles and scattering loose scrolls. It snatched at the book, spun the pages. I grabbed desperately at them, reaching to retrieve my place—

A bookmark. A page. I blinked and stared at the page, wondering why it was I had not turned to it before. A bookmark. A spell. I should have opened to it by the mark automatically. Unless my actions had been controlled—

A bookmark. An enchantment. A formula for . . .

"Immortality," I said aloud and looked up at him. "Immortality, on Lammas Night."

"Aloren—"

"You sonuvabitch."

It all crashed over me, hurting worse than anything I'd ever felt in any of the battles at the war. I just stared at him in silence.

"You *bastard*," I said, my heart hurting. "You—you tried to cast this, didn't you?"

"Aloren, you must understand—"

"And it backfired! And you were *stuck* here! Until I came along." The rage burned in my belly, the Light reacting to it. A light blue glow began to flower about me.

"Were you going to possess me?" I snarled, standing. A flash of Light crackled out of my hand and hit the book. I heard Jesamen scream, staring in horror at the ashes that had been his salvation. "Were you going to weaken me, and then try to overcome me? Or did you just want a partner?" I swallowed, and my voice fell into a dangerous whisper. Now the rage was controlled. I realized, belatedly, that I had destroyed *my* salvation as well, but I did not care. It didn't matter. *Nothing* mattered.

Save one thing.

"You *used* me," I growled. "You *preyed* on me, you bastard. And now I'm going to give you *exactly* what you wanted."

Jesamen's face blurred—fear, anger, astonishment. "If you destroy me," he hissed, "*you* die, too! *Anything* you do to me will echo back onto you! Don't you realize what you've done?"

I smiled coldly. "Jesamen, you know what?"

Fear flowered higher in his eyes, and I saw the realizations clicking into place there.

"This is the *second* time you've messed with something you couldn't control."

And then I opened my hands, sent my wish to the well, and released the Light upon us.

The clatter of dishes snapped Maakus out of whatever spell he had fallen into. He blinked, staring at the wall behind Benzamin until his sight cleared. Only then did he allow himself to look at the magus, who was smiling congenially at the young girl, busy at clearing away the dishes.

Maakus stared at her for a while, the flickering at the edge of his mind growing stronger. His glance flashed from Benzamin, to the scroll and the journal, to the girl—

To the necklace with the silver locket around the girl's neck—

"The child," he said abruptly. "Where did she get that locket?"

The High Lord smiled at him, and the madrigal felt a familiar chill. "It's her, isn't it?" Maakus asked as the child silently left the room. "She's actually—"

"Madrigal, listen to me. Did Aloren ever state in her journal why she went to the war?"

Maakus shook his head.

Benzamin closed his eyes. "She was . . . of all the *kioko* magi, she was the most powerful to be born in nearly a hundred years. When she went to the war, the High Lords found her to be an excellent weapon." The magus sighed. "She fought on the lines for nearly a year and a half, and killed fifty of the enemy *ni'ochi* magi single-handed."

"So why was she discharged?"

The High Lord's lips flattened. "What she told me was that one night, after watching yet another wave of the enemy sweep over her friends, her partners, her associates, and kill so many, she decided to end the war herself. And the next day, she brought down a flood of Light that blasted trees in a half-league long circle. It was then the High Lords decided she was too dangerous to use anymore, and had her transferred as far away as we could send her. To the east. She was expected to walk a circuit or settle in a village for a year. Those were her options."

Benzamin swallowed. "The High Lords had plans for her. They said that all she needed was rest, and then they would bring her back until she broke again. Even as it stands now, the war still is in no sight of ending. Students used to take twelve years to learn our craft, and now we rush them through in five. So long as they are at least sixteen, we send them."

"But the King and High Lords *must* see what they are doing is draining—"

"Draining? Only to the magi. We use a minimum of troops since most of the battles are magic-wrought. It is of almost no consequence to the majority of the realm. Just to the magi. And the *kioko* magi are all that we have to fight the *ni'ochi*. At this time."

The bard swallowed this silently. "And if they knew she lived . . . ?"

Benzamin sat, staring at the plate of food that neither man had touched. "I was the one who trained her. I was the one who told the High Lords she would make an ideal soldier. I am the reason she became dead inside. I will be the reason she will learn, in silence, from me. And by the time I finish teaching her, hopefully this war will be over."

"But what happened to her that she is so young?"

"Gods only know. It was what she asked for, I think. Aloren's greatest flaw was she was too forgiving at times. Perhaps she took pity on Jesamen. . . ."

Maakus shook his head. "What was . . . how did you make me see that vision?" The last thing he remembered seeing before the . . . memory hit him was the magus opening his hand at him, and then an explosion of Light.

"She left *you* a journal, and left *me* that," Benzamin said softly. "The pieces of this puzzle are now together. The riddle is solved. And now *you* have to do me a favor."

"What is that?"

"Leave the song as it is."

Maakus swallowed. "But it has no ending."

"Yes, but if the High Lords learn that she is alive, that she has not died but become a child without the memories of her past and all the power . . ."

The madrigal nodded. "I can think of several consequences." He stood quietly, and heard the door to the west open. The child peeked in again.

"Benzamin . . . if they were bound together . . . what happened to . . . *him*?"

"I'm not sure." Benzamin called softly to the girl, who walked to her mentor, eyes still on the madrigal.

Gray, Maakus thought, holding her gaze. *Now I know.*

"I must leave, sir," he said. "I thank you for your time."

"Maakus."

The madrigal turned back, brow raised. "Yes?"

"What of your song?" Benzamin asked. "And the *kioko* magus Aloren?"

Maakus glanced at the child, who stared back.

"The *kioko* magus Aloren? She learned that the spirit was one of evil, and died bravely in the process of destroying it." He swallowed a bit, and cracked a shaky smile.

"Indeed," Benzamin said.

"Long life, High Lord."

"Long life, madrigal."

Maakus never looked back.

Benzamin sighed as the door shut, turning to smile down at the child Allaya. It had been too dangerous to keep her original name.

"I'm gonna go study my books, sir," she said.

"Do that, dear." He thought for a moment. "Bring your friend in, will you?"

She nodded and ran out. Not a minute later, the door reopened and a boy entered. Green eyes met Benzamin's own, his young face solemn.

Benzamin sighed again. He had made so many mistakes in his life. Aloren had only been one of them.

"Is there something you wanted, sir?" the initiate asked.

Benzamin stared long and hard at the child, thanking the gods for the gift he had been given.

"No," Benzamin told the boy. "I just wanted to make sure you'd taken your bath. Dismissed."

Jesamen bobbed his head once, turned, and left.

A Choice of Dawns

SUSAN SHWARTZ

I forced out the last words of the invocation with the last breath in my aching lungs and stood panting. My hands were shaking, and sweat dripped down my ribs beneath my robe. The circle I cast glowed about me. Sweeter than the wine in the Cup, keener than the edge of the Blade I held was the awareness that my time of silence, of exile, of helplessness had passed. Even though the spell from the strange book I had found—or that had been found for me—was gray, and a darkish hue at that, I had not been blasted.

Not yet.

The fumes of herbs and incense burning at the cardinal points did little to ease my need for air, and other Words—either of Welcome or of Banishment—remained for me to utter. I had only to choose.

The months I had spent in the house of the wizard who was supposed to be dead, or lost, or borne off on dragon's back (depending on whom I asked) had completed my healing. It was not my strength to complete a Great Workings I feared: it was my judgment.

Would I compound an old folly with a new? Bad enough I had accepted the village's offer to bide here. Worse that I had not fled the first time I heard that voice whispering to me as I studied or swept or, worst of all, just before I slept—in the vanished wizard's

very bed. I might have recoiled when the bittersweet
fragrance of lilacs I had not cut wafted from my plate.

At least, see where you have journeyed. Curiosity,
as much a besetting sin of mages as pride, stirred in
me as it had when I first read the spell and a prickling
along my spine told me this was a ritual I could survive performing.

Again, I raised my arms. The sleeves of my robe
fell back, exposing the scars, paler now, that braceleted my wrists. Let them be a caution to me—please!

The mists outside my glowing circle wreathed up,
then faded. I stood in a clearing surrounded by dark
trees. A sickle of silver moon gleamed barely above
the treetops; other light seemed to rise from the land
to greet it. The circle was not of this world at all,
until I slashed it with my sword.

The Great Workings can be lonely, a loneliness that
can prove fatal if a mage must pause and wait
between incantations.

I heard no footsteps, but I knew when *he* drew
near. Wind blew, stirring, even within the circle, the
grains of sand and earth I had so carefully poured
out. It brought with it the scents of rain on lilacs and
wood ash, the scents of the wizard's house and the
flowers with which he had wooed me.

And was it all that unlikely? Even changed as I was,
I was surely not that uncomely . . . was I? Just because
one man, eager for power, had made me believe
power was the only reason anyone could want me
didn't mean someone had drawn a heated brand
across my face and soul—did it? Or was it that my
power was now *mine*, guarded against anyone who
might coax me into yielding it? I was more than an
instrument to gain power or glut desire: I was myself.

I saw him then, and that "myself" dwindled into a
feeble, malformed thing. He was slender, with eyes

as changeful as a troubled sea—with his troubles, or mine? He smiled at me, and his eyes flickered. Oh, he remembered too: the dreams, teasing at the edge of my mind and my body's awareness.

I had but to slash the circle with the Blade, hold out my hand, speak the Words, and bring him back to all he had lost. Before the rite, I had put lavender-scented linen sheets upon his bed (now mine). I had set out porridge and bacon (magecraft is hungry work) by the hearth I had swept. There was enough for two, not just for the meal, or for the winter, but for all our lives if I could trust him.

But if I chose wrong, ah, then he would own not just the bed and the food and the village that had welcomed me, not just me—body, heart, and prisoned soul—but all that he could seize and drain the life from.

Mages draw upon their souls in the Great Workings: the spell I had uttered tonight was neither wholly of sun nor shadow. Mages respect power itself; it had only been in my exile that I came to want the comfort of a sheltering god—as I did now.

Well, would I stand here forever until my strength failed and I was as trapped as he? A coward is not fit to be a mage. Not in arrogance or in folly, I hope I made my choice. I had to know. Always, always, a mage must know.

I slashed the circle with my silver Blade, opening a gate. His eyes brightened with such joy that my own eyes filled with tears. I raised the Blade, holding him off. Too easy, too easy by half to bring him into the Circle and have him, were he of the dark, seize possession of it.

I stepped outside my circle. A cord of silvery light followed me, binding me to my life and to my world.

Unlike the cord that binds babe to mother, cut *this* cord, and body and soul go free.

Similar light, much diminished, circled him. So he still possessed some tie to our world.

"Lady, I beg of you." No suppliant, he put out hands for the Cup, but did not fall to his knees. I offered it to him. A creature of the dark would recoil from the blessed wine. He sipped, his fingers brushing mine, his eyes hopeful, searching.

He raised the Cup again to his lips, but this time, it was my hands that he kissed. His lips were very warm; they moved with alarming speed to the scars upon my wrists. I jerked hands and Cup back so quickly that some of the blessed wine spilled. Never mind the dreams that had assuaged my loneliness, while arousing longing and far, far more. I would not be this easily won.

"My poor, wounded lady." It was the voice from my dreams, coaxing me so that, against my will, I smiled. "Will you not drink with me?"

Not he but maidcraft (though I had thrown maiden-hood away too) made me flush, made my eyes fill and fall—that and the remembered lilac fragrance of my shadowy suitor's gifts. I brought the Cup to my lips, my eyes searching. His eyes lit: he would have life again, a mage's powers, tempered by this ordeal, human warmth—perhaps he would welcome my pres-ence in this restored life.

Not only the pungent wine made my head spin . . .

Thunder rumbled out, and the earth shook. A high wind howled out from the sudden darkness of the sky. I reeled, knowing it had blotted out the circle I had so laboriously cast.

"So, I have me a pair of magelings now, sire and dam. You shall breed me more, teach me your crafts—or each watch the other writhe in torture till you submit!"

"Run!" cried the wizard. He seized my hand and dragged me from the clearing, from the ruined circle and my hopes of a swift return into the darkest reaches of the forest. Clutching the Blade, I ran, my heart pounding in my chest. Behind us, *things* howled and bellowed, their voices rising in pitch until I wanted no more than to clap hands over ears until the keening stopped drilling into my brain.

I staggered, and he flung an arm about my shoulder, drawing me along secret twists and turns in the forest until we drew up before a vast pine. Its lowest branches formed a canopy that brushed the ground. He pushed me through the branches, then toward the tree's massive trunk.

"Here," he gasped.

"Here" was a crack in the bark that turned out to be the entry to a tiny cave within the living tree. I sank down onto a carpet of needles. He leaned out, listening as the hunt raced past. The silver of our life force lit the cave.

"They do not see this?" I brushed my fingers through the light where it pooled together, then flushed at the gesture.

"The tree's life conceals us," said the other mage. He knelt and fumbled through bunched herbs. He tore off some leaves and arranged them at the portal, murmuring a warding spell.

"You seem to have learned to live here," I said, noting containers wrought of burl or leafy nets, some attempt to equip the woody cave with rudimentary comforts.

"I survive. When I first escaped the Master, all I could think of was surviving to return home. When you came . . ."

I raised a brow.

"I told myself I had found another reason to live."
He fell silent, his shoulder brushing mine, his mind
reaching out. We dared not exchange names, not in
danger such as had found us, but I knew that if I met
him elsewhere on the Planes, a hundred lifetimes
from now, I should recognize the touch of his mind.

"You know the stories in our world of the Wild
Hunt," he said. "This place has a Hunt of its own. Its
Master—" he shuddered "—is not one whose hospitality I crave. He wanted a tame mage or, better yet,
two from which to breed an army he can use to enter
our world and upset its balance."

"How does he know about our world—or about its
balance?" I asked.

He looked down. "Lady, you are not the only one
of the Wise who has been a fool. I thought I was wise
in appealing to you, but you have given me another
cause for fear. Forgive me for dragging you after me
into this world."

His shoulder flinched away from mine. Once, I had
thought I had found a companion with whom I could
stand side by side, neither mastering nor mastered.
This man's voice had made me dream a second time.
False dawns, both times.

I huddled in upon myself.

"How long do you think we can hide here?" I was
proud that my voice did not shake.

"The days are very short in this place. One man,
alone, could dodge the pack, but with you here and
the Master aware of you, I fear those days are num-
bered." He knelt to rummage among his meager
belongings. Then he turned back to me, holding a
battered blanket, shaped to make a crude cape.

"You deserve far finer, but this is all I have," he
said.

"I am your debtor in the other world," I made myself say. "Your house has been a refuge to me."

"Aye, and once I return, I shall never leave it—" he laughed. "That is what I say. But, lady, you tremble. I wish I had wine for you or a fire."

He spread the blanket over my shoulders, his hands pressing my shoulders briefly, his breath stirring my hair. A lump filled my throat.

"Oh, this is so good," he went on, and I realized that he spoke as much from relief at having companionship as from a need to explain. "One watches; one sleeps. Rest, my . . . lady. You are weary from the passage between worlds."

A howl from outside our fragile keep had waked me, the wizard's fingers at my lips lest I cry out, betraying us both. Now, my companion rested, his face turned toward me.

"Forgive me if I stare. It has been so long since I have seen another face," he apologized. Gradually, he drifted into sleep. The lines of strain, the lines of craft smoothed out until the sleeping man, his head so close to my knees, might have been a young scholar or fighting man. If he were such a man and I a weaver, say, or a broidress, or even a real lady . . . I sighed.

His eyes opened again, and he smiled. Then he flung an arm over his face—disappointed at the sight of me rather than another, or reminded of our danger? A silver bracelet gleamed on his wrist, where my wrist was braceleted with scars.

He reached for a covered vessel and offered me water in which herbs had steeped. I wrinkled my nose at the unfamiliar scent. How long could I go without drinking? Sighing, he exchanged the container for another, this one of clear water.

"We must get you back," he said. "There is a fane, less than half the night's travel from here. I found it when I escaped. It is near a river . . . near, too, to where the Master holds his court."

"Is there danger in venturing so close?"

"Lady, this land teems with danger! I was mad to venture here, madder still to draw another after me. We shall get you home."

"We? And then?" I hated myself for asking, as if I taunted him with the preservation of his life and soul.

"Perhaps by then I shall prove that you can trust me." He shrugged off what meant his return home and bent to scoop up dried pine needles. He crouched, shaping them into a small map of the land we must cross; we studied it, illumined by our own silvery life force.

We took the blanket-cloak with us when we left the tree, but left all else behind, silently aware that, come success or defeat, we would not pass that way again. I had Cup and Blade tucked into my belt. He had a club to which he had bound a sharp-edged stone that looked like flint.

The silver cords—mine vivid, his diminished by his long stay in this place—that marked our lives glowed about us.

And ultimately, they were what betrayed us to the Hunt.

We crept to the edge of the forest and crouched side by side, staring out into the clearing where shadows stalked and leapt as if about a central core. The moon was waxing now as if days had passed during the time we hid in the tree.

The mage shuddered. "*He* is there." He shaped the words without sound. I could imagine how he would know the Master of the Hunt from the time he had been his captive. I would have rested my head against his shoulder, but the Master of the Hunt's threat to use us to breed magelings still heated my cheeks. I pressed chilled hands to my glowing face.

"Was he not there before when he called out to us?" I asked.

"When you translated yourself to this place, the use of power drew his attention. Now, he has come to hunt us himself. I could do without the honor."

Even as a stranger in this strange land, I knew we could not remain where we were until dawn or our enemies caught us. *He* had resisted, had escaped, but could I? I had scarcely resisted the temptation to betray myself into another mage's hands and bore the scars of it, and I had succumbed to this man's entreaties. I did not think I would be able to withstand the Master of the Hunt.

And, in any case, could either of us stand to see harm done to the other? No: we must keep safe.

We started to withdraw into the slightly greater safety of the forest, when a howling went up. I gasped and glanced back. Shadows, the shadow creatures knew to ignore. But even the faintest glimmer of our life force, straying in its mere abundance into the clearing was enough to alert them—enemy, invader, *prey!*

"That's done it!" the mage whispered.

We ran, heedless of cracking twigs or scattered rocks. The time for stealth had ceased. Once, in what seemed like an earlier life, I had ridden with a man I had thought I had every reason to trust. I had heard horns being blown, but in my innocence—I was but newly released from Schola Magium—did not recognize hunters signalling the Mort. I had begged my companion to intervene, but he had not only laughed at my tenderheartedness, he had drawn me along to gloat at the death.

This time, I was the quarry. I drew breaths that

felt like spears piercing heart and lungs, but I ran and did not stumble.

Light erupted behind us, light and smoke and a reek of burning pitch.

"They found my tree," he muttered.

Would they burn down the entire forest to take or kill us? I had dwelt at the edge of a great woods and knew how swiftly such fires spread. One could dig a trench the fire might not leap, or retreat to the center of a clearing, or to the middle of a river. Any hope of safety led to exposure—which might lead to death or worse.

"They herd us," I gasped.

"Aye, unless . . . lady, are you resolved?"

I had the Blade, sharp enough to give us escape if all hope failed. I drew it. Faint moon-and starlight, much filtered by leaves and pine needles made it glow the silver of the lives it might have to drink.

"Now?" I asked. "There is strait payment for whose who end their lives before they exhaust every hope."

The other mage's eyes lit. "Honor to your courage, lady. I do not counsel death, but a great risk. Not far from here lies a gate. I do not know where it would take us, or even if it would work for us but . . ."

"Then we risk it!" I gasped. The reek of smoke grew stronger. Soon, we would have to leave the forests in any case.

The fire behind us cast a semblance of false dawn. Our shadows fled with us, silver light dancing with them, as we turned back to the clearing. To save time and our lives, if the fire spread, say, by a tree when its sap exploded, we must head for open space. I was greatly tempted to beg my companion to stop and guard me while I cast the circle that would take us back to our world, but I still feared that as much as I feared the Master of the Hunt.

The clearing stretched out before us. I headed for it. I heard only the crackle of the fire, closer now, frighteningly close. Those hunting us had ceased their cries.

"Along this path!"

Imprudent to flee across the clearing when a perfectly good way lay before us through a stand of trees into a barren spot. In its center stood two standing stones, topped with another. To each side, trees stretched out behind the stones. My vision could not pierce the darkness that lay between them.

But I could not miss the creatures, half hounds, half other, that raced toward the clearing, or the figure with its horned crown that urged them onward.

"Run for it!" The mage gave me a push. I ran, hearing him come after me.

Then they were upon us. I heard the hounds yelp and scream as he swung his rough-made club. Hot blood splashed upon my Blade, coating it to the hilt. It burnt my hand, but I forced myself to go on fighting, to force myself forward. I could hear my companion's voice chanting words of protection. His voice grew ragged, then more distant.

We were almost at the gate when he cried out in pain and fear.

Before the gate loomed the Master of the Hunt, the shadows from his horned crown falling upon us like dungeon bars. I cast the blanket-cloak from off my shoulders onto the hounds, entangling them.

The mage's blows should have been deadly, but they recoiled from the Master. At a gesture from him, as if the Master grew tired of a child's repeated attempts to play with him, the club snapped. The despair in the mage's face struck me to the heart.

Clever enough to be a mage I was, but I had bitter reason to know I was not wise. Light fell on the blood-smeared blade that had once been a sacred instrument. And at that moment, I was gifted with a revelation as keen as any granted to the very greatest of all mages.

"Your club," I gasped. "It is a creature of this world. It cannot destroy its master."

I darted forward, feinting and slashing in some parody of swordsplay. The Master's laughter hurt my ears. He evaded the Blade, then reached out and knocked me down. I went sprawling, but as I fell, I tossed the Blade.

Hilt over point, it spun in the smoky air until my ally, my . . . love? . . . snatched it and lunged forward. With the weaponscraft I lacked, he held the Master off long enough for me to reach the gate.

"Go on!" he urged me.

I planted my feet. "Not alone."

Perhaps, if he had not been weary almost unto death, he might have dodged about the Master and joined me in the shadow of the gate. But as he ran, the Master seized him and sank his fangs where neck met shoulder as if determined, could he not breed mages, he would feast upon the one in his power.

My scream matched his. I ran from the gate, beating on the Master's back, drawing his attention. The Master turned toward me. I knew a moment's bitter triumph: we would die together, mage and mage, like a ballad no one would ever sing. Then the creature shrieked and collapsed.

I saw my friend standing there, reeling, but still on his feet. Even as the Master sought to drain him, he had struck to the heart, piercing that unholy flesh with a blade that was not of his forging, not of his world; and it had proved mortal, or as mortal as anything might.

Now, my companion's blood coursed down his neck and chest. The light that pooled about him dwindled.

"Go," he whispered, and hurled the blade back to me. The black blood of the Master burned off it in flight. I caught it before it touched the trampled ground.

I ran forward then and caught him too before he fell.

"Little fool!" he murmured. "The hounds are only stunned. Let them rise, and they will seek us out. Take the gate."

"Not alone!" I tugged his arm over my shoulder, and staggered toward what might be a very dubious refuge. With every heartbeat, I could feel the warmth of his blood.

"Just one step more," I begged him. "Please." Another, then another, and then . . .

. . . we were falling through black night until a silvery light exploded about us. He crumpled against me, bearing us both down onto ground that did not reek of monsters' blood.

Behind us loomed yet another gate. Before us . . . ah yes, before us shone a river, crossed only by a bridge formed by a Blade like mine, only immensely longer and finer. The river shimmered with its own light. Across it, the sky lightened toward an unimaginable dawn.

We could cross, if I could bear him that far . . . but even as I watched, the sword bridge was withdrawn. The crossing was barred, at least to me.

I looked down at my companion's face. So pale it was, and so serene now. My eyes filled, shimmering with the light from the river. I knew what that pallor, that painlessness meant.

Not long indeed.

"Behind us," he whispered. "The fane I sought. I did not mean to enter it . . . quite like this." He coughed. Blood trickled from the corner of his mouth.

Drawing upon the strength that even the weakest man or woman finds at a moment of utmost trial, I drew him with me into the sanctuary.

Beyond the standing stones shimmered a pool. Beside it lay a stone as great as those that formed the gate. It gleamed as if it had been purified for some holy use.

"Bring me there . . ."

It looked too much like a bier for comfort, but we had the choice either of that stone or the cold ground. He slumped down onto the rock, propping himself with one hand, or he surely would have fallen full length. His reflection gleamed in the water, except for the spreading darkness from his wounds.

The silver light that yoked him with his native earth flared up like a candle end, then guttered out. In this new darkness, he still gazed at his reflection. Now it held more life than he. His blood dripped from his body down the stone. Tapers of light erupted at each end of the altarstone.

I stumbled toward the pool to fill the Cup. I set it to his mouth. At least, I could wash the blood from his face, wet his lips before he set forth on his journey, and I on mine.

"Light fails, light and life together. I would be *dead* at home," he murmured in quiet amazement. "I don't want this. I want . . ."

He let the water moisten his lips.

I set Cup and Blade aside and took his hands in mine.

"Stay with me," I begged. "I love you."

"I love you," he cried softly, "but I cannot stay."

So strange it was to hear a magus speak of love, not power. Anger flickered in me that we would not have the time we had earned.

"If I inscribed the circle now and you drew on me . . ." I faltered.

"We would not survive the passage. Listen . . ." His voice had sunk to a whisper.

I bent close. "My true name. Gereint," he said. "Remember me. And . . ."

His fingers tightened on my hands, raising them toward his lips as the sun rose. He kissed the pallid scars upon my wrists and they vanished. He drew his silver bracelet from his arm and ringed my left wrist with it, still warm with the last of his life.

"You must return now," he said.

Tears poured down my face.

"I don't want to leave you." There the admission was. I had another one to make, too. "Gereint, Gereint, *my* name is . . ."

He shook his head. "Your name was marred. And so I give you another. It is 'Beloved.'" Our lips touched, then parted.

"I will take that kiss with me into forever," he said, smiling. "I beg you, go. Already, your light grows fainter."

Gereint's hands gripped the stone as if he sought to hold onto life long enough to bid me farewell. I saw him glance at the river that he must cross, then back at me. He did not want me to see him pass.

I cleaned the Blade in the long harsh grass. I filled the Cup again, disturbing the shadowy reflection that I did not want to see dissipate when the ripples subsided. Then I drew myself up, saluted him, as befitted an adept of our order, inscribed the circle, and began, ruthlessly suppressing my voice's trembling, the Invocation.

No fumes of incense eased my throat or my passage home. Instead, light wreathed up about me. It hid Gereint from my sight—all the farewell we would have. I forced myself not to weep. I needed my breath for the rite.

Cascades of silver exploded about me.

I lay upon the floor of Gereint's house, which was now and forever mine by my love's gift, idly drinking in the fragrance of rain upon the lilacs. Finally, I opened my eyes. I lay wholly covered with blossoms.

I let myself curl up on the floor as if, lacking Gereint, I could embrace my grief. Bereaved I was, yet somehow fulfilled. What else in me had changed? I would not find out by lying here.

I struggled onto my feet. The fire was banked. I stirred it into brilliant life. I hung the pot of porridge over it and set the kettle on the hearth to boil water for herb tea. Soon I would be hungry, I knew that from other workings. Soon, too, people would come, to inquire how I fared, as they would say. I knew they came even more for healcraft and reassurance. They were Gereint's people: no, they were ours. His sacrifice had kept them safe.

I looked out the window and saw not the familiar garden, the familiar slope edging down to the riverbank, but, with the shimmering of my tears, another river altogether, bridged by a sword that even now my Gereint must have dared cross.

A life of work. A life of service, friendship, perhaps love again; I would face it all.

The years would not pass rapidly. I would not wish them lessened, nor would he. An end to our waiting would come, in the fullness of my years or the midst of some good deed. And when I too crossed that final river, Gereint would greet me on the farther bank, smiling at me in the fragrance of the lilacs.

Miranda's Tale

JASON HENDERSON

"We've thought about it, Miranda," said Master Kenton. "We talked for a long time about it, as you know." Kenton had his pipe in his mouth and rocked back on his heels, a perfect caricature of the people of Denwyck. He squinted, for the sun was in his eyes, but he was too polite to move.

Miranda stood awkwardly, her arms cramping with the weight of the victuals she had just bought at the market. She looked past Master Kenton and saw the path out of the square, out of the village, out into the woods. The road from and to elsewhere. Miranda was glad for a place to hang her hat. But she had not expected the place to become—what would the word be—official? Permanent? *Home?* But here was Master Kenton nevertheless, trying ever so hard to appear not to be uneasy around her. Non-wizards were so *odd*, Miranda decided. The magic had to be taken care of and so one needed a wizard. How nice to be a necessary evil. Miranda balanced the basket on her hip and reached up to move her hat from her eyes a bit. "And what did you decide?"

Miranda could envision the meeting without needing the answer, and it required no clairvoyance. She had wandered into the village of Denwyck because that was where the road had taken a wizard needing a village. And in she came, around the bend and through the wall, walking under trees that bloomed as if in defiance of the spiritual living death of Denwyck. And that first week, when the marauders came, casting spells and killing sheep, and she used her powers, the gossip started. Portly women hung over window sills and whispered audibly about the new wizard. New wizard! As if she'd come to fill that hole.

Fifteen years! She mourned inwardly, and then berated herself: *Come along, Miranda, don't you think it's about time you settled down? This is what you're made for. Take the village.*

"We talked about it, and obviously everyone feels we've been long enough without a wizard," Master Kenton continued.

"Yes." Old Stephen must have died, what, eighty years ago, by all accounts? Before Miranda's wandering even began. Just her luck she'd land in a starving village.

"And of course we feel you have the qualifications." Master Kenton stopped now to see if Miranda would respond. Miranda nodded, to acknowledge the compliment, such as it was. Master Kenton continued: "Has the inn suited you?"

Miranda nodded, wanting to get her groceries home, "Of course, thank you." As if they were paying for it.

"Well, excellent, then," said the old man. "Jacob Deferish will be very happy to hear it. He has remarked that you have been a model, if silent, guest."

This warranted a smile. "Thank you again."

"But I trust you would prefer not to remain at the inn, Master Deferish's hospitality notwithstanding. The council and I—we feel you should take Stephen's old house. It's not much, of course, and the place needs work. I understand there's quite a library. Haven't seen it myself, of course."

Miranda couldn't help it. She wanted to say: *No, I wander, the stars are my ceiling,* some sort of nonsense like that, but she simply could not help her eyes lighting up with excitement at the prospect. Somewhere she heard Jemuel say: *Good girl. You have a spark of ambition after all.* "I will," she found herself saying, and it wasn't to satisfy Jemuel or anyone. "I would be very pleased to."

So much to learn, Miranda thought as she approached the house of Stephen, the Wizard of Denwyck. *So much I've put off learning.*

Jemuel had been shocked, she recalled, as she curled up by his fire and drank his chocolate, he in his ostentatious chair, a book resting beside him. *Shocked.*

"You have never been placed in a village. Fascinating." the older wizard had said. "You received your training at what age?"

"I was eight when the Circle found me."

"Right," he said, and he handed her a biscuit, and she kept from laughing, feeling as she did like a circus animal being handed a herring. But Jemuel was so sensitive. "Eight, which is very late. Very late," he repeated.

"Well, I wasn't available until then. I was shipwrecked with my father."

"He was a wizard?"

"Not a very good one, but yes." Miranda snuggled herself in the blanket Jemuel had given her. She felt comfortable. No way in the world she'd be here long. "He taught me spells, but mostly it was my own ability that I worked on; I made up my own uses for magic. I didn't really know what I was doing. I talked to a few ghosts, of course, and had some unpleasant experiences with dead pets."

"All part of growing up," Jemuel said drily. He lied well for a man. No wizard pupil would be allowed anywhere near living subjects until she'd learned the ground rules; Miranda knew that, now. Father was careless, but he never could say no to her.

"We were returned to the mainland when I was eight and I was snatched up by the Circle."

"Did you ever see your father again?"

"No."

"And how did your training progress?" Jemuel's voice was always soft, like a father, but different. His voice made you want to go to sleep, but it made you talk instead.

"I was a difficult student, I think," Miranda smiled, dunking her biscuit in her mug and nibbling at it. "The Circle wasn't sure if I could be retrained, as they liked to call it, and God knows I fought them every inch of the way."

Jemuel nodded. Miranda tried to ignore his probing eyes. She wanted to stay in his house and drink chocolate and eat biscuits by his fire, and she had no desire to get complicated. "So when you graduated they didn't try to place you?"

Miranda let out an embarrassed laugh. "Oh, I was placed. The village of Senkevvin."

"Mmm-hmm . . ." Jemuel surely had heard of this. Did he know everything?

"I lasted three months."

"And then what?"

"I pleaded with the Circle to put me on special assignment, and that seemed to suit me. I spent some time in the Far Corners, looking for a few unwizards who were practicing magic."

Jemuel closed his eyes. "Unpleasant business."

"I hated it."

"Why?"

Miranda leaned forward and put her arms around her knees. "Jemuel, this is a magical world. I learned to use it on my own before the Circle ever found me."

"Natural talent."

"Right. So what if they hadn't found me?"

"I don't understand the question," Jemuel said, lying well again. The man seemed entertained by her. Clearly.

"Was I a wizard or wasn't I?"

"Before your training?"

Miranda nodded. The chocolate was running out. "Before my training by the Circle."

"The Circle would say no."

"And if I had returned to the mainland and gone to some village and set up shop solving problems, controlling weather, whatever, what would I be then?"

Jemuel tilted his head. "I see. You would have been an unwizard."

"Right." Miranda waited for a moment but Jemuel was still silent. Finally she said, "I shut them *down*, Jemuel."

"And how did that make you feel?"

"When? At what point? When I went into their minds and fried their brains, as I'd been ordered to do? Or when they refused to beg for mercy? Or maybe you mean before that, while I was still trying to gain their trust? Rotten, Jemuel. Rotten to the core."

"This doesn't do you any good," said the wizard, by which he meant he didn't want to discuss it.

"All I'm saying—and then I'll drop it, I promise, because I don't have any assignments right now anyway and I like your company—all I'm saying is, what if we're doing something wrong?"

"Wrong?"

"What if there could be more wizards? What if we're controlling the magic when we should let the magic control itself?"

"Danger," said Jemuel. "That way lies great danger."

But of course, she couldn't ask questions like that anymore, Miranda told herself over and over again as she watched the kind and sheepish village men carry her goods into the hall of Stephen's house. She was a real, honest-to-god village wizard now. Miranda, Wizard of Denwyck. She was part of the establishment. So much for the stars, her ceiling.

From the outside, the house was indeed the wreck that Kenton had warned her about. But the inside! Dust, God, yes, plenty of that, but such a vast collection of *things,* models physic and spiritual, texts and tomes and treatises on every concern, scattered throughout, laid on chairs idly, stacked haphazardly on shelves and in corners, on the table in the kitchen. (Interesting, Miranda noted, that there were knife-and-fork scrape marks on the kitchen table. She got a good feel for Stephen's habits from that.)

It was when she turned away from unpacking her few things and trying to move some of the collected dust around that she sat down in Stephen's old chair in his library. Then, as she ran her fingers along his desk and began to take in the sheer enormity of his collection of books, she felt the wind stir. As if the wind itself awakened, and feeling her, approached and touched her, and touching her, spoke:

You know our crimes are many, Miranda, don't you?
Open the magic. Unlock the chains.
On Lammas we give the bread.

Miranda had dealt with hauntings before. That was first-year stuff. And it was clear, from the way the spirit watched her as she rose in the morning and went about her business setting up shop, that the resident spirit was not immediately intent on doing any mischief. And by the time the spirit was guiding her hand clearly to *this* stack and not *that*, *this* book and not *those*, that she knew who her guest was. As if there were ever a doubt. What remained was to find out about him.

From Stephen's journal:

November 14

I have of late been struck by a disturbing realization, and it came to me thus: there is, in this village, a man not terribly on in years but nevertheless past his prime. His intelligence is not esteemed among the villagers, but it has been my habit to employ him as something of a handy-man. Dervish is his name.

Some weeks ago I asked Dervish to try to bring the old well back to health, so full of cobwebs and refuse as it is, and this task naturally took the man a goodly amount of time to complete.

I did not know the well was haunted. Fool, fool! I should have surveyed it, but the decrepit thing had been on my lands for so many years and I had never had cause to suspect it of any impediment other than the annoyance of its physical uselessness.

Dervish came to me where I sat—I have taken of late to spending my early evenings by the pond, where I watch my ducks—and he told me that the well had a spirit trapped in it, that had long ago stopped the well from working, to attract attention, so that perhaps some wizard would come along and free it. Again, I point in contempt at my own prodigality. But

*what intrigued me was that Dervish had managed to
get a handle on the whole situation. He did not solve
it—that took my doing, and a simple spell it was. But
that evening when I paid Dervish his weekly wage, I
saw a look in his eyes that told me that perhaps,
with a try or two, he could have accomplished it.
Somewhere, back there in the man's childhood, had
things been different—and never in this journal would
I so flagrantly dispute the Circle in its wisdom—had
things been different . . .*

Dervish could have been a wizard.

*Not now, perhaps. We don't allow the magic that
is used by all to be actually manipulated by all, and
Dervish is long past his prime, too late for the Circle's training.*

How many are out there, O Circle?

Do they know our crimes?

Have we known all along?

Miranda put down the volume. The passage must
have been written a century ago, at least. She shuddered despite herself. *Are you here, Stephen? Can
you tell me about this?*

It was all so familiar. The Far Corners unwizards
had tried to feed her their legends: *There was a time
when magic was free, not controlled by a chosen few.
It will be so again. It must be.*

"But that way lies danger," she said aloud,
repeating Jemuel.

Does it? spoke the spirit. *What kind of danger,
Miranda?*

"You talk a good game, you who would set the
magic free," she said. "But consider it. Breaking the
locks on spells the Circle has set, opening up the
magic language, and what would you get? Maraunded
villages, sunken navies. . . ."

Cured sick, fed people. . . .

"All of which the wizards can do."

But should they? You sound like Jemuel. I know you better than that. I brought you here for a reason.

"You brought . . ." Miranda stared at the wall of books. She felt silly, like a child, talking to one of her fellow castaway imaginary friends. "No. I refuse to believe that."

Believe what you like, Miranda. What you've always wanted. Open it. Break the chains on the magic, the chains on the spells.

"Why don't you?"

I no longer have that ability. Not like this. But you can help me, Miranda. I have made preparations. Let me show you the way.

"It can't be done. Open the magic? Even if I wanted to, even if you wanted to, that's a hell of a spell."

I have made preparations.

"Go find someone else, Stephen."

The wind erupted in the library, papers exploding on the desk. Something invisible hit the bookshelf and dislodged a pile of books. The spirit screamed, *Find someone else! Years! Years I spent deriving the spells to be cast! Fellow wizards died to provide me with the parts I needed! In life I tied myself to the fabric that runs through the spells of the Circle. But I was not able to finish my work. There is no one else! You have the training! You have the want! You . . . have . . . the . . . need!*

Miranda looked down at the table. "It's too much, Stephen."

One spell you must cast! One only! One out of two, your choice!

"I will hear no more!" Miranda cried, and with that,

she stormed out of the library and out of the house. *I didn't ask for this.*

Miranda sat by the duck pond and watched the creatures there.

Dervish could have been a wizard. Ridiculous.

What if we're controlling the magic when we should let the magic control itself?

That way lies danger.

But at Far Corners, you felt wrong, didn't you? They'd moved in on the Circle's territory and you shut them down! That could have been you.

You would have been an unwizard, then.

When she returned to the house, she said, "All right. Tell me more."

They talked as days turned to weeks, Miranda reading Stephen's work and then asking the spirit about them at night when he came to her. His writing was gentle, open, and the thought that at the end of each period of study she would be visited by and could converse with the author made her excited to learn more.

Sometimes the spirit, it seemed, had to be guided to his particular words, so long had it been since he had written them, but he opened the theory to her in a way Miranda had never imagined conversing with the Far Corners amateurs. Yes, there was danger in the opening, but the danger was offset by such opportunity. Yes, it would mean the end of the Circle, but what were they, anyway, but hoarders of power who kept their subjects in ignorance? And all the while she felt the living Stephen of the books moving in her, addled perhaps, but lucid.

And Stephen had a spell for her to cast. Two spells, in fact, differing by one word. One was a spell of banishment, to let the poor spirit rest forever. But the one Stephen pushed her towards, in his voice and in his writing, was the other—the opening of the magic—and with it, the gift of flesh for the attendant spirit.

Open it, and we will be together. Or else set me free. For I am tired, Miranda. But I think you know the choice you want to make.

It was true, though, that Miranda felt a duty in any event. Poor, trapped spirit! To grant it rest, or to grant its wishes, and bring Stephen back—and there was something else, wasn't there?

We can see the new world together.

Her choice. And the day of casting loomed: Lammas Night, the night when Peter's chains were broken, the night when the new harvest is celebrated by the baking and offering of the season's first loaves of bread.

Tired, Miranda pressed her hands against the bookshelf and lay her forehead against the leather volumes. She was sick of reading yet still eager to learn, and she half wished that the knowledge would burst from the leather spines of the books and into her head.

"Are you still there?" she whispered.

Another whisper, not her own, and now a breeze touched her open robe and it fell a bit, the cloth sliding past her knees. Miranda closed her eyes and felt something touch her hands, fingers interlacing with her own, and she kept her eyes closed so that they stayed real.

Ghostly fingertips on the backs of her hands, brushing at her wrists. It was Stephen; he was behind her. Don't look. Don't break it. The hands that were and were not there caressed her arms, and then she felt them at her face, soothing, and Miranda opened her mouth as the hands brushed against her lips. The hands came to her neck, gliding along its length, and she gripped the shelf firmly and swayed with them. Yes. . . .

Then she felt his fingers playing at the base of her spine and she heard a rustle as the robe lifted by some unknown power all its own, up and over her head and against the bookshelf. Miranda's breath echoed in the cloth that surrounded her head, and she did not open her eyes, but pressed her head against the spines as he explored her, pressing, relaxing. Warm. She tightened her grip on the shelf.

On Lammas we give the bread, the bread is the flesh, the flesh is the life. . . .

Miranda felt him pressed against her, felt herself opening to him, arching her back, and the hands glided back to her breasts as he entered her.

The flesh is the life. . . .

She found herself grinding against him, wanting him fully, still not opening her eyes, not even to stare at the dark books, and all she could hear was the echo of her own breath inside her lifted robe, *don't look, don't break it.* Miranda moaned and gasped, afraid for just a moment, his hands tightening at her throat and her closed-eye vision going white and speckled, but yes. . . .

Miranda gasped again, no air, and the sensation grew in intensity. If she could breath she would only say yes. . . .

But then, a thought, an image in her brain, of Stephen and Dervish and the well, the well empty, Stephen casting a spell there, and Dervish. . . .

Hands gripping the small of her arched back, anger uncontrolled, strangling her, the robe high above and around her head, no air—

The bread is the flesh, and the flesh is the life. . . .

Oh, god, oh, god. . . .

Dervish—

Brilliant colors and flashes of white stars, swooning and exploding at once, flooding with warmth and pain and tortuous pleasure. Miranda shook, vibrating head to toe, the explosion rocking her to the core, no air and none needed, God, oh God, shaking violently as it reverberated through her until the shake was just a quiver at the base of her spine, and she felt herself as outside her own body, falling to the floor, crashing to earth.

You're not him! You're not him!

Alone, Miranda dug her fingernails into the floorboards and gasped, her eyeballs relaxing into her skull, lungs exploding with new air. Alone. Alone. Alone.

Oh, god, oh, god.

On Lammas we give the bread, the bread is the flesh.

The flesh is the life.

Jemuel was still in his nightcap when he came to the door, thrusting a candle before him. He looked out and sighed, as if in exasperation. "I heard you calling as you rode," he said.

"Please, can we talk?"

"Of course." Jemuel rubbed his eyes and turned, and she followed him into his study, where he set a fire burning and she took a seat. "Chocolate?"

"No. Thank you. Did you know Stephen?"

Jemuel was stoking the fire with a poker and raised an eyebrow. "A little before my time, but he was alive when I came to this village."

"Was he in trouble?"

Jemuel replaced the poker in its stand and wiped his hands on his gown, and took a seat in his chair. "Aren't we all, at some time or another?"

"I want to show you an image, and I want you to tell me if it is Stephen."

Jemuel nodded, slowly. "All right."

Miranda lay back and whispered something, and brought the image forward, of the wizard whose spirit she had been talking to so much, and of late had shown such ardor in the library. The wizard she saw fighting with another man at the well on Stephen's land. She saw the images and drew from them, one after the other, here a profile, there a badly lit front view. An image from a mirror. She extracted the details and set them in the image of a man, and cast it at Jemuel.

Jemuel sat, receiving the image, and studied it. After a while he turned the image away. "Hmm."

"Is it Stephen?"

"This is the spirit in Stephen's house?"

"Is it Stephen?"

"Of course not," Jemuel snapped. "You knew that, too, or you wouldn't have come all the way out here to ask me. Wrong question. Try again, Miranda."

"Who is it?"

Jemuel smiled and wagged his finger as he got up from his chair and went to his shelves. "You know, I spent some time on special assignment with the Circle as well, before I received placement. If you pay attention you can find out interesting things. Secrets are hard to keep among wizards." He pulled out a book and held it at an angle, and Miranda could read the title, in gold: *Roster, under Fredren*. "Fredren was the head of the Circle when I was young, this is a roster of the Inner Circle. I think we'll find what we're looking for here."

The older man flipped through the pages, and letting out a small exclamation, lay the book on his desk. He beckoned to Miranda. "Here's your Stephen."

Miranda looked. She had no surprise to gasp out, either. There, in a woodcut of the Inner Circle of Stephen's time, was the image she had carried here. Pointed chin and wide cheekbones, a good, hawklike nose. And under it, the name. "Dervish," she said.

"You know him?" Jemuel asked.

"The names of the Inner Circle are kept secret, aren't they?"

He nodded. "For the period in which they serve, yes. I got this much later."

Miranda thought for a second. After recounting what she could from the journal entries, she said, "Why would the Circle have sent one of their own to pose as a village idiot and get into Stephen's good graces?"

"More than that," said Jemuel, "Why would he then allow his wizard abilities to show?"

Miranda sat back on Jemuel's familiar rug. "To entrap Stephen. Maybe they thought he would preach the Gospel of the Opening, as it were, to Dervish."

Jemuel said, "And how do you feel? Do you feel entrapped?"

"In what way?"

"Have you been doing a little preaching, Miranda?"

Miranda leaned forward. "What we speak of must never be mentioned again."

"Of course, " Jemuel said. "I'm too old to go about burning witches. At any rate, I trust you to keep what must be kept to yourself."

"I understand. This spirit, Dervish apparently, wants me to cast a spell. I have two choices, come Lammas Night."

"And they are?"

"Banishment, or flesh."

"I don't see the problem."

"There is a spell attached to the flesh spell. I

understand Dervish wanting to be flesh again, but the attached spell is not the kind of thing I think such a die-hard Circle man would approve."

"I'm not sure I want to know its nature," said Jemuel, in all seriousness. "Is it the kind of spell Stephen would want?"

"Yes."

"But . . ."

"But it doesn't add up. If these two were enemies in the end, why would Dervish's reward be tied to Stephen's?"

"Things are not always as they seem."

"Indeed," said Miranda.

"I think if I were you, I'd try to talk to the real Stephen," said Jemuel.

Miranda was staring into the coals of the fire. "I think I know just where to go. I must excuse myself, Jemuel, you've been very helpful."

"Always happy to aid and abet," said Jemuel, but by then Miranda was already on her way out.

Miranda heard the ducks at the pond and placed her hands on the well. Her mind burrowed down deep, down the slimy bricks into the dank water far below. She gasped as she made contact and finally spoke, "Stephen."

There was something like the drawing of breath, ethereal. "Miranda."

"I thought it was you in your house; I was going to set this wizard free."

"To do so . . . would accomplish my life's work."

She saw images then: Dervish and Stephen at the well; Dervish revealed, discovering Stephen's plan; Dervish banishing Stephen to the well; Stephen banishing Dervish to Stephen's spell; the cold water mocking Stephen, and both of them reaching out for just the right wizard, who would surely come along in time.

"But how did you know I would find you?"

"I did not," said the spirit in the well. "Things have worked out better than I had planned in that regard. The choice is still yours, Miranda. Say the words, as I have prepared them."

"I don't want to set Dervish free."

"But so much more will be set free if you do so. What is he, after all, compared to our revolution?"

"A hypocrite, a liar. He preached your philosophy to get himself flesh."

Silence. "I understand."

"I want *you*, Stephen, not this revolution, not if it means losing you."

"You do not know me."

"But I do. The words he spoke were culled from your books. He learned your arguments, but I read them in your hand."

"Then you know what you have to do."

"Why did you do this?"

"To punish him. To break him, to force him to speak that which he did not believe. To make him my servant, if you will. Cast the spell."

Miranda stepped back from the well. The ground was damp against her feet. "If I cast the spell of banishment, your spell of Opening, taking down all the safeguards, all of that is lost?"

"Yes."

Miranda turned back to the house. Lammas in a fortnight. She had to think.

It was Lammas Night. The circle smoked on the floor where Miranda had drawn it, and in its center she sat, her palms held up, and she felt the spirit near by:

Yes, now. . . .

"With the word Kadbin, formed with care by Alexander, who died to make it, I call."

Kadbin, by Alexander. . . .

"With the word Nednal, formed by Roderick, who died to deliver it, I call."

Nednal, by Roderick. . . .

"With the word Cyphertan, formed in his last breath by Cedrick, I call."

Cyphertan, by Cedrick, yes, spoke the spirit, *bring me and our new world!*

"With the word Lanhadruf, formed by James, who carried it leagues before he succumbed, and delivered at last by his son Hal, I call."

Lanhadruf, by James!

"With the word Mannivandal, formed by Edmond, I call."

Mannivandal, yes. . . .

Miranda stopped for a second and breathed.

Nartedil, by Lucas.

"All these things I speak in remembrance of the formers, but now cast I the word Gremfnel, by Stephen."

What?

"And all the work of Stephen's comrades remembered, I banish this resident spirit."

But they can only be spoken once! This is . . .

"Be gone, Dervish," Miranda whispered, and the spirit howled and Miranda saw images of a dream disappear with him, gone, and she was alone.

And when morning came, Miranda rose and went to the well. For she had another spell to cast, and years and years of work before her.

Lady of the Rock

DIANA L. PAXSON

"Like I was tellin' ye, Mistress Erne, there's not much left of the old place now—" Sean McMurtry's voice grated on the words. His son Luke hauled back on the reins and the pony halted.

My fingers clenched in the folds of my traveling cape as I looked at the ruins of Carricknahorna Hall, trying to reconcile these rotting timbers with my father's stories of the warm and welcoming house in which he had been born. Blackened timbers rose from a rubble of masonry, stark against the gray stone of the escarpment from which the place took its name. On my left, to the west, the land fell away into a tangle of wood and farmland, and to the east I could see the blue glitter of Lough Arrow through the trees.

My poor father, I thought with a sorrow worn to a dull ache in the months since I had left India, *perhaps it was a mercy you died without seeing what has become of your home.* But Carricknahorna was all he had possessed to leave me. With neither the beauty nor the wealth to attract a suitable husband even had I desired one, what was I to do now? I could feel McMurtry's concern like the slow warmth of a peat fire, and the hotter flare of his son's sympathy.

"The agent wrote there had been a fire," I said carefully, using disciplines I had learned in the East

249

to banish panic. "But I thought that the rest of the house—"

McMurtry shook his head. "It was seven years ago, and what the fire left the weather's done for. The coasts of Sligo can breed fierce storms, though you might not think it now with the sky so smiling. It's been over a dozen years since we've had such a wet summer, and if the harvest fails again—but such talk is foolish . . ." he broke off, shaking his head.

I looked at him and shivered. My father's fellow officers had joked about how cold they found Ireland when they came home on leave. I, who had been born and raised in India, felt chilly even in June. This land was green as India during the monsoons, but instead of the hot embrace of the sun, a veil of silver mist wrapped the land. I had come here eager to learn what mysteries that veil might conceal. But at this moment the cold was all I could feel.

"A blackguard the agent is not to have told ye, but he's not been here himself in many a year." McMurtry grimaced. "And you are the last of the Family. I suppose now you'll be selling off the land. . . ."

I sighed. My friends in India had advised me to do so. I could have stayed there as part of the circle who were carrying on the work of Madame Blavatsky, but ever since I had read W.B. Yeats' first book of poems, I had been fascinated by the old lore of Ireland. He was a Sligo man himself, I had heard, and his writings filled me with a longing to learn about the magic of my own land.

He nodded to Luke, and the younger man began to rein the pony around. He was, I gathered, about my own age, with a shock of reddish-fair hair and bright blue eyes. But even if our stations in life had been the same, there was an innocence in his face that I had lost when my father died. In spirit, he was far younger than I.

"We'd best be getting back to the village," his father said. "Ye can sit snug by my fire until time for the Dublin train—"

I shook my head, for the money I had left would not keep me long in town, and besides, I was wearied of journeying. "Is there no place here where I can stay?"

"There's no inn, and no gentleman's house I can take ye to, for Lord Skein's place is all closed up while he is in London, but—" he looked at me narrowly. "Ye seem a brave lady, to have come all this way from India and have lived with those black savages they have out there."

I thought of the wise brown face of my old teacher and suppressed an ancient exasperation at McMurtry's insular prejudice.

"There's the priest's house. It's on your own land, lady. Ye might stay there."

I raised one eyebrow. My father had never mentioned this, but he had been sent away to school young and then joined the Army. "What happened to the priest?"

"He . . . died," said McMurtry, "and we are a small place here, so the bishop has not sent us another man."

"And why," I went on, "should I need to be brave?"

"Well—" he eyed me uneasily, "There may be ghosts. Father Roderic was a strange man, always after digging up old stones. There've been some odd stories about the cottage since he was taken. But my old woman has kept the place dusted, and the roof is sound. And there are the books—he was a great reader of old tales and collector of dusty volumes. It seems a pity to have them mouldering away for lack of care."

I grinned. When I was a child I had visited Madame Blavatsky's house, and heard spectral singing and seen spoons dance through the air. I did not think one Irish ghost would trouble me. And there were the books. I wondered how the old man had known the very thought of them would draw me, even if there had been anywhere else for me to go.

As we turned up the lane, another vehicle, a two-wheeled trap being driven far too quickly for the road, flashed in front of us. Luke McMurtry hauled back on the reins, swearing, and the old horse half reared in the traces.

"An' the same to you, me bucko, if ye'll not learn to give way when your betters have the road!" The driver of the trap drew breath to continue, then stopped, having noticed me at last.

"This is Miss Erne, Bailey, and I'm thinking that even the lackey o' an English lord'll acknowledge that *she* is your better, and grant her the right o' way!" Young McMurtry's voice thinned, then steadied as the other man, a thickset fellow with a brush of black hair and a striped scarf tucked into the neck of his tweed jacket flushed red.

"Ma'am—" he lifted his hat to me. Luke slapped the reins on the pony's neck and we trotted smartly past.

"And who might *that* be?" I asked as we left the stranger behind.

"A da—" the lad recalled to whom he was speaking, blushed in turn, and tried again, "a dirty, misbegotten rascal—"

"He is Lord Skein's factor," interrupted his father.

"And not much liked in these parts, I see—" I replied.

"Man or master, there's not much choosing between them," McMurtry sighed. "His lordship will not mourn if we're all driven from our homes by one more bad harvest. He's been buying up land all around here for the sheep, ye understand. No doubt ye'll be hearing from him as well."

I nodded. The remnants of my family's lands were rented out to local farmers, and brought in barely enough to pay the taxes. My father's agent had written already with an offer from Lord Skein. Common sense counseled me to accept, for what use was the land to me when I could not afford to rebuild the hall? But the beauty of those green fields was like a sword to the heart. How could I let them be trampled by this John Bull?

McMurtry had spoken truly. The cottage, though it had the musty smell of a place long disused, had been cared for as if its owner might at any time return. At first I was surprised that McMurtry, who carried the post as well as running the taproom and seemed to function as village headman here, had suggested I live there, but my family, though less prominent than that of Lord Skein, the biggest landowner in the district, had been longer on the land. I supposed it comforted him to have an Erne, even a sallow, skinny girl who seemed destined to be an old maid, living here. Then I found the trunk into which they had carefully packed the former occupant's books, and I began to suspect that perhaps the place had been tended so carefully because they were afraid.

The old priest—or perhaps I should say the former priest, for Father Michael Roderic had been in his thirties—had been a man of catholic tastes, and not in the sense used by the Church. It was fortunate, I thought as I turned the pages of a Latin treatise on magic, that I was not pious. My family were of the old gentry that held to the Roman faith, but when my mother died my father had abandoned his religion, and I had grown up learning more of my *amah's* Hindu gods than of Christianity. The trunk was a treasure trove for me. In addition to the grimoires, there were a number of volumes published by the Irish text society, and several tattered issues of *Béaloideas, Eriu,* the *Archivium Hibernicum,* and other journals of folklore.

During the lengthening evenings I pored over them eagerly, but during those days it was not raining I took long walks, learning the countryside. It would have been misleading to call any part of Ireland truly prosperous in these days, but the land around Carricknahorna had a curious air of desolation, as if all the luck had gone out of it a long time ago. It had been a little over a dozen years since the harvests had begun to fail here, in some seasons a little better, but in others disastrous.

The farmers who came in on market day seemed to fear this was going to be one of them. I could not help overhearing some of their talk, though they would doff their caps and smile when they saw me watching. I would nod and smile in return and go my way, conscious of their eyes on my back, and surprising sometimes an odd look, almost of hope, on their faces if I turned to look back at them.

One afternoon as I passed the little church, it occurred to me that as I was enjoying Father Roderic's books, I ought to pay my respects at his grave. Many of the stones in the churchyard were cracked and lichened, but the newer graves were still welltended, with here and there a drying posy of flowers.

It was there I sought, for by the dates on his books, the priest could not have died before 1882. But though I found the graves of my own ancestors, there was nothing with Father Roderic's name. No doubt he had been taken away by his own kin, I thought then, but an old woman swathed in a black shawl was raking leaves, and it would do no harm to ask her.

I was not prepared for her laughter.

"Buried? No, not he! Or if Father Roderic lies beneath the earth it is in no consecrated ground! He was taken by the fairies, have they not told you? Fourteen years ago it will be, come this Lammas Eve, there on Stirring Rock below the hill!"

"On Stirring Rock?" I was careful to keep my tone level, but my gaze went to Carricknahorna. I could just see the big rock below it through the trees. "My walks have not yet taken me that way."

" 'Tis safe enough now, and on Bilberry Sunday, when the lads and the lasses go to picnic there, but it can be an uncanny place after nightfall. There is a cave there, they do say, that opens to the Otherworld."

I must have shown my reaction then, for she began to cackle once more. Wondering if the story had been meant to intrigue or to frighten me, I gave her a penny and walked on. That night I dreamed of a young man in black who went ahead of me across the hills. I tried to go faster, but somehow I could not come up with him, and then he disappeared into a crack in the hill. I stood listening, but heard only an echo of laughter on the wind.

The next morning I had meant to walk up to Stirring Rock, but it was raining, and I busied myself trying to find places for the contents of the trunks that had followed me from India. It was then, sweeping out the back of the old wardrobe, that I discovered the diaries.

The first volume bore the date of my birth, twenty-one years ago. It must have been started, I thought, shortly after Father Roderic arrived to take up the living here. He had come, it seemed, with aspirations very much like my own—a craving for old tales and old ways. Father Roderic was a disciple of the eighteenth century English divine, Stukely, who had first charted the mysteries of Stonehenge, convinced that Hibernia held mysteries to equal those of ancient Greece and Rome. He had even, it appeared, been introduced to Madame Blavatsky once when she was in London. I found myself wishing I could have met him. We would have had a great deal in common, it seemed to me.

The name of Carricknahorna caught my eye and I paused, moving the lamp so I could see the faded handwriting, precise and angled, with an occasional irrepressible flourish that revealed the writer's romantic soul.

"I walked out this afternoon to Stirring Rock, an alluvial boulder below the escarpment called in Gaelic Carraig na Eornan. It is an impressive feature, as if a giant had been playing ball and dropped it there, but more interesting is the folklore in the district regarding the stone. They say that in the old days it was the site of a combat between the god of light and the black bull that devours the harvest, for the favor of the lady of the land. On Lammas the people would go there to make their offerings to the ancient powers. This was done up through the Middle Ages, though the bishops preached against it. But since the English came to rule here the old customs have declined, and now the old rock is honored only on Bilberry Sunday at the end of July, when the young people go to sing and dance."

There was more along these lines, with reference to articles in various journals. Father Roderic appeared to be in disagreement with Wakeman, and contemplated an article of his own. I wondered if he had ever written it. I flipped through the pages, seeking the scholarly reflections embedded in the references to parish fetes and visits to the sick. One year led on to the next. My grandmother's death was noted; he wondered when my father would return to claim his inheritance—a disturbing comment there—

"The people miss their old lords as well, though they will say only that it's not 'right' without an Erne to dwell below the Rock. I fear that Lord Skein is not an acceptible substitute. In the old days, it would have been the Druid, their priest, who spoke for the absent king. . . ."

That night my sleep was troubled once more. I saw the young man I had followed, but now it seemed to me that he stood before a shadow that might be the entrance to the cave. His hair was as bright as young McMurtry's, but more knowledge than one man ought to bear haunted his deep-set eyes.

"Come—" said his gesture, *"Lady of Carraig na Eornan, come to me!"*

Looking into those eyes, I knew that this was the kindred soul for whom my own had been longing. I scrambled up the cliff, straining to grasp his hand. For a moment, it seemed, our fingers touched. Then, as I gained the ledge, he was snatched suddenly away into darkness and I was alone. The wind tugged at my dark hair, bringing a hint of music. It was a song I had heard a girl singing last market day. But the words were different—

> *"The fair god fights the dark god's reeve,*
> *For corn the Lady will receive;*
> *Both lad and lass,*
> *Let all ill pass,*
> *On Lammas Eve, on Lammas Eve!"*

*   *   *

I woke exhausted, as if I really had spent the night climbing, and found on my pillow a posy of the blood-red poppies that grow among the grain. It was the last week of July. It seemed to me there had been something about Lammas Eve, that the ancient Irish called *Lughnasadh*, in Father Roderic's diaries. Pulling on my wrapper, I began to search through the yellowed pages.

Bilberry Sunday dawned with a spattering of rain against the window panes. Gray skeins of clouds were unravelling across the sky, stained pink by the rising sun. I had asked McMurtry whether there would still be dancing at Stirring Rock if it rained, and he had laughed at me. Wet weather was traditional, and the festivities would not be stopped by a few showers when the Sunday was also Lammas Eve.

Especially, he had added more soberly, when this might be the last festival. "Another failed harvest, lass, and we'll all be taking ship for America. And I do not think Lord Skein's sheep dance. . ."

I had slept badly, haunted by dreams of blood and fire. The priest had been there; it was his need that had called me. I remembered my own sorrow and confusion, but not what had caused them, only his appeal—

"I can save this land, lady, if you will call me back again!"

There was no point in going back to bed. I pulled on my walking skirt of dark green twill, did up the buttons of the matching jacket with its high neck and flaring peplum, and looked around for my cape and hat. By noon no doubt I would be envying the local girls in their stuff skirts and shawls, but they would expect me to dress like a lady, and at least I would be warm.

When the trap drew up at my door I was surprised to find McMurtry driving. But seeing his scowl, I decided against asking after his son. According to the folklorists, Lughnasa celebrations were a traditional time for courting. Perhaps Luke was sparking a girl of whom he did not approve. I wondered why the thought should give me a pang.

Clouds still hung behind the escarpment, but the meadow below Stirring Rock was ablaze with sunshine. A blue trail of smoke from the bonfire hung in the bright air. As we drove up I heard the lively lilt of a fiddle; a few of the merrymakers were dancing. Cheerful voices hailed McMurtry as he reined in, faltered as they saw me and altered to a more sober tone.

"It's welcome you are, lady," said Rose Donovan, whose mother cleaned for me. "Come and sit if you will. The first of the new potatoes are roasting and will be ready soon."

I nodded and clambered down. The girl had always been guardedly friendly, but now there was a kind of grave courtesy in her manner that reminded me of ancient tales. I looked up at the gray bulk of the rock with the odd sense that all of us here were moving back in time. In this ancient place we were bound to old relationships of lord and leige that this new century had forgotten. My ancestors had ruled here. What did that mean to me?

The weather was changeable, blue sky half-veiled by opalescent cloud that thickened at times to release a misting of rain. They had stretched canvas near the fire to protect the fiddler, and someone set a wooden milking stool there for me. I was finishing my first, ceremonial bite of the new potatoes when shouts and laughter erupted from down the hill.

The girls ran towards the noise and I got to my feet, wishing I could kick off my shoes and join them. In a few moments they reappeared, dancing around a heaving knot of young men, McMurtry's son in the lead, who were hanging onto ropes tied around the neck of a young black bull. It was not entirely clear who was leading whom, but someone had tossed a garland across the curving horns. I thought suddenly of the sacred bulls I had seen in India.

"He's a fine beast, my son," said McMurtry, "but not from my byres. Where does he come from, and why have you brought him here?"

"As to his origins, where he comes from he will not be missed, and I left compensation," said Luke. "As for his destination—was it not you yourself who told me of the great bullfeasts they used to have on these heights? It seemed to me that maybe if we made the feast in the old way our old luck would come again."

"That's heathen talk—" McMurtry began, but the boy shook his head.

"We shall eat and drink in the name of the lord of glory and his blessed mother, and where's the shame in that?" He laughed, and at that moment the sun came through the clouds again and blazed on his hair. I blinked, and a voice I remembered from my dreams seemed to whisper, Now it begins. . . . I shivered despite the brightness of the sun.

"If you mean to feast this evening you'd best be butchering him now," said Rose. "And we'll be needing more wood for the fires—"

"Take the beast back, lad. There's no good can come of this—" McMurtry interrupted. But Luke was hauling on the ropes, laughing. Bright hero and black bull—I had read something of this in one of Father Roderic's diaries. I stared, trying to remember.

Before the memory could come into focus we heard hoofbeats, and Lord Skein's factor careened around the bend. Something seemed to click into place in my awareness. McMurtry turned to his son, the high color fading from his cheeks.

"Luke, lad, ye've never gone and stolen this bull from Lord Skein?"

The young man stepped between his father and Bailey, who had leaped from his cart and was advancing with fists balled, looking himself rather like the bull. Some of the girls covered their ears as a stream of profanity curdled the air.

"'Tis a sale and no thievery!" exclaimed Luke. "I left the beast's price behind him!"

Bailey's hand plunged into his pocket and came back with a small pistol. "I'll take the bull *and* the money, for damages, and you yourself to the magistrate to answer for the crime—"

"Lady of Carricknahorna—" McMurtry turned to me, his face working. "Stop them—"

He had invoked the ancient contract between lord and people, and though the law of this time gave me no authority, I could not deny his appeal. But as I walked towards the antagonists, I felt myself becoming part of a pattern that was older still. The clouds had drawn in again, stealing the brightness from the day. From beyond the hills came a mutter of thunder.

The crowd stilled. I took a deep breath, let it out slowly as my guru had taught me, and felt the familiar shift of awareness. Consciousness floated on a plane from which I could observe all things, myself included, a state, I noted with a detached wonder, in which I could also remember my dreams.

"The bright god and the dark must do battle to

release the harvest. The Goddess will judge between them. . . ."

I felt Father Roderic very near, as if I need only turn my head to see him. But vision was fixed on the two men before me.

"This is the assembly of Lammas Eve. I invoke the ancient law of the *feis,* that supersedes all others," I said clearly. "Let the two men fight, body to body, for possession of the black bull." I reached out, and Bailey, as if mesmerized, dropped the pistol into my hand.

With a care that had become ceremony, men assisted the two combatants in taking off their shoes and upper garments while others marked out a circle. With the same deliberation, I took my seat on a boulder at the base of Stirring Rock.

"Let the combat begin."

Bailey set his feet and with a growl threw a cut that would have shattered Luke's chin if he had not danced out of the way. He responded with a swing that glanced off the factor's bicep. For a few moments they circled, feeling out the ground; then came another flurry of blows.

At first it seemed an even matching. Bailey's stocky frame was heavy with muscle, his efficient punches proclaiming the victor of many taproom brawls. But young McMurtry fought with a gaiety that exasperated the older man, and most of the time his whipcord quickness kept him out of trouble. Still, as the fight went on, the factor's blows began to land, and red blotches appeared on Luke's fair skin.

"Soon the lad will tire," said the voice in my head. *"As I did. I knew nothing of fighting then, but I have had fourteen years to watch and learn. Call me, Lady, and I will join with him. For the sake of land and*

*people, he must win. And when he has won, my dear
one—then, wearing his flesh, I will come to you. . . ."*

It was true. In the ancient rites the priest of Lugh
was required to win in order to release the harvest,
and surely if this year's yield was ruined the people
here would be destroyed. And I had come to know
this man, reading his books and his writings, sleeping
in his bed. The possibility of meeting face to face as
well as mind to mind was a temptation that could not
be denied.

"Michael Roderic—" I whispered. "I summon you.
Into the body of the man who stands where you stood,
who fights the battle you fought, I call you to descend.
Wandering spirit, take flesh again and win the
harvest!"

Luke McMurtry stumbled; Bailey's next punch
caught him full in the chest and he reeled. Then
he blinked and pulled himself together, both less
graceful and more focused. He lifted his fists to
defend once more, and the smile with which he
faced his foe transformed Luke's youthful features
into a face full of passionate self-mockery. I had
seen it in my dreams.

Laughing, he began to beat back his enemy. The
part of me that was Miss Anna Erne exulted, but that
part that floated above all this was one with the gods,
and as Bailey began to falter it came to me that this
too was wrong. The fight must be a fair one, whether
man to man or god against god. I resisted the knowledge, but my teacher had trained me too well. In
India they teach that a human soul can become one
with its god; it was the Goddess within me, the Lady
of the Land, who spoke now.

"Crom Dubh, Dark Lord of Land-wealth, arise to
defend your own. . . ." The words seemed to reverber-
ate between the worlds. "Lugh, Lord of Light,

descend to challenge him. To the winner the fruits of the earth shall belong!"

A spear of flame shattered the world into patterns of dark and brightness; hearing exploded into thunder. In the next moment the heavens opened. Through veils of rain I saw the struggling figures distorted, towering above the earth in interlocking spirals of light and shadow. Around us raged the storm, but its fury was less than that of the spirits that strove beneath it. I was on my feet now, arms lifting. Lightning bloomed again, and as the thunder followed I felt the charge flare through my outstretched hands and down to earth beneath my soles.

I saw Lugh's long arm strike, his fist smashed into the Dark God's chin. He reeled back, and then, like a tall tree falling, went down. Shadow swirled around him. The victor turned, his radiance sending rainbow flickers through the storm, and the goddess in me saluted the god.

"Bright One, my thanks to you—" I murmured. "Go now, and release the body you have worn. You have the victory." His smile, like the world seen by lightning, was imprinted on my soul. Then he swayed and gently crumpled to lie beside his foe.

Wind whistled around me, and then suddenly the rain was lessening. I ran to the fallen men, and the others, sensing something beyond their understanding, gave way.

"Michael. . . ." I whispered, recognizing the gleam in the blue eyes that met mine. He lifted one hand to touch my cheek.

"Lady—I have done it. I claim my reward. I claim you—"

My own grasp tightened on his. I wanted that. Feeling the spark as skin touched skin I knew that my body wanted it as well as my soul. But I had been trained too well. My eyes pricked with new tears.

"Michael, this boy has his own *karma* to work out. You must give back this body and go on—"

"I was a poor priest," he answered. "The Christian god would not have me now."

"Seek rebirth then, as the Druids, like the Hindus, believe, or perhaps the old gods will release you from the Wheel."

"Do you not love me?"

I nodded, swallowing. "Too well, my love, to hold you here."

He nodded, and the mockery left his smile. "Pray for me." He gave a little sigh and his eyes closed.

"What is it? Is he dead?" I heard a step and McMurtry's voice behind me.

"He is exhausted." I tried to stand, feeling as if I had fought the battle myself, and the old man reached out to help me. "Your son will come back to you, as will the other one. They need rest, that is all." I moved aside, and he followed me.

"You were here," I held his gray gaze, "when they fought fourteen years ago." I saw in his eyes the flicker of recognition, and of fear, but he could not look away, and I thought that some of the goddess must be in me still. "Where is Father Roderic's body, McMurtry? Is it in the cave?"

Sweat beaded on his brow, but he nodded. "How could we have explained it, him coming up here on this day? He fought one of Lord Skein's farmhands, and hit his head when he fell. We panicked and hid the body, and nothing has gone right for us since that day!"

"It will be all right now," I said, looking around me. Already the clouds were blowing eastward and the world was suddenly full of sunshine, refracting

back from grass and leaves in a crystal dazzle of light.
A great peace began to fill me, and I realized that I
had spoken truly. This harvest would be a good one,
and not only for the village.

I had come home.

Note: For more information on the traditional folklore
of Lughnasa I recommend *The Festival of Lughnasa*,
by Máire MacNeill, Oxford University Press, 1962.

Publisher's Note: The sometimes strange syntax and editorial elisions are intentional in this homage to Faulkner.

Before

GAEL BAUDINO

All this happened before you were born.

The intersection of Jefferson and DeWitt, unpaved from the beginning and not likely to see brick or even common concrete in the near future, sent up a haze of dust in the late July heat, though it would have sent it up even in the first blush of April, when everyone knew that spring was coming, and the women and girls were looking at Easter dresses and hats, and there had been rain maybe—not ice, not sleet, but real rain—the kind that made the tautness of one's skin let go not so much from humidity as from simple relief that winter was past and soon there would be flowers: bulbs coming up, and apple and peach and dogwood blooming outside of town in the forest that Vinty White had never been able to develop for that mill he had wanted (though his son, working more nocturnally, had been much more successful when he had showed up at her bedroom window and scratched just like her cat wanting in).

But this was July, and when old Mrs. Gavin (childless throughout her sixty years, and everyone thought that she should have had at least *one* in there somewhere, seeing as how Clinton Gavin, her husband, dead and gone now ten years, was known to have been as randy as a stoat) pulled her old DeSoto somberly along the street, stopping at the stop sign more out of condescension to than fear of the law, then driving on through as though she were steering not a heavy green car but a black-clad and sable-bedecked hearse, she left behind her a white pall that must have cloaked the intersection, stop sign and storefront alike, for five minutes or more, and it made Greta turn away from the big plate glass window that Willie McCoy, the owner's son, had spent twenty minutes cleaning that morning because his father had thought that a clean window might attract more customers to the soda shop than a dirty one, even though, in her opinion, the heat would bring customers enough whether the window was clean or not.

She turned away because the whiteness of the dust outside the window reminded her of the whiteness in her mind that she had struggled to maintain for considerably longer than five minutes, struggled to maintain, in fact, for almost four months now, being partly but mostly successful, save for times like this when she was reminded not so much of the presence as of the maintenance of the whiteness by some external event, in this case old Mrs. Gavin's DeSoto and the pall of dust it raised.

No. And something else, too.

Out of that pall, appearing gradually, as he had appeared out of the silver of that moonlit April night, came Jimmy White, cruising up Jefferson in his Ford pickup, slowing down hardly at all at the stop sign and then, swinging left on DeWitt with a scratch of rubber on dirt without even waiting for the car coming the other way (which had the right of way), and it was a good thing for Jimmy that Sheriff Wallace was not around that day, but then again it really did not matter whether he was around or not, for Sheriff Wallace was a first cousin of Vinty White, Jimmy's father, and Sheriff Wallace would have had no more luck writing Jimmy a traffic citation than Greta would have had convincing anyone that Jimmy had come to her bedroom window scratching like her cat wanting to be let in. But she had not tried in any case.

But with another scratch of rubber on dirt and another cloud of white that reminded her of a different white, Jimmy slewed his truck around like the flap of a hand so that it faced in the opposite direction and in the opposite lane; and then he pulled over, parked, and came into the soda shop where he lounged up against the wall by the door, looking at her (there were no customers in the soda shop just then, and Willie, having finished his useless cleaning of the front window, had gone in search of a boy's adventure while his father was away down the street buying cigars at the tobacco shop), appraising her from beneath his dark hair, his thumbs hooked in the pockets of his jeans so that his fingers pointed at and echoed the pubic saddle that lay beneath the blue cloth, and

"Mornin', Greta," he said, and she looked up from the rag she had been using to polish the countertop, but not really, because she had been looking up all along, though not so that anyone would have noticed (or so she had hoped), and she said

"Can I get you anything, Jimmy?" And he, thumbs still hooked, fingers still pointing, shook his head.

"I jus' come to check on my little one."

"You don't even know there *is* a little one."

"My father would've had a little one, and I'm like my father, girl. We's all magic men in my family. My father was a magic man, my grandfather was a magic man, and I'm a magic man, too. Just like in the song."

She turned her head away. That was what had been playing on her radio when he had come to her window that night, silently, like a cat, and scratching like her own cat waiting to be let in, except that when she had unlatched the fastening and slid the lower sash up, standing in her nightgown with her hair all loose around her shoulders and not even underwear on, she had seen, instead of white cat paws, a man's hands reaching for the sill and she had not had time even to think (though she was still not sure, between the forced episodes of whiteness, what she should have thought at the time, or what she could have done except say *no*, and even that would have been as nothing since it had been Jimmy White coming in through her window, and everyone knew who his father was and how his father had, in his prime, like his father before him, sired child after child upon any number of women scattered throughout Oktibushubee County, sired them perhaps in just this way [the shameful births hushed up and secret, families raising the cuckoo birds as their own so that by now no one knew who might be related to whom], just as everyone knew—just as she knew—that her father worked at the bank that Mr. Gavin had left in trust to his wife until she died and then to the faceless and nameless group of investors and backers in Chicago who administered that trust, who, upon her death, would acquire ownership of it, and that Mr. Gavin and Vinty White had in common a great-grandmother somewhere up north) before Jimmy had been in her room.

"You puttin' on weight?"

"Maybe I am, and maybe I ain't. None of your business, anyway." And he, still lounging at the door, his thumbs still hooked in his pockets and not having moved an inch, said

"It's my business, all right. That little one, boy or girl, is *mine*, and you'll take care of it." And she, not looking at him, or rather, keeping herself from looking at him with anything more than the corner of her eye

"There ain't no little one."

And he laughed and said

"Sure there ain't."

"There *ain't*."

"You jus' take care of it. Boy or girl, it's mine. And I'll tell you, it's a boy, too. I know, 'cause I'm a magic man. All the men in my family are magic men. I know it's a boy, and I'll know if you don't take care of him."

And before he left, he went to the jukebox at the side wall, stuck in a quarter, and paid for three repetitions of the Heart song so that she would have to listen to it again, and again, and again, the engine of his truck roaring behind the music, his tires scratching and sliding on the unpaved street as he pulled out, slewed around, and headed on out of town toward the highway and the house of his father.

She heard a siren later on, but she did not think much about it, because there were always a few things that would make Sheriff Wallace turn on his siren, even if he would not turn it on for Jimmy White no matter how often he drove like one who had been snakebit. More than likely it was something simple, something common: someone from out of town who had run the stop sign that everyone knew was hidden behind the ivy bush at Duncan and Main, maybe, or a cat up a tree somewhere, as her own cat had been that April morning when she had gone out to look for it and had found it hanging terrified from the high, leafless branches of the frost-rimed maple into which

Jimmy's attentions had driven it the night before when he, afterward, had come scratching at her window, imitating it perfectly as though he had been listening to it for days, planning for just the evening when her mother and her father would be out at the movie theater, planning it so that she herself would open the window so that even if she said anything (and he knew she would not) he could say that she had let him in herself, planning it and waiting and then doing something to the cat to keep it out of the way and coming instead himself.

But when Mr. McCoy's cigar, fresh from the tobacco store (his son Willie having, by adolescent prescience, arrived back in the soda shop just ahead of him so as to continue the deception that he had been on the premises and working the whole time) had driven her into the bathroom to kneel at the stained toilet and heave dryly from a stomach that had already been emptied from just such heaving an hour before, she could not help but think of the wished-for, enforced whiteness in her mind that had been shattered now by Jimmy's visit, by his questions, by the hook of his thumbs in his pockets and the point of his fingers at his crotch, and of the inevitability of what would happen to her, a dictated fate just as inescapable as that which had, last April, been forcing the buds into existence on the branches of the peach and the apple and the dark dogwood of the forests that even Vinty White could not put a mill in for the quicksand that was there; nor could she forget his words that had conveyed that morning, as they had conveyed that April evening when he had come in through her window, that same inevitability: his magic, shared as though consubstantially with his father and his grandfather; his arrogance and his willingness to plant his seed widely and even indiscriminately among

the women of Oktibushubee County, knowing as he
did so that that same magic, or maybe a different
kind of magic—the magic of money, the pollinating,
fertilizing touch of coin and bill and draft—protected
him from all consequence and repercussion; his declaration (for it was a declaration, not a wish, a promise
rather than a hope) that there was a child (and there
was) and that it was a boy (and it would be); and
his unspoken pronouncement, felt by her rather than
uttered or maybe even thought of by him, that, as his
father was like his grandfather, and as he was like his
father, so the child would be like him, and that she
would see that child grow to a swaggering manhood
in which he would drive a truck and scratch at windows and plant his seed with as much arrogant skill
and inevitability as Jimmy himself

or maybe not, for near closing time, when Mr.
McCoy had left the soda shop once again, this time
to journey up the street for beer with his friends, and
Willie McCoy had vanished again too, Mrs. Gavin's
old DeSoto came back down the street. But instead
of driving by, solemn and funereal, leaving behind it
only a white pall as though in token of oriental and
cryptic mourning, it pulled to the curb right in front
of the soda shop and stopped. And now Mrs. Gavin
herself was getting out—furs despite the heat and dia-
monds maybe because of it (flashing icy in the pall of
whiteness)—and coming into the store.

But she was a lady, and she would not sit at the
counter like a man or a hoyden, and so she took a
chair at one of the marble-topped tables that Mr.
McCoy had had trucked in all the way from Biloxi,
trucked in and placed on the scuffed linoleum check-
erboard of the soda shop floor like tombstones imper-
vious to the chrome and the jukebox; all the colder,
perhaps, because of that, and therefore all the more

attractive to Mrs. Gavin who was obviously hot and upset. And Mrs. Gavin sat down in the wrought iron chair and stared at the cool marble tabletop as though she would have liked to have laid her flushed face against it and rolled it from side to side so as to bring her sweating cheeks to its cool, polished surface but could not because she was a lady, childless but a lady. Instead, she reached into her purse and extracted a handkerchief that could not have been more than eight inches on a side, dabbing thereafter at her temples like one who wished that she could just damn all and swipe at her dripping, fevered forehead like a convict on a summer labor gang might swipe at his forehead with a bandanna that had perhaps eight times the area of Mrs. Gavin's embroidered and lace-work instrument.

And Greta brought her a glass of ice water because Mr. McCoy had said that that was good business (though not for the boys and girls attending summer school down the street who came in at 3:15 sharp every day with nickels and dimes and quarters, clamoring for Cokes and Pepsis and 7-Ups and some cherry syrup with that and some chocolate in that because they were just children and Mrs. Gavin was a lady), and Mrs. Gavin ordered a strawberry phosphate as though she were herself a girl in school, (though not from any school now, a school, rather, that gave its lessons fifty years ago, when no one had heard of any such thing as an atomic bomb, and people still believed that world wars did not need numbers after them so that you could tell them apart); Greta taking her order with respect but thereafter hurrying to the big book of recipes that Mr. McCoy kept in the back room because for the life of her she did not know what a strawberry phosphate *was* much less how to make it, which was doubtless because this was only her first summer in the shop, a first job fresh out of high school with nothing before her but a looking forward to—

But she found the book and the recipe, and repeating the litany of ingredients and quantities to herself silently, she went behind the counter and spooned and pulled levers and pushed plungers and mixed until the strawberry phosphate was finished. Then, conscious that Mrs. Gavin's eyes were on her (seemingly looking at her a little more than one might ordinarily look at someone, as though she were, with sixty childless years behind her, seeing something that might have remained . . . no, probably *did* [no, more than that, probably *had to*] remain hidden from most people in the town, remain hidden from all who knew nothing of April evenings and scratchings at windows and the stunned disbelief that gave way to an incontrovertible reality that had to be because it *was* as no cat paws but the hands of a man grasped the sill and a foot swung over and a face followed it in; remain hidden because, alien thing that it was, it could not be grasped, remain hidden because she was Greta Harlow, remain hidden because her father was respectable and worked at the bank, remain hidden because her mother was respectable and kept house like a proper woman), she brought the strawberry phosphate to the table, and, setting it down before Mrs. Gavin, heard her ask

"Did you hear the news?" And Greta, having knelt at the shrine of her nausea and stood at the employ of the soda store all that afternoon, unable to eat for the first and hoping all the time that she did not have to think for the second, said

"No, ma'am." "I saw it," said Mrs. Gavin. "Terrible. Just terrible. But I always knew he was going to end up that way."

"Ma'am?"

"Sheriff Wallace kept me there because I was a witness." And then Mrs. Gavin took a sip of her strawberry phosphate that became more than a sip, became, in fact, a large swallow that set her coughing for the better part of a minute before she found her voice again. "Terrible. Just terrible. He came out on the highway without a thought, and that big truck ran right over him. The driver stopped, of course. And he had one of those . . . what do you call them? The radios?"

"CB radios, ma'am."

"Yes, and he called the sheriff and the sheriff came, and I stayed because I'd seen the accident and I didn't want the driver to get into trouble even though I probably didn't have to. Everybody knows how Jimmy White drove."

The night: a smoldering hot thing that hung about the town as a dipsomaniac vagrant might linger on the corner of an otherwise unremarkable neighborhood. But she did not notice the heat, for across the town square that was deserted but for those few who had come through the simmering night to see the last showing at the movie theater and who were now returning to their cars to go home to outlying towns even smaller than this one and to the tiny farms that dotted most of Oktibushubee County (their size both a relic of the Reconstruction that had burst the wide plantations asunder and a defiance to the agricultural practices of the future which would see those same plantations reestablished under different names), visible through the lamp and firefly-lit darkness was the library, itself deserted because not even the cool floors and the vaulted ceilings that held the heat high and away from the books and the reading tables could tempt the town from its televisions and its air conditioning and its fans and along through the July heat that was slowly preparing to transform itself into August heat (there being but a few hours now remaining before the shops and the homes and even the library itself would tear one more page from the calendars that were both almanac and advertisement for a hundred things, from motor oil to shoe polish to light bulbs to insurance).

"It was Jimmy White, wasn't it?" Mrs. Gavin had said, and Greta, on the other side of the marble table that Mrs. Gavin had made her sit down at because there were no other customers in the soda shop (and if Mr. McCoy wanted to say anything about it he would have to say it to Mrs. Gavin, and anyone who knew either Mr. McCoy *or* Mrs. Gavin would know that he would therefore not say anything at all, even if he had at that instant walked into the soda shop, which he did not), broke down because Mrs. Gavin had looked at her and had, with sixty years of childlessness behind her, *known*.

"Yes, ma'am."

"About four months ago."

"How . . . ?"

"I know," Mrs. Gavin had said. "I know."

And into the library now: past the front desk with its own marble top that had been set upon its oaken pedestal at least one hundred years before the electronic things that now occupied its surface, that scanned magnetic strips and bar codes with sensors and lights, had been thought or even dreamed of; the librarian looking up first at her and then at the big clock that registered twenty minutes to closing time (and that was all the hint that she was going to give and she assumed that it would be enough), across the floor that had, years ago, been wood but which now

was linoleum because the wood had stained and warped
with the heavy rains coming in through the roof
during the big storm when she was a girl and there
had not been enough money in the town to redo it
properly, up to the ranked rows of the card catalog
that was much larger than might have been expected
just as the library was much larger than might have
been expected, but the town was the county seat and
had wanted a big library to rival the one going up in
Magdalene on the other side of the county line.

And Greta had looked at Mrs. Gavin, and then she
had understood.

And Mrs. Gavin had nodded.

"It's going to be like him," Greta had said, and her
voice had been hoarse, husky as, no doubt, Jimmy
had wanted it to be when he had demanded that she
ask for what he was going to give her in any case,
demanded that she ask in the accents of a seductress
who would take anything he had to give, who would
ask for his arrogance and his manhood in the way that
only a woman who had been weaned and raised on
the saccharine milk of motion pictures and syndicated
television could ask; or maybe he had not wanted that
at all, maybe he had wanted instead exactly what he
had gotten: a terrified acquiescence, a hoarseness and
a huskiness as sexless as fear. "It's going to be just
like him. He said—" And Mrs. Gavin, taking her
strawberry phosphate that was as dated and as decep-
tively simple as herself, sipping at it, and then holding
the cold, dripping glass against her hot cheek

"They all say that. My Tom was the same way."
Another sip. "And I believed him. And so . . ."

And with fifteen minutes to closing time at the
library (and the librarian at the desk not looking up
every minute or two, because she had given the only

hint she was going to give and that was that), Greta was kneeling at a bottom shelf in a dark corner, pulling out a book that, according to the stamped date on the library form pasted on the flyleaf, had not been pulled out for twenty years (and the card in the pocket, she saw, bore among its five or six antique signatures that of Mrs. Gavin herself), standing and opening it to the color plates, turning page after page until she found what she was looking for, thereafter closing the book and taking it up to the desk as she fumbled in her purse for her library card.

Mrs. Gavin had put aside her empty phosphate glass and had leaned toward her. "They all say it. And we all believe them. Sometimes we believe them until it's too late." And Greta, as though her hands were suddenly around something of which she had not dreamed five minutes before, something of which she had not dreamed since that April evening with the scratch of what she thought was her cat on her sash window

"Ma'am?" And Mrs. Gavin, shaking her head, taking out her handkerchief to dab once more at her temples

"You'll have to learn, too. Just be careful. Don't take too much."

They all say it. And we all believe them. And the next day, when she called Mr. McCoy and told him that she was not feeling well and could not come to work, and when she lied to her mother and told her that she was feeling quite well and was going to work, she found that she could not forget even a particle of Mrs. Gavin's words, could not forget either the precious or the (seeming) dross of what had been said over the table in the soda shop, the two having become so commingled that the second had taken on the nature of the first, the knowledge of a certain weed growing in a certain place and steeped in boiling water in a certain way (and it was imperative that she have the book, because one weed might look much like another, and only the right one would do) infusing with something of a quintessential imperative the knowledge that all men believed that they were magic, that all of them believed that their offspring would be boys when they wanted them to be boys and girls when they wanted them to be girls, believed, too, that their boys would be like them down to the last baseball glove and bottle of hair tonic and even desire for women.

But if that were true, then Jimmy's belief was indeed one with his father's and his grandfather's, one with, in fact, the belief of all men; and Mrs. Gavin had said that it was belief *only*, that experience (and she had sixty childless years of it) had taught her that the belief was unfounded. And, suddenly, the fluttering in Greta's belly (even as, book in hand and knee on the warm forest floor, she was finding what she was looking for, finding it and gathering it in, filling a paper bag that had, three days before, brought ice cream home from the supermarket) took on a different meaning, for all men thought they were magic, and none of them were, and Jimmy's now-dead thumbs hooked in the pockets of his jeans and his driving and his words seemed to be now no more than a small part of the continuing protestations of men everywhere, no more than a few urgent but obscure words in that unspoken language of masculinity that attempted to deny what was, that tried, with every resource, to declare what was not: that children belonged to them and to them alone, that fantasy would make reality kneel to them as Jimmy had made Greta, shaking and in her nightgown, kneel to him before he had reached down and lifted her and carried her to her own bed.

And, taking the filled bag home, walking along the road and knowing that, as her father would be at work when she returned, so her mother would also be out of the house (playing bridge and drinking tea at Mrs. Sandhurst's), she found that she could not but dismiss Jimmy's statements and predictions as untruths that had not so much sullied his mouth as confirmed him in his place: that as he was man and she was woman, so it was his lot to believe, and it was hers to know. And she did know. Even with the water boiling in the white kitchen of her father's house, even with the weeds lying rinsed in the tin colander, ready to go into the water for the precisely three minutes of boiling needed to produce an infusion that was neither too weak nor too lethal, she knew, and she knew that she knew.

But then, Jimmy's surety shown for the dust that it was, the poison cup brewed and waiting for the touch of her lips, that deliverance in which she had not dared to believe for almost four months (for the doctors in town all knew her and her father and her mother, and she could not, *could not* ask for such a thing or reveal what had to be revealed in order to ask for it) within the reach of an arm, she realized that there were other possibilities. No, she *knew* with all of her fertile womanhood that there were other possibilities, possibilities inherent in the basic, vivific mixing of sperm and egg that no high-school biology textbook, no matter how explicit in its descriptions or protested against by Mr. Burke's Baptist congregation, could adequately or even partially reveal; for as there was falsehood in Jimmy White's cocksurety, so there was also truth, for he was magic, as all men were magic, and therein lay the real magic: the magic of women, of children, and of nurture, of men who worked a job and came home one day to find a baby turned into a child or a child turned into a woman or a man with no help or interference or even faint suggestion from them.

But it was his. And she had not asked for it or wanted it. What grew within her belly came not from love, not from even a passing acquaintance, but only from the lust of a young man now dead twelve hours and an April night that had given him the opportunity he had wanted.

And yet, still. And still. And maybe. And then, again, maybe. And in her mind she saw Jimmy at her window, and Jimmy in the soda shop; and she saw, too, Mrs. Gavin, childless and alone save for the money her husband had left in trust for her, the money she would never own but only use until she died, and all of it out of her own choice and a book she had, by chance, found in the public library forty years ago, the same book that now lay on the kitchen counter beside the still-steaming pot and the tin colander and the cup that would make her one with Mrs. Gavin, even as Jimmy White had insisted that he was one with his father and his grandfather.

And so, after looking at the cup with its cooling poison for a long time, she picked it up, and she